This book is due for return on or before the last date shown below.

D1630784

For my grandchildren
Benjamin, Mark, Natalie, Samuel,
Andrew & Naomi

There are five books in the Oswain Tales series

Hagbane's Doom
Gublak's Greed
Surin's Revenge
Tergan's Lair
Feldrog's Sting

Collect them all!

www.oswaintales.co.uk

THE OSWAIN TALES

HAGBANE'S DOOM

JOHN HOUGHTON

STARSHINE
Books

Published in the United Kingdom by Starshine Books in 2007

Cover picture – Matty Tristram

First published 1984 by Kingsway Publications
Revised 2001 as Oswain and the Battle for Alamore
This new and fully revised edition 2007 by Starshine Books

ISBN 978-1-905591-16-9

Printed and bound in Great Britain by
Antony Rowe Ltd, Chippenham, Wiltshire

STARSHINE BOOKS
Brown Cottage, Glynleigh Road
Hankham, East Sussex BN24 5BJ
www.starshine.co.uk

Contents

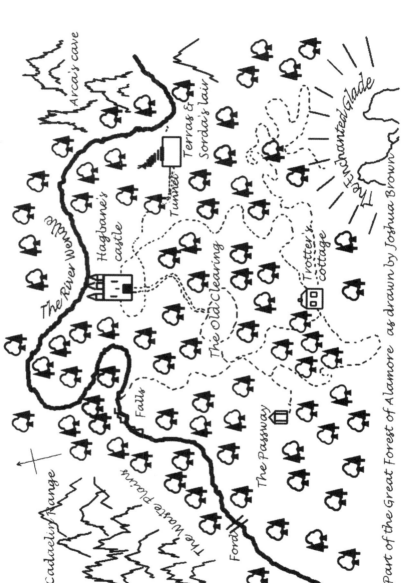

Arca's cave

Tervas & Sorda's lair

Tunnel

Hagbane's castle

The River Wenn

The Enchanted Glade

Trotter's cottage

The Old Clearing

Falls

The Passway

Cadaelin Range

The Waste Plains

Ford

Part of the Great Forest of Alamore   as drawn by Joshua Brown

1
Dreaming of Adventure

Our story begins with a young prince who had an unusual dream. It took place one night in the realm that some call The Land Beyond the Far Places but which, like many such lands, is maybe closer than you think – the wondrous world of Caris Meriac. The prince's name was Oswain and this was his dream.

A single candle burned in the empty night. The flame beckoned Oswain and he drifted towards its hypnotic glow until its light filled the dark dream space in which he floated. Three faces swam into the light – a freckle-faced boy, then a girl with deep, dark eyes, and finally a smiling young lad, each one so alive, so real that he wanted to speak to them; but they simply faded away into the flame.

Oswain wondered who they could be.

A gust of wind blew on the flame so that it flickered in a wild confusion of light. Another image began to form and his heart beat faster; never before had he seen such an evil-looking face. For a brief moment it hovered before his gaze, the glaring, red-rimmed eyes so hateful that he would have turned and fled if he could. But our dreams do not let us run away, and so he watched, staring in horror as the face slowly dissolved into ashes, until only the flame burned on.

With a quiet hiss, the tongue of fire parted down the middle to reveal the deep space that lay beyond the stars. It seemed a lonely place. Then Oswain spied a single dot of light in the far distance. The light grew in size, rushing towards him at such a speed that almost at once it filled the screen of his mind with its dazzling brightness. A splendid jewel hung before his eyes.

'The Merestone,' whispered Oswain.

He awoke with a start and found himself lying on the floor of his bedchamber. Trembling slightly, he rose and crossed to the window. His room was on the third floor of the palace and faced south over the royal gardens. Beyond the starlit lawns and shadowy trees the sleeping city of Castelfion lay quiet and still. Oswain gazed thoughtfully at the shimmering starry skyline of the homeland he knew and loved so well. Then, almost without his being aware of it, he looked up into the night sky. Hanging like a pearl in the velvet blackness, one star gleamed more brightly than the rest. He glanced at the gold ring on his second finger. It was set with a silvery fragment of stone that flickered in response.

He breathed the night air deeply and felt a thrill run through his body. The moment that he had waited for throughout his young life had finally come.

'My destiny calls me. Elmesh has spoken.' He uttered the words quietly but firmly to himself, and then the prince turned to prepare for the journey that lay ahead.

* * *

'If you do that again, Andrew, I'm going to thump your head in!'

Joshua Brown was crouched busily polishing his bike in the back yard. The paving around him was littered with pieces of rag and chrome cleaner and spanners, and the metallic smell of polish hung in the warm spring air. For the fourth time that morning he shoved the annoying football away from him.

It wasn't that Joshua had anything against footballs. If you asked him what his favourite hobbies were he would say riding his bike or kicking a ball – or even both at once. In fact, he had recently suggested to his teacher, Mr Pyle, the idea of cycle football using bikes with engines rather than pedals so that the players' legs were free to kick the ball. Mr Pyle had muttered something about buckled wheels and broken legs and him taking early retirement – and no, it was unlikely to become a new Olympic sport!

No, what irritated Joshua about football on this particular morning was the fact that his brother Andrew kept seeing how close he could dribble the ball to where Joshua was polishing his precious bike and he was fed up with it landing among his spanners and cleaning materials.

His brother laughed at him and ran to retrieve the ball. 'You shouldn't be in the way of the goal. Anyway, I was here first.'

'No you weren't. I was,' Joshua countered.

'Yeah, but you went indoors.'

'So?'

'So it's my turn to play on the patio.' Andrew retorted.

'But I left my bike here. You had no right to move it.'

'Did.'

'Didn't.'

'Oh, will you two shut up arguing. You'll frighten the frogs away!' Their sister Sophie was crouched over the nearby garden pond and was peering intently into the greenish water to see if frogs would eat fish food.

Her brothers ignored her and carried on bickering until in the end Andrew shrugged his shoulders and wandered off, dribbling the ball back down the garden.

Joshua turned his mountain bike upside down so that he could polish the spokes. The bike was a birthday present from his parents and it was his pride and joy. Perhaps it wasn't the best mountain bike in the world, but it was his and it was new with lots of gears and chrome and bright yellow paint work, and much better than the second-hand bikes that belonged to his brother and sister. He recalled how thrilled he had been when he first set eyes on it. Concentrating hard now he polished away at the wheels until they sparkled like diamonds in the sunlight.

Sophie watched patiently as one frog after another popped its head out of the water. The flakes of fish food drifted across the surface and she willed them to eat it. At least the commotion had died down. After all, she thought, frogs are very shy creatures.

But things didn't stay quiet for very long between Joshua and his brother. Andrew's football hit the wall with a resounding smack just to Joshua's right. Then again, and again, only this time closer. Joshua began to seethe with anger and Andrew knew it, but he carried on kicking the ball nearer and nearer, just to make his point.

Of course, it was bound to happen sooner or later – one of his shots went wide and the ball struck the back wheel, knocking the bike over with a noisy clatter of metal on concrete.

Joshua was absolutely furious. 'That does it!' he yelled and with a cry of rage he sprang after his brother. Moments later the two of them were wrestling on the ground like a couple of wildcats.

'Mum, the boys are fighting again,' Sophie called out.

Mrs Brown appeared at the back door with a tea towel in her hands. 'Now just you two stop that,' she ordered. 'Joshua move your bike to that end. Andrew you go and play at the other end. I've had enough of your squabbling. Do as you're told or I'll make you both come inside. Do you understand?'

The boys broke off their fight and nodded sulkily. As soon as their mother's back was turned, Joshua glowered at Sophie.

'Sneak.'

'I heard that, Joshua,' his mother called. 'That's your last warning.'

Joshua yanked his bike upright. 'I've had enough of you lot,' he muttered to nobody in particular. 'I'm going for a ride.'

With that he mounted the machine and pedalled furiously down the drive, deliberately skidding the wheel on the gravel as he span off into Winton Drive. He hadn't even bothered to put on his safety helmet.

Sophie huffed. Her shy frogs had disappeared. 'You can be so irritating, Andrew,' she snapped, and with that she stomped off indoors. Andrew shrugged and carried on kicking the ball against the wall. Moments later, Sophie's music blared from her open window until her mother yelled to her to turn it down. It was just another Saturday morning in the Brown household.

Joshua peddled wildly down the street, imagining that he was riding a world class Superbike in a Grand Prix. Now that would be an adventure! He began dangerously and stupidly to weave on and off the pavement and into the road, dodging between parked cars and the trees that lined the route. Braking hard, he slithered round into Green Lane and pounded up the slope towards the rise and then, crouching low over the handlebars, he freewheeled down the winding hill towards the park. Ignoring the no cycling signs he shot through the pedestrian gate and sprinted towards the T-junction where the path met the main walkway ahead. He would show them!

Then it happened. A mother pushing her baby buggy appeared out of nowhere. She was right in front of him. Horrified, Joshua slammed on his brakes, but it was too late. The bike skidded and squealed and with a sickening, horrifying clunk smashed into the side of the buggy. There was a moment of shocked silence. Time seemed to slow down as he flew over the handlebars. Then he heard a woman scream and a baby's cry and he felt a jolt of pain as he hit the tarmac.

The next thing he knew he was picking himself up, surrounded by a crowd of people shouting at him and scolding him for his stupidity. The buggy lay skewed on its side, as did his shiny new bike. He looked around for the baby and saw that it was in its mother's arms and crying loudly.

Joshua didn't know what to do. Dazed and dismayed, he simply stood there with his head spinning until a grim-faced park warden strode across and took charge.

The mother was badly shaken and close to tears as she comforted her baby. An elderly bystander stooped and examined the buggy. 'A bit scratched, but it don't seem to be damaged,' he announced. 'Lucky it weren't one of them prams they 'ad in my day. All polished coach work, they were. And you, young lad,' he said turning on Joshua, 'You would have got a good clip round the ear!'

The park warden looked Joshua over and decided he wasn't badly hurt. 'You had better apologise to the young lady,' he said sternly. He reached into the inside pocket of his green jacket and brought out a notebook and a silver ballpoint pen. 'Then I shall want your particulars.'

Joshua, shamefaced and almost crying, mumbled 'Sorry.' to the mother as best he could. Then he added, 'I didn't mean it.'

The young mother, still pale from the shock, nodded silently and snuggled her baby close. She didn't look at Joshua again.

'Now then, young man,' said the warden. 'Riding a bike in a prohibited place. Riding dangerously. Damaging property. You are in big trouble, my lad. And you're not even wearing a helmet.' He sucked in a breath between his teeth. 'You can thank your lucky stars the young lady was carrying her baby at the time. I dread to think what would have happened if he had been in the buggy.'

'I-I'm sorry,' Joshua blurted out. 'I didn't mean it.'

'No doubt you didn't. But you didn't think about other people, did you?' the warden replied.' That's the trouble with you kids these days. You've no sense of responsibility. I shall have to report the incident, of course, and I had better warn you that you may be hearing from the police about the matter.'

Joshua was aghast. It was the last thing he wanted to hear.

The warden was speaking again. 'I need your name and address, and your parent or guardian's name,' he said.

Numb with shock Joshua said, ' Joshua Brown. My dad's name is, um, Michael, Michael Brown.' Then he gave his address as 32 Winton Drive.

At last the bystanders began to go their different ways, some of them still muttering among themselves about 'kids these days'. The park warden had put his pen and paper away and Joshua made to pick up his bike. 'Oh no you don't. You can leave that,' said the warden. 'I'm confiscating it. Your father can come and speak to me about it if and when he's ready. And by the look of this front wheel it's in no fit state to be ridden anyway.'

Joshua tried to protest but the park warden was having none of it. 'The best thing you can do my lad is to get off home and tell your parents what's happened before you get yourself into any more trouble,' he said. 'Now go on, be off with you.'

But Joshua couldn't face going home. 'How can I tell my parents?' he said to himself. 'Mum will go spare, and Dad'll kill me when he finds out.'

The thought that he might never see his bike again, his birthday present of only two weeks ago, upset him even more and he was really struggling not to cry. Then aware that he was still standing at the scene of the accident and people going past were looking at him curiously, he shoved his hands into his jeans pockets and shambled off along the path that led to the lake.

'What a mess. What a stupid, stupid mess!' he thought to himself. 'And it's all Andrew's fault. If he hadn't kicked his stupid ball none of this would've happened.'

By the time he reached the lake, Joshua had planned to puncture his brother's football, his bike tyres and his head, but then realised that he wouldn't do any of that because it wouldn't solve the problem. What was he going to tell his parents? He thought for a moment of lying. Some kids had stolen his bike and ridden off with it. They had caused the accident. Well, that wouldn't work. Obviously.

How about brake failure? 'I don't know how it happened, dad. I pulled on the brakes as hard as I could but they didn't work, and the next moment...' He could hear the question now: What were you doing riding on the path in the first place, son?

No, he would just have to tell the truth and be done with it, he decided.

But what was the truth? He had ridden his bike in a rage and crashed into a mother and her buggy. Supposing the baby had been in the buggy? He could have killed the child. The park warden had spoken about the police coming round. The more he thought about it the more gutted Joshua felt.

He had reached the railings of the lake by now and there were lots of people feeding the ducks and generally enjoying themselves the way people do on a Saturday morning. Joshua was hardly aware of them but suddenly someone shouted.

'Hey, there's that kid who smashed into that push chair.'

He glanced to his right. A bunch of boys were pointing at him and laughing.

'Looks like he's lost his bike, don't it?'

'What a nutter!'

'Yeah! Head case!'

'Going for walkies, then?'

Joshua glowered and clenched his fists. They were asking for a fight. Well, if they wanted one, he would give them one. Right now.

He opened his mouth to shout back at them, but then he thought better of it. There were a lot of people about, and he was outnumbered about five to one by the gang. His scuffed hands were sore as well. That might not have stopped him from laying into them, but then he spotted the park warden coming back along the path towards the lake. The last thing Joshua wanted was to be in more trouble. He turned and stalked off, muttering 'Bog off!' under his breath while several old ladies tutted at him.

To his relief no one bothered to follow him and he soon found himself walking in an unfamiliar part of the park. Not that Joshua really noticed. The boys' taunting had reminded him that his precious bike, his best ever birthday present, was wrecked and had been confiscated. He would probably never see it again. The more he thought about it, the more upset he felt and, because no one was about, hot tears came into his eyes. Everything had gone wrong. This was the worst day of his life. He stumbled across to the shelter of a tree and began to sob bitterly.

How long he remained like this Joshua neither knew nor cared but at last he stopped crying and began to wipe his eyes. Slowly, he became aware of his surroundings.

He was standing on the edge of a small grassy clearing surrounded by trees just starting to show their bright spring leaves. On the far side under a canopy of trees he could see a two-bar iron fence, and beyond that a cemetery. Wiping his nose on the back of his hand and sniffing as he did so, Joshua wandered over to the fence. Anything to delay going home to face his family.

The cemetery looked pretty overgrown and the gravestones were so old and crooked that Joshua thought the place must have been neglected for years. Maybe it was just his mood but it looked as sad as he felt. Hardly thinking about it he climbed over the low fence and began to wander among the graves, glancing idly at the faded epitaphs on the weather-worn stones as he did so.

He was just on the point of turning back to the park when a much larger tomb caught his eye – the sort that he had heard were called mausoleums. This one had an arched roof and green marble walls. Joshua decided out of curiosity to see who was buried there.

Following a narrow sandy path he walked round to the entrance where he found an unusual archway of grey stone. In the centre of the arch he saw carved in stone an eagle in full flight and above that a single star. The pillars of the arch were rounded and were wrapped around with animals like squirrels and rabbits and stoats and badgers, all climbing up towards the eagle and the star.

None of this interested Joshua very much – until he peered inside the archway to look for the name of the person buried there.

What he saw absolutely took his breath away. In clear gold letters on a black plaque against the green marble he read, unmistakably,

The tomb of Joshua Brown

and written below it was today's date.

2

Through the Passway

'What the…?'

Joshua could hardly believe his eyes. Surely this couldn't be his grave. He was still alive and anyway the tomb looked as though it had been there for years and years. It must belong to someone else and it was just a coincidence that whoever it was had the same name as himself. Then a wild thought came into his mind. Perhaps his parents knew he was soon to die and they had built this tomb ready for his funeral. But the plaque had today's date on it. Did it mean he was going to die today? He felt the skin prickle on the back of his neck at the thought.

'Don't be stupid,' he muttered to himself.

But the thought wouldn't go away and the longer he stared at the plaque the more he began to ask himself what his life was about. Bikes and football and computer games didn't make much sense if you were going to die today. So, what did matter?

It was not the type of question Joshua could answer, so he said to himself the first thing that came into his head. 'I want to have a real adventure. That's what.'

At that very moment he had the most eerie sensation that he was being watched, and he could have sworn that he heard a voice, though as far as he could tell he was quite alone. The voice was mellow, a woman's voice he thought, though he couldn't be certain. It was almost as though the arch itself was speaking to him.

'Then you must pass beneath the arch of unknowing and walk the seeker's path,' it said.

At that moment something even more uncanny occurred. The plaque began to dissolve into mist. In fact the whole wall under the arch rapidly became a grey fog. Joshua's heart beat faster. Was he dying right now? Was this what it felt like to die? Did all the pictures just fade into nothing?

The fog began to clear and Joshua thought it must have been a trick of the light, or maybe he had banged his head when he came off his bike and his eyes were playing up. But what he saw next almost made his stomach turn a somersault. Instead of the wall with its plaque bearing his name, he could see a short passage, and beyond the passage, trees – trees all winter bare and drab looking under a sombre, grey sky that stretched into a mournful distance.

Joshua didn't know what to make of it. He glanced at the pillars of the archway and with a shudder he saw that the stone carvings were moving, the stone animals intertwining with each other as they climbed upwards towards the eagle – and surely the eagle's wings were slowly flapping. So shocked was he by all this that Joshua staggered back and stared around wildly just to make sure that the rest of the world was still normal.

Satisfied that he wasn't going mad or about to die, he approached the tomb again. The forest scene was still there, where the wall should have been. Tentatively, Joshua reached his hand forward. It passed into thin air. With a gasp, he withdrew it and felt it tingle the way it sometimes does when someone comes into the warm after being outside in the cold. Cautiously, he tried again and once more his hand passed through. Withdrawing his hand, Joshua stared at the scene before him. The bare branches were moving slightly in the wind. This was no photograph.

Then the penny seemed to drop. 'Hah, I know what this is. It's a hologram!' he exclaimed aloud. But why would anyone want to set up a hologram in a derelict graveyard in the first place? Then there was the matter of his name on the tomb? It was too much of a coincidence, and nobody knew where he was, so it couldn't be a practical joke.

Looking around him Joshua could see no sign of anything electronic like an infrared sensor that would trigger the illusion when somebody came near.

Puzzled, he made up his mind; he would try stepping right into the picture and see what happened.

Taking a deep breath, he strode forwards – and smacked his nose on the wall of the tomb! The winter scene had vanished and he was face to face with an unyielding green marble wall. Even the plaque bearing his name had disappeared.

'Weird,' he muttered, rubbing his nose. 'Very weird.'

Joshua was disappointed, and even more puzzled. Had he really just imagined it all?

Deep inside he hoped not, but there was nothing more to be done. So, being none the wiser, he heaved a sigh and started out for home. The tomb was a puzzle, a mystery all right, but now he had a more pressing matter on his mind. What was he going to tell his parents about the accident?

A lot of serious talking took place in the Brown household that evening. Telling his mum what had happened and then later on having to repeat it all to his dad was just about the worst thing Joshua had ever had to do in his life. Never had he felt so ashamed of himself, or so stupid. Over and over he asked himself the same question, 'Why?' And that was followed by the regrets. 'If only I hadn't done it. If only.'

Of course, if only Andrew hadn't wound him up...and if only Sophie hadn't called their mother... Both of them kept their heads down that evening and said very little, and nothing at all to Joshua. And when they spoke to their parents it was very quiet and respectful indeed.

'I'm disappointed in you, Joshua,' said Mr Brown. They sat alone, opposite each other in the front room, while Mrs Brown busied herself in the kitchen and the other two watched television in the back room. Meal time had been a tense affair and neither Joshua nor his parents had eaten much. 'You should know better at your age.'

Joshua nodded glumly.

'I mean, for crying out loud, what got into you? You know cycling isn't allowed in the park. That's bad enough, but you must have been racing like a lunatic not to stop in time.'

Joshua fiddled with his fingernails. 'I was annoyed with the other two,' he mumbled. 'They just got me wound up.'

Mr Brown huffed. 'That's all well and good, but you must learn to control yourself. Life's full of people winding other people up but you can't just go charging around like a madman because of it. You could have injured that baby and the mother, or worse. Then what would have happened? It doesn't bear thinking about.'

'Do you know if they're all right?' Joshua asked lifting his eyes.

'Thankfully yes. Your mother made enquiries,' Mr Brown answered.

'I'm very sorry, dad. I won't do it again,' Joshua ventured.

Although he had been very cross, Mr Brown was a kindly man and he was mostly relieved that no real harm had been done.

'Well, I hope not,' he said. 'But it's no use me just letting you off, is it? I'll see about getting your bike back from the warden but mum and I have decided as a punishment that you won't be allowed to ride it for the next six weeks. From what you've told me it'll need repairing, anyway. You will also write a letter of apology to the park warden, and to the mother. I've got the names and addresses. I will send her a cheque to cover any damages, but you will be paying that back out of your pocket money for a good long while. Is that fair and understood?

Gloomily, Joshua agreed.

Mr Brown sighed. 'Just be more careful in future, son. And for goodness sake grow up! Go on, off to bed with you. I've had enough.'

Unlike his sister Sophie, Joshua didn't often dream but on this night he did. It wasn't very pleasant. All he could see were cogs and wheels and bits of bike flying all over the place and a horrible sound of screeching metal filled the air. Then he heard a baby screaming and he was being chased by a mob of angry mothers, but the mothers turned into pieces of his bike and he was running for his life as bits of metal crashed all around him. With a cry he jerked awake and lay among the bedclothes, wishing that none of it had happened and wondering if he would ever really see his bike again.

Almost everyone knows that the best way to get rid of a nasty dream is to think of something else more pleasant. So, Joshua tried to imagine what it would be like to be on holiday. His mind drifted to long sandy beaches and adventure centres where you could abseil down rock faces and go white water rafting. At length, he began to doze off again. 'I fancy an adventure,' he yawned sleepily to himself. 'A proper one.' The image of an archway and a bleak forest beyond flashed into his mind, but before he knew it he was fast asleep.

*   *   *

High in the night sky, though many miles and many worlds distant, in the stark emptiness of the snow-covered mountains, a mighty white eagle felt a light tug in the wind. It was nothing more, but Arca, whose senses were tuned to the finest degree, knew that he had received a command. His time had also come, and from that moment he flew steadily south.

If Joshua Brown had but known it, the adventure really was about to begin.

*   *   *

Joshua woke in a surprisingly good mood the next morning. Maybe it was because the worst was over. He had told the truth and although his parents had been cross they had treated him fairly and he knew that his mum and dad would sort out any problems. The only thing he had to do was write his letters of apology. Mind you, he wasn't sure quite how to begin. 'Dear Madam, I'm sorry I crashed my bike into your buggy and might have hit your baby if he had been in it,' might be true but it didn't sound quite right somehow. Maybe his dad could help him.

His thoughts were interrupted by Sophie and Andrew

coming into his bedroom. Both had solemn expressions on their faces.

'We've come to say sorry,' Sophie explained.

'Yeah, sorry I wound you up and knocked your bike over,' said Andrew.

'S'alright,' Joshua answered. 'It was my own fault, really.'

'Yes, but we didn't help,' said Sophie. 'And I'm sorry your bike got ruined. That's really rotten luck.'

'And it was real mean of that park warden to confiscate it,' Andrew added.

Joshua shrugged his shoulders. 'Well, it's done now. I'll just have to get on with things.'

'Why don't you show us where it happened?' Andrew ventured.

Joshua flashed him a glance. 'What, so you can laugh?'

'Sometimes going back to the scene can help you get over it,' Sophie suggested. 'I read it somewhere. Anyway, we'd like to come with you.'

'Sorry, I didn't mean to sound ungrateful. Thanks. Yeah, let's do that.'

'And we'll leave our bikes here and walk,' said Sophie, giving Andrew a meaningful look.

An hour later, after they had all washed, dressed and eaten breakfast, they set out for the park. Joshua had put on a Manchester United sweatshirt and jeans, and though he had combed his brown hair his mother told him it still looked as though he had just got out of bed.

Sophie was wearing her favourite black trousers and a sea-green jacket over a World Wildlife Fund T-shirt. She had put her blonde hair into a ponytail and tied it with a poppy red hair band.

Andrew, the youngest of the three, strode along

wearing a denim jacket over a green check shirt and jeans, and as usual a cheeky grin. When they reached the park he tried out his latest joke on them: 'What do you call someone who kills bikes?

'Go on,' Joshua sighed.

'A cycle path!'

'Andrew!' Sophie exclaimed.

'What?'

'Duh! Not exactly tactful, considering what's just happened to Joshua!'

Joshua took a playful swipe at his brother. Andrew ducked and yelled sorry.

Before long, they reached the T-junction where the incident had taken place.

'You can still see the skid marks,' said Andrew, pointing. 'You must have been going at a billion miles an hour.'

'Well, more than ten, anyhow,' said Sarah sensibly.

'This is where I hit the buggy,' Joshua said. 'Look at those scratches.'

The three children spent the next ten minutes examining each tiny mark on the tarmac, discussing which bit had caused which mark.

'So, what did you do after that?' Sophie asked. ''Cos you didn't come straight home.'

Joshua didn't want to admit, even to his sister, that he had cried, so he said instead. 'Oh, I just went for a wander. You know, to chill down.'

Sophie nodded. She understood how he would have felt.

'There was something else, though,' Joshua said, suddenly bright with the memory. 'I found this really spooky place on the edge of the park – some old graveyard. Do you want to come and see it?'

Sophie and Andrew had no objections, so after walking for a while and taking a few wrong turnings, Joshua brought them to the iron fence.

'It's just a sleepy old graveyard,' Andrew observed. 'What's weird about that. Unless, of course, you come at midnight when there's a full moon and all the ghosts and ghoulies are holding a party on the gravestones!' he added with a laugh.

Joshua ignored his brother's attempt at humour and addressed Sophie instead.

'I came here yesterday,' he said. 'I found this old tomb and…well, you'll see.'

It took Joshua some minutes to find the green marble mausoleum again. Somehow it didn't seem to be in quite the same place as it was yesterday, and that puzzled him.

'There it is,' he said, pointing. 'I thought it was nearer than that.'

'Doesn't look very special,' Andrew observed as they approached the tomb.

'Wait until you see whose name's on it.'

All three crowded under the arch and looked at the black plaque on the wall with its gold lettering.

'See,' said Joshua, unable to prevent the catch in his voice. 'It's my name, Joshua Brown.'

His brother and sister were strangely silent. Then all at once they both said, 'No, it's not, it's mine!' And Andrew said 'Andrew Brown', and Sophie said 'Sophie Brown'.

'Don't be silly,' Joshua replied, looking perplexed. 'It says Joshua Brown.'

'But it doesn't,' Sophie insisted. 'It says my name!'

'No, it doesn't. It says mine!' Andrew exclaimed.

It took a few minutes of arguing before it fully

dawned on the three children that they really were each reading their own names, and for Joshua to realise that the date had changed as well. Sophie shuddered and went pale while Andrew simply stared hard at the writing, trying unsuccessfully to make the name change.

'I told you it was spooky, didn't I?' said Joshua. Then he added, 'There was something more,' and he told them about the vision of the winter forest that he had seen – though he didn't mention the voice.

'Well, it's not here now, is it?' said Andrew. 'I mean this name thing is really odd, but you must have been dreaming the other bit, or something.'

Joshua was just about to remonstrate with his younger brother when Sophie gripped his arm. She looked as white as a sheet and he could feel her trembling.

'Look!' she cried.

All three stared in amazement as the wall of the tomb misted over and once again the arch opened out into a short passage and a grey forest beyond.

'I told you,' Joshua whispered.

'Is it some kind of illusion, do you think?' Andrew asked. 'You know, the way they make things like whole jet fighters and elephants disappear on telly.'

'I thought it might be a hologram,' Joshua replied.'

'But that doesn't explain why we all see our own names,' said Sophie. 'I think it must be magic – except that nobody believes in real magic any more, do they?'

'You can put your hand into it. I tried that yesterday,' said Joshua. 'It kind of makes it tingle, so maybe there's electricity in it.'

Each one tried putting their arm into the scene as Joshua suggested and all agreed that it did make you tingle.

'If you can do it with an arm, you must be able to

walk right into it,' said Andrew.

'Tried that yesterday and I just walked into the wall,' Joshua replied.

Sophie had a faraway look in her eyes. She was a thoughtful girl who enjoyed watching waves beat on the seashore or the way the rain fell on her eyelashes. Everyone said she was a day dreamer, but she preferred to call it imagination, and said it stopped her getting bored in lessons. Her best teachers had the sense to tell her to write down her day dreams.

'I've got one of my feelings,' she said, and before the boys could say, 'You and your feelings!' which they often did, she explained.

'I…I think this is some kind of gateway in time, only it's not a game or anything like that. It's real and…and because we can read our names I…I think we're meant to go through the arch.'

'Yeah, right – but like I said, I tried it and it didn't work,' Joshua protested.

'Well, maybe we're meant to do it together,' Sophie replied. 'That's why we all see our own names.'

'D'you reckon it'd be safe?' Andrew asked.

'I don't know,' she answered frowning slightly. 'But I still think we should give it a try and see what happens.'

'There's something else,' said Joshua. 'I thought you'd laugh at me, or say I was crazy, but yesterday I thought I heard a voice.'

His brother and sister wanted to know where the voice had come from and what it sounded like, and especially what it said.

'I'm not quite sure,' Joshua answered, 'but it was something like you have to go through the arch and find the path.'

'Well, that's it,' said Sophie full of excitement. 'We've

got to do it, then.' She shivered in anticipation and added, 'But I feel a bit frightened, all the same.'

'We'll do it together,' Joshua decided. 'Come on, let's hold hands and step forwards – but watch out for your nose in case it doesn't work!'

But there was no blank wall this time and with one simple stride the three children crossed the threshold from their world and stepped into the unknown.

They found themselves standing in a dimly lit, arched passage, feeling slightly dizzy and tingling all over. Ahead of them stretched the mysterious dead forest and whatever mysteries it held in store for them.

'Let's go,' said Joshua as the tingling feeling wore off. Stumbling slightly, he led the way to the end of the passage.

They emerged from a bank in the side of a hill and found themselves at the head of a short flight of moss-covered stone steps. The steps looked ancient, as did the rickety handrail that ran down the left side.

Before venturing further they scanned the scene before them. They had entered a vast forest of ancient, grey trees whose winter bare branches reached up into a cold pale mist. Many other branches lay broken on the ground. The sour smell of decay hung in the dank air and all was silent. Lifeless – as still as death.

All of a sudden Sophie felt far less sure of herself.

'Wh-where are we?' she stuttered. 'It's like some kind of petrified forest. I don't think I like it after all. Maybe we should go back?'

'Just a minute,' said Joshua, trying to gather his wits. 'Let me think. You know what I think's happened? It's like what you said, Sophie. We've found a gateway in time. You know, like in science fiction when you go into a para...what-do-you-call-it?'

'Parallel universe,' prompted Sophie.

'That's it. One of those. Anyway,' he continued, 'if that's what's happened to us then we had best try and find out what it's all about.'

Andrew was all for it. 'Yeah, let's take a look round. But watch out for aliens or robots with death rays.'

Joshua nodded thoughtfully. 'Maybe it's just that we've gone back in time – or maybe forwards'

' We could still be in the same place, but centuries ago or…or centuries to come,' Sophie offered.

'Except that…except that things like that don't happen in real life, do they?' Joshua replied. 'There's got to be a better explanation. Come on, let's take a look round.'

They walked down the steps until they stood on the barren floor of the forest. Sophie was feeling less panicky. 'Well, I suppose…I suppose these things can happen,' she mused. 'I mean, why not? Everyone imagines it, so why can't it perhaps just be real?'

Joshua shook his head. 'Yeah, but I can imagine a…a…I know…an elephant playing a guitar on top of the school building, but that doesn't make it real,' he said.

Andrew laughed and said Joshua was nuts.'

Sophie waved her hands helplessly. 'Well, I don't really know. We're either dreaming it, or we're actually here, wherever here is,' she said. 'We'd better have a look round and see if there's anyone else. But let's be careful, just in case.'

They wrapped the red ribbon from Sophie's ponytail over a small branch of a nearby oak tree to help them find the entrance again. Andrew wished he had a laser gun but he had to make do with a broken stick and just pretend.

'There's hardly a sign of life anywhere,' Joshua noted. 'The forest is almost dead. Just a bit of moss and a few bushes growing here and there. I wonder what happened to it?'

'Mmm, it's not dead but, well, as though someone has taken all the life out of it.'

'Well, it must be dead then,' laughed Andrew.

'No, that's not what I mean. What I'm trying to say is...'

Before Sophie could explain there was a sudden rustling and crashing from the dead undergrowth nearby and, in a twinkling of an eye, the three children found themselves surrounded, not by aliens or robots, but by a gang of fierce-looking animals all armed with spears and clubs.

'One move and you die! Stay right where you are.' The speaker was an important looking stoat.

Joshua, Sophie and Andrew could not have moved even if they had tried. It's bad enough to find yourself where you did not, even in your wildest dreams, expect to be. But to be confronted by animals that are the same size as you and that speak, well, that is a bit too much. Robots might have made more sense.

Sophie screamed.

'W-what...!' Joshua spluttered.

Andrew looked wildly about him, trying to see if they could make a run for it.

The ring of animals closed in – rabbits, foxes, weasels, moles, squirrels. Their fierce eyes and bared teeth made it quite clear that they were far from friendly. And the prods and pricks that the children received were real enough to prove that this was no dream.

'Talking animals! What is this? Narnia or something?' Joshua gasped.

'D…don't be silly,' stuttered Sophie. 'Th…that's just a st…story. Anyway, there's no sn…snow.'

'I hope there isn't a witch, though,' said Andrew.

'Silence!' ordered the stoat. He flashed a look at the other animals. 'You know what to do. Tie them up and take them away,' he commanded.

At once, the animals swarmed over the children, pushing them to the ground. Sophie started to scream but a gag was thrust into her mouth. Rough ropes bound their hands behind their backs and, in spite of their frantic struggles, it seemed only a matter of seconds before they were all quite helpless. Quickly, they were dragged to their feet and, encouraged by the spears, were shoved along a narrow twisting pathway that led off into the barren undergrowth.

As they stumbled along, Joshua began to pull himself together. Wherever they were, and whether they had been brought here by science or by magic, one thing was clear – they had fallen into the hands of hostile creatures and they had to escape as soon as they could. That wasn't on at the moment, so he tried instead to keep track of the twists and turns and ups and downs, hoping that when they did escape they might find their way back to the passageway.

It proved impossible; many paths criss-crossed their route and often they would be forced to the left or to the right down yet another winding track through brambles and hawthorn bushes. Soon he was totally confused.

He noticed that the pace was hotting up and many of the animals were casting nervous glances over their shoulders as though expecting to be chased. Perhaps there was someone who would come to their rescue, Joshua thought, and this cheered him up a little. For one crazy moment he just wished they had their bikes with them.

The company was almost running by the time they reached the end of the trail and they came at last to a panting halt in a small clearing.

The children fought to get their breath through the smelly gags. If only they could speak!

The stoat, obviously in command, nodded to their closest captors and the three children were pushed forwards in the direction of a tall, imposing elm tree. At first, they couldn't see why. Then they noticed a dark hole near the roots. Sophie wondered if it somehow led back to their own world. Andrew thought it might be a prison. Prods from behind soon had all three crowded reluctantly in the entrance and staring into the gloom.

It was Joshua who saw them first. A pair of slant yellow eyes glowed out of the darkness and began to move towards them! Panic welled up inside him, and his mind filled with all kinds of nameless dreads about child-eating monsters. Maybe they really would die today. Sophie screamed into her gag and Andrew struggled for all he was worth. Wildly, they turned to run but were met squarely by a mass of sharp-pointed spears that would allow them no escape.

Slowly but surely the helpless children were driven backwards into the black hole, there to meet whatever unknown horror awaited them in its depths.

3
Mr and Mrs Trotter

'What do you want done with 'em, Aldred, sir?'

The owner of those slant yellow eyes spoke, and materialised into the form of a smart-looking fox. Andrew noticed that he was wearing body armour made of metal and leather. He realised for the first time that many of the other animals wore armour as well, though none of it could be described as a uniform. The fox also carried a bow and a quiver full of arrows.

'Are they spies? More of *her* work, eh!'

'That's right, Foxy,' Aldred the stoat replied. 'Caught them up by the old Passway.'

'Strange looking creatures, aren't they?'

'Hmm. Not like her usual work and not very strong either. We overpowered them with hardly a struggle,' the stoat explained.

Realising with relief that they were not about to be eaten alive Joshua tried to say something through his gag but it just came out as 'Mmmmffff.' He struggled to free his hands.

Andrew and Sophie stood side by side behind him. Glancing at each other they tried to reach each other's hands behind their backs to see if they could loosen the ropes that bound their wrists. However, a sharp smack on the wrists from one of the spears soon put paid to that idea.

'What weapons did they have, sir?' asked Foxy the guard.

'That's the odd thing, they've got none. Unless it's some secret magic we don't know about. That's why I want Trotter to see them,' Aldred replied.

'Very good, sir. I'll fetch him.'

The children were pushed through a door at the end of a short dark tunnel and found themselves standing in a small bare room that was lit from a window high up on one pale yellow wall. All the other animals had remained outside, with the exception of a hedgehog who continued to menace them with his fearsome looking bristles. The room appeared to be quite civilised and he hoped that this Trotter, whoever he was, would allow them to explain who they were.

They waited only a few moments before another door opened and in walked an ancient badger.

Andrew had done a project on badgers at school but he had never seen one like this. Trotter – at least, that's who he assumed the badger must be – wore a dark faded green jacket with an old red tartan scarf wrapped round his neck. A pair of wire-rimmed spectacles were perched on the end of his snout. He was obviously very old because even his black stripes were turning grey and he walked with a slight stoop as though he were very weary. Compared to the other animals Andrew thought the badger looked unimportant.

To his surprise, however, Aldred the stoat stepped forward smartly and saluted the badger with great respect.

'Strange spies, Trotter, sir. We caught them by the old Passway. Truth is, sir, I don't know quite what to make of them, so I brought them to you as soon as possible. What do you think she's up to this time?'

Sophie was squirming with frustration as she tried to free herself. Who was this 'she' that the animals didn't like? Was it a girl, or a woman? Or even another animal?

The badger stepped forward and peered at the children through his wire-rimmed spectacles. Sophie thought he had kind eyes. For about a minute, he looked them over, not saying a word. Then he spoke in a low voice.

'Loose their bonds and remove those gags.'

Aldred raised an eyebrow but much to Sophie's relief obeyed at once. She took a deep breath as the gag was removed and then began to rub her chafed wrists. Joshua stretched his arms with equal relief while Andrew waved his hands to get the circulation going. All three were full of questions and they gabbled one on top of the other.

'Who are you? Where is this place…?'

'What are we doing here? Why did you tie us…?'

'Who is this 'she'? How do you know we're not…?'

With a smile the badger held up a paw. Then, to the amazement of everyone in the room, he slowly went down on one knee before them.

'Children of Time Beyond Time, for that is who you are, is it not?' he asked gravely.

The children looked blankly at one another. The badger's words made no sense at all.

'My name is Trotter,' he continued. 'I bid you welcome to the Great Forest of Alamore in the world we know as Caris Meriac.'

'Allie Moor? Carries Merry Yak? Who…I mean, where on earth is that?' asked Andrew looking puzzled.

'I've got a horrible feeling it's not anywhere on earth,' Joshua muttered.

'You mean, we're on another planet?'

'I don't…I don't know what I mean. Not yet, anyway,' Joshua answered.

'Let's listen to what else he's got to say,' Sophie interrupted and she gave the badger her best sweet smile.

If Trotter the badger was confused by the children's response, he didn't show it.

'You have come as it is written,' he said. 'May Elmesh be praised! I ask you to forgive us for the rude welcome that we gave you, but these are perilous days, and we did not know the hour of your coming.' He wagged a fore claw knowingly. 'Nor would it have been wise for us to know, lest our enemy were to discover it. My guards were only doing their duty.'

Andrew sniffed and was about to say 'Huh!' but Sophie slapped him on the arm and gave him a warning look.

Before anybody else could speak, Aldred blurted out, 'But are you sure, sir? Are you really saying these creatures are on our side? That Elmesh has sent them?'

The badger's eyes twinkled. 'Of course. Did I not tell you that I had received indications of their coming and of what to look for?' He rose from his knees and turned to Joshua. 'Is it true that you are the Children of Time Beyond Time?'

Joshua found himself stammering. 'W-w-well, y-yes...maybe. I-I don't really know. We aren't usually called that – we're just people, kids, that's all. Listen, what is all this? Where are we? How is it you can speak? I don't understand what's happened to us. Is it all some kind of a dream?'

'And who is this enemy you keep on about,' Sophie added. 'She? Her?'

Trotter rumbled a deep laugh in his throat. 'Too many questions at once. And I thought you were coming with answers! Never mind, never mind. Elmesh has strange ways. I will answer your questions as best I can. But first, I think, a cup of nettle tea would be in order. You must come and meet Mrs Trotter. She will be most interested to see you.'

'Nettle tea!' Andrew exclaimed. 'It sounds horrible. It'll sting our mouths to death.'

'Shh, Andrew. Don't be rude,' Sophie scolded. 'I'm sure it'll be all right. Anyway, I've heard of people drinking it in...in our world.'

Andrew scowled but said nothing.

Sophie decided that she liked the badger. 'A cup of, um, nettle tea would be very nice,' she said, 'and we'd love to meet Mrs Trotter.'

With great politeness the badger ushered them through the door by which he had entered.

If the world had seemed strange up until now, for a moment at least it became almost normal. They found themselves standing in a delightful cottage room complete with gleaming brasses and glowing copper kettles, wooden beams and soft armchairs. A small log fire burned in the smoke-blackened fireplace and flowery curtains decorated the leaded windows. They had entered by a kind of back door into the badger's home.

'What a pretty house!' exclaimed Sophie. 'It's beautiful!'

'I'm glad you like it, my dear.' Mrs Trotter bustled in, wearing a frilly apron. 'You're very welcome to our house. That is, if you're not friends of *hers*.'

'My dear, may I introduce you to the Children of Time Beyond Time – um, people. They have come as I said.'

Rather quaintly, Mrs Trotter cocked her head to one side and gazed at the children in turn. 'My, my. Well, pleased to meet you, I'm sure, but is that the only name you have?' she enquired. 'It's quite a mouthful, my dears.'

The children took to her at once and Andrew replied cheerily, 'It's nice to meet you, too, Mrs T. Can I call you Mrs T – because you're going to make the tea, even if it is nettle tea, and it's the first letter of Trotter?

Mrs Trotter looked flustered for a moment. 'Well, yes, I suppose so. Never been called that before, but it...well, it doesn't really matter what you call me, I suppose.'

'I'm Andrew...Andrew Brown, and she's Sophie, and that's Joshua.'

Joshua and Sophie glowered at their younger brother because he was so annoying, but Mrs Trotter laughed. 'Andrew. I can see you and I will get on just fine.' She reached out a paw and shook his hand with mock solemnity and then turned to Joshua and Sophie. 'So you're called Joshua,' she said. 'And you look as though you've seen the most summers.'

Joshua mumbled something indistinct and shook her paw rather awkwardly.

'And...what was it...Sophie? That's a lovely name,' said Mrs Trotter as she shook Sophie's hand. 'Well, you are all welcome, that's for sure. And now I expect you would like that cup of tea,' she said. 'Make yourselves at home. Sit down, my dears.' She turned to Trotter. 'Look after them while I make the tea, husband – and don't be too serious with them!'

She bustled back to the kitchen as they flopped into the armchairs. Aldred joined them.

For a moment everyone sat in silence. Mr Trotter seemed unsure what to say next, so Joshua broke in. 'Um, I think we're all a bit confused,' he began. 'I mean, everything's happened...like...suddenly. We don't know how we got here, or where we are, and...well, you're animals but you talk and live in houses…'

'It's all a bit confusing,' Sophie explained.

'Yes, of course,' replied the badger settling himself more comfortably into an old sofa by the fireside. 'So, you do not know where you are, or why you are here?' He nodded. 'I suppose that's to be expected. Elmesh would have wanted your identity kept secret, but that is very secret: not even to tell the deliverers who they are!' He smiled to himself.

'Um, excuse me, but who is El…Elmesh?' interrupted Sophie.

'Elmesh, who is Elmesh?' exclaimed Trotter. He sat up with a blink of surprise that made his spectacles jump. 'You don't know? Elmesh just is. Without Elmesh there would be nothing, nothing at all. No sun, no stars, no Caris Meriac, not even the Great Forest of Alamore.' The badger shook his head in amazement. 'Nobody has told you that? Goodness gracious me! Yet, it is surely obvious that Elmesh has sent you!'

'But all we did was walk under an arch and along a passage,' said Andrew.

'Well, not quite,' Joshua interrupted.' 'I mean it was a path through a tomb!'

'Whatever. Anyway,' Andrew continued. 'We came out at the top of some steps and then your gang jumped us. I just don't get it. And what did you say this place was?'

'Ah, those steps and that entrance! There is something special about that place, you see. We call it the Passway. It is a doorway, though it is only open on very rare occasions, I believe.' He nodded sagely and looked at the three children in turn. 'You have entered the world of Caris Meriac, what the wise also call The Land Beyond The Far Places.'

'You mean, we're in some kind of fifth dimension,' said Andrew.

'Fifth dimension, eh?' Trotter answered with a smile. 'Well, maybe, but I think you will find there is a lot more to it than that.'

'We're not dead then...or dreaming?' Sophie queried. She had begun to wonder.

'My goodness me, no. Why should you ever think that?' Trotter chuckled. 'No, you'll probably feel more awake than ever once you grow used to things!'

Sophie smiled.

'You said we were to be deliverers,' said Joshua. 'What did you mean?'

Trotter's answer was delayed by the entry of Mrs Trotter laden with a tray of tea and cakes. Andrew's eyes lit up. He could see, and smell, fresh doughnuts and fruit buns and rock cakes and reckoned that he could even cope with nettle tea with a few of these inside him.

For a few minutes there was nothing but the clatter of cups and saucers and plates as everyone sorted themselves out and helped themselves to what they wanted. Once they were all served, Trotter said he would try to begin at the beginning.

'Years ago, before the troubles began, the Great Forest of Alamore was the most beautiful place imaginable,' he said. 'Birds sang in the trees, scented shrubs bloomed everywhere. The forest folk were free to go about as they pleased and there was plenty of food for everyone.' Trotter's eyes gazed into the distance.

'We were young then,' said Mrs Trotter. 'My, what great times we had! Not a care in the world.'

Trotter nodded and smiled at his wife. 'The secret lay in the Enchanted Glade. You see, Elmesh had gifted the forest with the Merestone and that was what made the place so magical.'

'What's the Merestone and where is this glade?' Joshua asked.

'Oh, we must take you there. It's wonderful, even now,' said Mrs Trotter.

'The Merestone is a special jewel of great size and power,' Trotter explained.

'Why, if you hurt yourself, just to go to the glade made you better,' said Mrs Trotter. 'I remember the time when I twisted one of my back paws so badly that I could hardly walk. I hobbled to the Enchanted Glade and as soon as I got within sight of the jewel the pain went. I actually scampered home.'

'And then there were those who sought wisdom and spent hours gazing at the Merestone and learning the ways of Elmesh,' said Trotter.

'Did you do that?' asked Sophie eagerly.

'Yes, I did, but as I say it seems a long time ago now, for, alas, all that has changed.' His face filled with sorrow as he spoke. 'A great tragedy fell upon us. *She* came one fateful day and stole the Merestone.'

'*She*? But who is she?' Sophie asked.

'Hagbane!' Aldred, who had been listening, spat the word out. 'Hagbane the Crone!'

At his words Sophie felt a chill run through her veins.

'Andrew's eyes were wide with wonder. 'Wow!' he gasped.

'Yes, Hagbane the Crone,' Trotter nodded. 'Stealing the Merestone was bad enough but then one day she returned to enslave the Great Forest and our happy days came to an end.'

'The forest began to wither and die; flowers ceased blooming and almost all the birds fled,' Aldred explained. 'Food has become scarce and the forest folk live in fear of their lives. That is why we have to defend ourselves.'

'Aldred is right,' said Trotter. 'She controls us from her castle and nobody can touch her while she holds the Merestone. We are almost helpless.' His shoulders sagged and the children could sense the sorrow of a brave creature fighting on but knowing he had lost the war.

'Well, I'm not afraid of any silly Crone, whatever she is. We'll just go and kick her door in and get your Merestone back!' Andrew declared stoutly. 'Anyway, what is a Crone? I bet she's just some silly old woman, like Mrs Clackey down the road.'

'Oh, shush, Andrew!' exclaimed Sophie. 'Listen.'

'Alas, I do not think it will be quite that simple,' Trotter continued, shaking his head. 'Yes, I do believe you will help deliver us from Hagbane's power, for it is written that it should be so, but you will find that she is a very dangerous enemy.'

'Many of our folk have tried and as a result now languish in her dungeons, or worse,' said Aldred.

'What's languish mean?' Andrew wanted to know.

'Well, if you were languishing in prison you would be slowly losing hope and rotting away, like hanging in chains with no food,' Joshua explained.

Andrew went very quiet at the thought of no food. Perhaps tackling a Crone wouldn't be so easy after all.

'It's not just the troops that she has,' said Aldred. 'It's something worse. I don't know how to explain it but she throws a shadow over your inside. You just want to give up and die.'

'Where do we fit into all this?' Joshua cried. 'Because we seem to be the most unlikely Crone fighters I can think of – whatever Andrew says.'

Andrew glared at him but said nothing. This Hagbane creature was sounding worse than he had thought and he wished he had kept his mouth shut.

In answer to his question the badger ushered them out of their armchairs and into another room filled with dusty brown books and parchments.

'I have studied the ways of Elmesh all my life,' he said. 'Many hours I have sat in the Enchanted Glade and gazed into the pool that we call Elmere. Often I have looked upon the light of Elrilion as it reflected in the water.' Seeing their puzzled frowns, he explained. 'Elrilion is Elmesh's special star. When you see it rise you'll understand why.'

Aldred took up the tale. 'Trotter was entrusted with the ancient scrolls of the Great Forest of Alamore,' he said proudly. 'We recognise him as the one true lore-master among the forest-folk.'

The children looked at the old badger with renewed respect.

'Five nights ago I had a vision in my sleep in which I saw your faces by the light of Elrilion,' Trotter explained. 'I knew then that the time had come for matters to change. You see, many years ago a wise elder brought a revelation to our people.'

'A revelation? What's that?' Sophie asked.

'It's a mystery revealed,' Trotter replied. 'And among other things it referred to you.'

Seeing their mouths hanging open in amazement, he smiled. 'I suppose you want to see what it says.'

'Yes, please!' chorused the children.

Trotter showed them across to an old-fashioned and dusty desk piled with brown covered books and parchments. After a few moments of searching he selected an old yellowed parchment covered in strange symbols.

'It is written in an ancient script but I will translate it roughly for you,' he explained. Then, adjusting his spectacles on the end of his snout and clearing his throat, he began to read:

Children come from time beyond time,
And then the Merestone will mend;
To judge the dark Crone's evil crime,
Passway steps they descend.

True the king who comes to his throne,
Through a path of fire and pain;
But let him not struggle alone;
Together his crown we'll gain.

Rise up and take heart for the fight,
We must set the forest free;
Dispelling the dark with the light;
Giving life to fur and tree!

'I confess I do not understand more than a part of this, especially the bit about a true king, but it is obvious that you have come, and we must start from there.'

'But are you sure it's really us it's talking about?' Joshua asked.

'You might be mistaken? After all, we're only ordinary children,' Sophie added. She was beginning to wish they had never gone to the tomb in the first place.

'We've no magic powers or weapons, or...or anything,' said Andrew. 'What can we do against this horrible Crone creature?'

Trotter looked each one of them straight in the eye.

'Elmesh does not deceive. It is you, and inside I believe you know that it is so.' He spoke with such gravity that Joshua felt he could only nod in agreement. Sophie and Andrew, in spite of their misgivings, found their heads nodding, too.

'As for weapons, I do have one that I can give you,' smiled the badger.

As he spoke, he unlocked a small chest by the side of the desk and from it drew what looked like a large powder compact covered in green tarnish. He handled the object with great reverence. 'This is Gilmere, mighty mirror of the Merestone. My father, Rufus the Strong, entrusted it to me. I have kept it for this day.'

He looked at each of the children in turn.

'You are the eldest, Joshua, so I guess I should give it to you,' he said at last, as though not quite sure.

If Sophie felt that the mirror should have been given to her instead she said nothing but when she caught just a trace of smugness on Joshua's face her heart was filled with misgivings.

Trotter handed the object to Joshua who took it gingerly. 'What do we do with it and how will it help us?' he enquired.

'If you press the clasp it will spring open and let forth its secret. But do point it away from us all, and use it wisely.'

Joshua held the mirror in the palm of his hand and did as he was instructed. The lid flipped open, releasing a blaze of dazzling light that filled the room with a terrible but wonderful radiance.

Joshua's ears were filled with the whine of a powerful motorbike. He was astride a machine made of liquid fire and hurtling along a vast desert road. The speedometer told him he was doing three hundred miles an hour.

There were bikes ahead of him and he was closing fast. Hardly aware of what he was doing his finger closed on a button. With a buzz like an angry bee, bolts of laser fire shot from the fiery frame and zapped those in front of him, blasting them out of his way. He gritted his teeth and wound up his speed even higher.

Andrew felt his stomach lurch and then found himself riding a wild roller-coaster of sparkling golden fire on tracks of shimmering silver laser beams. He could feel his hair streaming out behind him and crackling with electricity as he swooped up and down and side to side. Every nerve in his body seemed to tingle with fire.

Everything began to spin for Sophie. The cottage room disappeared and in its place appeared fiery angels spinning flying webs of rainbow coloured jewels all around her. She shielded her eyes against the power of the light. So dizzying was the sight that it was something of a relief when Joshua snapped the lid shut.

All three children felt wobbly at the knees and reached for items of furniture around them just to steady themselves as the light faded away and their senses returned to normal.

'Wow, impressive! What is it?' Joshua gasped.

'Nobody really knows,' said Trotter who, like Mrs Trotter and Aldred, was removing his paws from his eyes. 'We believe the mirror was formed in Elmere by the hand of Elmesh.'

'Elmere – that's the pool in the..the Enchanted Glade, isn't it?' said Joshua.

Trotter nodded.

'I've always thought the mirror is a shard of the Merestone,' said Mrs Trotter.

'The only thing we do know is that it has captured some of the light of the Merestone,' Trotter said.

'Although it has not the power of the jewel itself, we believe it will still serve those who use it rightly in the battle against evil.'

'Why didn't Hagbane steal this, too?' asked Andrew.

'Because she doesn't know of its existence,' Trotter replied. 'My father gave it to me on his deathbed and we have kept it hidden ever since.'

'You could have used it yourself,' Sophie suggested.

Trotter shook his head. 'A weapon such as this is not for the likes of us forest folk. We are peace loving and don't willingly take to arms. This would be a dangerous thing in our hands and in the end we might even be tempted to use it against our own kind.'

'Besides which we felt the time for its use was when the prophecy began to be fulfilled,' Aldred added.

'And now we've turned up and it's all starting to happen, I suppose,' said Joshua.

'Use it carefully, won't you,' said Trotter. 'Always remember that the power belongs to Elmesh and not to you. You must respect that fact.'

The children gazed in awe at the innocent looking object in Joshua's hand.

'Thank you for trusting us, Mr Trotter,' whispered Sophie. 'We'll do our best to look after it, and use it wisely.' She looked at her brothers, but before they could agree a bloodcurdling shriek rent the air and struck a chill to the marrow of their bones. The next instant, the door crashed open and in stumbled Foxy.

'It's Hagbane!' he gasped. 'She's down the path and she's caught Sam Squirrel. I think she's killing him!'

4
Captured!

The shock of hearing such a scream followed by Foxy's dramatic entry left everyone stunned. It was Joshua who snapped out of it first.

'Come on,' he cried. 'Let's try and stop her.'

Sophie tried to shout wait, but before she or anyone else could protest he was out of the door, urging Foxy to show the way, and rapidly followed by Aldred the stoat. Andrew and Sophie glanced at each other then made for the door themselves. Trotter followed more slowly, looking extremely worried.

'Which way?' Andrew cried as they burst from the cottage.

'Not sure,' Sophie gasped, looking around wildly. 'No... yes...I mean...his way. Come on!'

Joshua, Foxy and Aldred were out of sight but Sophie and Andrew sprinted down the winding path in hot pursuit. Trotter lumbered along behind them just as fast as he could.

Running hard, Sophie and Andrew neared a rocky outcrop where the path swept out of sight. Sophie slowed and motioned Andrew to do the same. She could hear the sounds of a struggle just ahead.

Moments later and panting heavily, Trotter caught up with them.

'Hide!' he growled. 'Whatever you do don't let her see you.' With that he shoved them off the path and behind the rocks and indicated that they should follow him as quietly as possible.

Keeping well hidden, the badger led Sophie and Andrew around the outcrop to a place where they were within sight of the disturbance.

Sophie stifled a gasp. A squirrel was hanging in mid-air and struggling for all he was worth in what seemed to be an invisible grip. She stared, horrified by the sight of his bulging eyes and the choking sounds that came from his mouth. With an effort she tore her eyes away. Then she looked again.

A vague shape began to materialise; in the middle of the path appeared a shadowy twisted figure whose bony fingers clutched the squirrel about his throat. Sophie stared with horror as the vile creature took shape before her: the long black cloak that seemed like darkness itself, the greasy grey hair tumbling wildly about her shoulders, the cruel eyes and long, distorted nose covered in warts, and the mouth twisted in a snarl of hatred. A stench of evil hung in the air around her, and it felt icy cold. Worst of all, Sophie seemed able almost to see through her, as though the creature wasn't quite solid.

She had come face to face with the Crone – and so had Joshua. He stood panting alongside Foxy and Aldred, mesmerised by the sight.

The Crone glared at him and her hard eyes glinted red. She dropped the squirrel to the ground where he lay whimpering in a limp bundle of fur at her feet.

'Well, what have we here?' she snarled. 'A new friend of these pathetic subjects of mine? Or what? And how many?'

She flashed a long black rod from the folds of her cloak.

Foxy reached for his bow and Aldred went to draw his sword, but they were too late. There was a blinding flash and a cloud of smoke. When it cleared the two animals found themselves frozen to the spot. Totally paralysed, they could only watch in dread as the Crone advanced upon them.

But not Joshua.

'Hello,' he said.

For Joshua Brown was seeing differently from everyone else. What he saw was not an ugly crone but the most beautiful woman he had ever set eyes upon. She had long auburn hair that cascaded over a dress of finest silver lace. Her almond eyes were dark and her full lips ruby red.

With a subtle smile she beckoned to Joshua come closer.

The others watched, horrified and helpless as the hypnotised Joshua was drawn towards the horrible darkness of Hagbane. Sophie tried to cry out from her hiding place, but Trotter gripped her firmly with his paw and motioned her to keep silent.

Hagbane cast a glance to her right hand and Joshua's eyes followed her gaze. His face broke into a smile of pleasure, for there he saw her hand resting on the finest mountain bike he had ever seen. It was brand spanking new and gleaming with chrome and bright red and blue paint.

'Yes, it's all yours,' she said in a voice that was husky with invitation.

Eagerly, he rushed forwards with his eyes now riveted on the bike.

'It...it's got everything,' he gasped with enthusiasm. 'All alloy frame, triple chain set and...and front and rear suspension. Yes, 21-speed grip shift, V-type brakes

– it's all there.'

Thinking of nothing else, he reached eagerly for the handlebars and, as he did so, his fingers let slip the precious mirror, Gilmere.

The Crone glanced to where it had fallen on the path and sneered. Then, with a cackling laugh, she ground the mirror beneath the heel of her shoe. In spite of her shadowiness her foot proved solid enough and the onlookers heard the splintering of a thousand shards of glass. Poor Trotter felt his heart break at the sound. The fight was over before it had even started.

Taking Joshua's hand in her own, Hagbane whispered, 'Come with me.' Then she led him away, mesmerised, into the depths of the Great Forest and in what the animals knew only too well was the direction of her own castle. As he walked hand in hand with Hagbane he held his other hand at an angle, just as though he were wheeling a bike. Yet, as the others could see all too clearly, no such machine existed. It was all in his own imagination.

As soon as Hagbane and Joshua were out of sight Trotter and Sophie and Andrew rushed from their hiding place and tried to revive Sam Squirrel and his would-be rescuers. As the paralysis began to wear off, their limbs regained movement. They found that they could speak again and the full horror of what had happened began to sink in.

Trotter groaned. 'Oh dear, dear me. How dreadful this is! If only he had used Gilmere wisely instead of rushing ahead like that. Now everything is lost and ruined.' He sat down on the ground, a heap of despair, his hopes as shattered as the pieces of mirror that lay at his feet.

'That's not fair' Andrew whispered to Sophie. 'How was Josh to know?'

Sophie took a deep breath and sighed glumly. If only Trotter had given the mirror to her, she thought.

Aldred and Foxy seemed at a loss as to what to do.

At last Aldred went across to where Trotter sat and breaking the silence with a polite cough said, 'Shall I round up a party to go after them, sir?'

The stoat's tone of voice said it all – it was hopeless. Trotter shook his grey head slowly.

'No, that will not do. You will never catch her now and it would harm the boy in any case. No, let me think for a moment.'

Sophie, though she felt sick with worry for her elder brother, went across and stooped down beside the badger. She put her arm gently around him.

'Come on, Mr Trotter. Don't give up,' she said. 'I'm sure there's an answer. I mean, you said that El...um, Elmesh has sent us, so maybe somehow this is all meant to happen as well. I suppose.'

Trotter looked up into her face and smiled.

'Anyway, somehow we've got to get Joshua back,' she added fiercely. 'We've just got to.'

He patted her hand. 'Yes, of course we must and we will if it's at all possible. Silly me. I just felt so taken aback by the turn of events. So excited to see you and then crushed by...by all this. I'm getting old, my dear. Maybe I'm losing my touch. You do understand, don't you?'

Sophie smiled and kissed the old badger, suddenly feeling she loved him.

He rose onto his hind paws.

'I know Hagbane well enough; she isn't going to kill Joshua, otherwise she could have done so at once. My guess is that she will keep him as a hostage, to find out more about him, and that gives us a little time to make some plans.'

His eyes turned to the smashed mirror and he made a decision. 'First of all, we must gather up every fragment of the mirror, for tonight we shall need it all.'

He performed this task himself, placing each piece with care into a red spotted handkerchief that he drew from the pocket of his jacket.

Aldred and Foxy tended to poor Sam Squirrel. Fortunately, they had reached him just in time and he seemed to be making a quick recovery.

'Sh…she just appeared from nowhere and grabbed me,' he gasped. 'I don't know why. I wasn't doing anything.'

Grim-faced, Aldred looked across to Sophie and Andrew.

'It appears to have been a deliberate decoy to get us here,' he growled. 'I think she knew of your coming.' The stoat's eyes narrowed suspiciously and Sophie and Andrew knew at once that he did not trust them. That, and the possibility that Hagbane could read the signs too – that she could know – made them feel very uncomfortable.

Sophie shivered, realising that it was growing dark.

'Can we go back to your house, please?' she asked quietly.

Trotter glanced at the dying sun and the lengthening shadows of the gaunt trees. He nodded, seeming to understand how the children felt.

It was almost dark by the time they reached the cottage door and already the first stars were appearing. Trotter stopped and pointed with his paw to where there was a gap between the treetops. A bright star lay just above the horizon glittering like a globule of molten silver. The sight of it brought an unexpected trickle of hope into Sophie's heart.

'Elrilion has risen,' whispered Trotter. 'All will be well, you'll see.'

* * *

High in an empty mountain pass, Prince Oswain saw that same star and was glad.

For several days he had trudged through the foothills of the Cadaelin range of mountains until he had begun to climb a high pass known as the Dragon's Claw. Once he made it through to the other side he knew he would be in sight of the Great Forest of Alamore.

It was then that the blizzard had struck. Visibility was reduced to zero as the snow beat against his face and the line between sky and mountain disappeared in a complete whiteout. Fierce winds seemed intent on tearing him from his path and dashing him on the rocks far below. Before long he was struggling knee deep in snow.

Night fell, but still he battled on.

'I can't give up now. I mustn't give up,' he muttered to himself.

He reminded himself over and over of his dream as he struggled on. Other forces might want to turn him back, but this was his destiny. Gritting his teeth, he yelled defiance at the wind and pressed on.

Almost faint with exhaustion, he came through the storm at last. Now, high up in the cold, clear, air he saw sky again – and Elmesh's star, Elrilion.

Beneath its light he made his crude camp. It was simply a blanket in the lee of an overhanging rock, and a far cry from the comforts of home, but it would do. Oswain was tough and well trained in the rugged skills of outdoor life.

As he lay, drifting into sleep, he recalled his departure from the palace. The king and queen had not questioned his going, or the time or the way, for it had long been known that he should.

As long as he could remember, Oswain had been taught about a journey he must one day make – a journey
that would take him away from the comforts of the palace. He was to perform a special mission, though no one could tell him quite what it was. He remembered as a child asking his teacher about it.

'All in good time. All in good time,' he was told. Oswain smiled at the memory. He had asked the same question year after year, and always received the same answer. But now, after twenty-one years, it seemed the time had come at last.

When he set out, his father, King Argil, had laid a firm hand on his shoulder.

'Be brave, son,' he said. 'And don't forget to send word when the task is done.'

His mother, Queen Talisanna, had gazed steadily into his eyes, her own grey eyes serious.

'Elmesh go with you, my son,' she murmured. 'Let your heart be strong, for I see not only enemies around you, but a battle that will take place within you. I pray and trust that you will conquer both.'

Then, with a quick kiss for his little sister, Princess Alena, he had left the security of the city of Castelfion with as little fuss as a man going about his daily duties.

With a yawn he settled for the night. Tomorrow he would take the track down to the Waste Plains that he must cross before reaching the forest.

*   *   *

'Come in. Come in, my dears. What a to-do. Dearie me. Anyway moping's no use. Sophie, come and help me in the kitchen.'

Mrs Trotter was one of those extremely sensible folk who know just the right thing to do when they are worried. So, when she heard what had happened she didn't stand around wringing her hands. Instead, she stoked up the fire, put the kettle on and enlisted Sophie to help her prepare something to eat.

'As for you, my husband, get these good folk comfortable. And don't look so gloomy or you'll curdle the milk!'

Trotter gave his wife a wan smile and ushered everyone into the living room.

Ten minutes later, instead of everyone pacing the room and eaten up with anxiety, they found themselves sitting by a cosy fire taking their fill of nettle tea and crumpets and feeling a whole lot better.

Trotter especially was back to his old self.

'Before we attempt anything else,' he declared, 'we must have Gilmere repaired. It was the only real weapon that we had.'

'That's more like it, dear,' said Mrs Trotter, nodding her approval.

'But I thought it was too badly smashed to be mended,' said Andrew through a mouthful of crumpet. 'How could anyone fix that mess?' He indicated the pile of twisted metal and shattered glass in Trotter's handkerchief. 'I think I'd just throw it away.'

'Young man,' replied Trotter, 'you will learn one day that when a work of art is broken it should be returned to its creator. He will do with it what he can. He may decide it is beyond repair and scrap it, or else he may remake it; but that should be his decision, not yours or mine.' He smiled at Andrew's glum face. 'We shall return the mirror to Elmesh and hope that it will be repaired.' He glanced at the others. 'If you are ready, I will take you to the Enchanted Glade.'

'I'll stay behind and look after the house,' said Mrs Trotter. 'Folks will be wanting to know what's going on, so I'll give them the latest news.'

'I'll lead the way then,' said Trotter. 'Aldred you bring up the rear and keep your eyes open for danger.'

Andrew noticed that Aldred was carrying his short sword at the ready.

It was by now quite dark and Sophie and Andrew's eyes, not being as keen as those of the animals, were as good as useless as they stumbled blindly along the twisting path.

'Ouch! That's the second time I've twisted my ankle,' Sophie exclaimed. She hobbled for a few steps before the pain eased.

It was only when they came to an occasional clearing that they managed to make out the shadowy shapes of the trees but it told the children nothing.

Andrew was feeling tired. 'How much further do you reckon it is?' he asked his sister.

'I've no idea,' she answered. 'It feels like we've gone miles but it's all this twisting and turning. We must be very deep into the forest.'

'I hope it's not much further,' said Andrew. 'My head's feeling funny.'

'Do you want to hold my hand?' Sophie offered.

'No, s'alright,' he said.

Sophie sniffed the air. 'I can smell something. It…it's like scent. Flowers…and…and like the fruit counter at the supermarket. It's sweetish,' she said.

Andrew breathed in and agreed. 'But I thought this place was all dead?' he said.

'The word's petrified, I think,' Sophie replied. 'You have petrified forests in our world. Anyway, it doesn't smell like that here.'

At that moment, the little group broke from the undergrowth and came into the pale light of a starry night. Before them loomed a mass of dark rock outlined against the night sky.

'We have arrived,' Trotter announced. 'Welcome to the Enchanted Glade.'

The air around tingled with life and mystery. Now there was no mistaking the sweet and exotic tropical scents that carried on a warm breeze. It was so different from the rest of the forest with its sour gloomy mosses and dormant branches? Here everything seemed so wonderfully alive.

Trotter led them through a narrow pass between two tall stones. Before Sophie and Andrew's wondering gaze there lay stretched out before them under the starlit sky a lush grove filled with a vast array of plants whose night-muted blues and greens spread in all directions.

'Wow, magic!' Andrew gasped.

Sophie was entranced.

Slowly, they entered the glade.

'How come this place is still alive?' Andrew wanted to know.

'That's because Hagbane can't find it,' Aldred explained. Andrew noticed that the stoat had sheathed his sword.

'Why not? I thought Hagbane had come here to steal the Mere...'

'Merestone,' Sophie prompted.

'True enough,' said Aldred. 'The thing is, since then a special protection has fallen on the glade.' He laughed. 'Whenever she tries to find it she just goes round in circles.'

'This place is the source, you see,' Trotter cut in. 'That is why things still grow here as in the days of the elders. Hagbane's magic just cannot stop it.'

Sophie nodded. She felt glad that there were some things the Crone couldn't do.

'Come now. I will take you to Elmere itself,' said Trotter.

Eagerly, they followed the badger into the depths of the glade.

Over to one side they saw a high, overhanging rock covered in grey-green moss. Trotter indicated that they should make their way towards it. Beneath the rock they found a stone shelf in which was set an oval pool about a metre across. The children's wonder at the glade and their awareness of its magic grew stronger and stronger as they drew near to it.

Andrew was grinning to himself and Sophie felt like laughing out loud.

'What a wonderful place,' she exclaimed. 'I feel so happy here, I could burst.'

'Me, too,' said Andrew, nodding as he took in the scene.

From the overhanging rock droplets of water formed themselves like pearls and fell one by one, with a bright *plip* into the pool below. Yet no dewdrop glistening in the morning sun could match these droplets for silvery brilliance. Each one, when it fell, glowed as if the light of Elrilion itself had been trapped within it. Luminous shadows from these watery jewels flickered and darted about the glade, and the water shone with their captured light.

Slowly, the two children advanced and peered into the pool. Their faces were pale and ghostlike in its limpid light. Awe-struck, they said nothing.

'This is Elmere, the Star Pool, beside which the Merestone once lay,' whispered Trotter. 'Alas, the Merestone is no more, but the pool still captures Elrilion's fire, as you can see.'

'It's just wonderful,' Sophie breathed.

'This is also the origin of the mirror,' said Trotter. 'Remember what I said, Andrew. We must trust that what was created here can be repaired. Aldred, pass me the pieces, if you will.'

The stoat obliged and, with great reverence, Trotter unfolded his red spotted handkerchief to reveal the fragments of the mirror.

'Come closer, Andrew,' said Trotter. 'Why don't you drop the pieces into the pool?'

'Go on, Andy,' Sophie urged.

Andrew approached the old badger. He could smell the animal warmth of Trotter's fur, and behind the badger's spectacles he could sense a deep and ancient wisdom. Earth and rock, and tree and root, starlit skies and flowing streams – and things far older still. It made Andrew feel very young but at the same time as though his life really mattered.

Gingerly, he took the handkerchief with its precious contents and laid it on the rock beside the pool. Feeling he was doing something very special, one by one Andrew dropped the broken pieces of Gilmere into the water. A crackling sound, like the breaking of ice, accompanied his action and blue flashes of light flickered in the depths of the pool.

'There, it is done,' said Trotter when the last piece was gone. 'That is all we can do here for tonight. But back at

61

home we must have a proper council of war to determine our best course.' The badger spoke with fresh resolution, his eyes sparkling behind his spectacles.

Sophie and Andrew shared the feeling, and, though reluctant to leave Elmere, they were almost dancing with excitement as they retraced their steps to Trotter's house. This time the children had no difficulty in seeing their way, even on the darkest stretches of the path.

5
Fumble, Mumble and Grumble

Back inside the cottage they found a weasel awaiting them. Like Aldred he wore light armour made of leather and metal.

'This is Stiggle,' Trotter announced to Sophie and Andrew. 'He is Aldred's second-in-command.'

'I came as soon as I heard the news, sir. Mrs Trotter has filled me in on all the details,' said the weasel.

'We need a council of war,' Trotter said decisively.

Andrew stifled a yawn. It had been a long day and he felt like dozing off but no one was prepared to consider sleep just yet. Late as the evening was, the six were soon huddled together around the fire, drinking steaming mugs of cocoa.

'It seems to me,' Trotter began, 'that our first object must be to rescue Joshua from Hagbane's clutches. To do that we must discover his precise whereabouts in the castle dungeons, for that is where she will have taken him.'

'That's assuming he's still alive,' interjected Aldred.

Trotter nodded. 'True enough. You may be correct in thinking that somehow Hagbane knew of the children's coming. If so, you may be sure that she is hatching some evil plan, using Joshua as a hostage.'

'Then no doubt she will question him thoroughly,' said Stiggle the weasel. 'Now, this Joshua may be strong-willed but few can hide anything for long once

Hagbane has them in her grip.'

'That is why our rescue attempt needs to be made soon,' said Trotter.

'Oh, this is just too awful,' Sophie cried. 'To think of that horrible old Crone hurting my brother. It's evil! Can't we do something *now*? I mean, she may be questioning him and doing all sorts of terrible things. Oh, *please*, let's not just sit here talking! I want to go and get him out.'

Aldred held up a paw. 'It's not as simple as that, Sophie. For one thing, the castle is heavily guarded by Grogs and Grims, and just to charge the walls would be fatal.'

'Grogs and Grims?' questioned Sophie and Andrew in unison.

Stiggle nodded. 'Most of our folk are scared even to go near the place, let alone inside.'

Aldred agreed. 'No, we must use our cunning and trust that Joshua is all right, at least for the moment. Assuming that's all there is to it,' he added with a knowing glance in Trotter's direction.

'I think you're being very unfair not trusting us,' exclaimed Sophie, who had noticed his look. 'I mean, do you really think that we're on her side or something?'

'I'm just a soldier,' Aldred snapped. 'All I know is that you turned up out of the blue and then your brother went off with Hagbane. And our only good weapon is ruined because of him.'

Trotter frowned and Sophie was just about to have a go at Aldred when her brother intervened. 'Leave it, Sophie,' he said. 'It won't do any good. We've got to help Joshua, and I want to do something tonight. It's no use arguing about whose side we're really on.'

Sophie huffed and folded her arms, glowering from

beneath her lowered brows. She hated it when people didn't think she was telling the truth.

Stiggle the weasel coughed politely. 'I believe there are three forest-folk who could discover Joshua's whereabouts for us. They could pass the word to him not to lose hope.'

All eyes turned on Stiggle.

'Who are they, Stiggle?' Trotter queried.

'Why, three who are small enough to escape the guard's notice, sharp enough to find their way in and stupid enough not to be afraid. I'm thinking of Fumble, Mumble and Grumble,' the weasel answered.

'Not those incompetent mice! You really must be joking,' exclaimed Aldred. 'Why, they can't even find their way out of their own nest without making a mess of it. Quite useless as fighting troops. I remember the time when...'

'Hold on Aldred,' interrupted Trotter. 'Stiggle's idea is not bad. Unless, of course you have a better one.'

Aldred thought for a moment, 'No, I don't,' he admitted. 'But let's face it, it's a bit risky, sir.'

'Risky or not, we've got to take a chance if we are to reach Joshua at all,' Trotter insisted. 'If we are to succeed, any rescue attempt will have to be made without a hitch and that means we must know where he is, and he must expect us. As far as I can see these three mice are our best hope.'

Aldred agreed with some reluctance, while Sophie and Andrew were just glad that something was being done. So it was decided that Stiggle should fetch the three mice.

*   *   *

The spell that Hagbane had cast over Joshua wore off within sight of her castle and he came to his senses with a start of horror as the vision of loveliness transformed itself into the vile form of the Crone. He realised, too, that there was no shiny mountain bike.

Instead, his arms were pinioned to his sides in the painful grip of two foul creatures with olive green, reptilian skin and vicious-looking teeth.

'Do you like my Grogs then?' Hagbane cackled. 'Nice creatures, aren't they?' She laughed at his plight as she strode on ahead of her captive. 'Come on, keep him moving,' she ordered.

Joshua felt sick from the stench of his captors and couldn't bring himself even to look at their faces. His heart sank even lower when he saw the gaunt stone fortress with its tall turrets and grim battlements. He could see at once that this was no pretty fairy castle but a place of dread where even the dark slit windows seemed to have eyes.

The Grogs dragged him under a gloomy archway and a massive, iron-studded oak door swung noiselessly open at Hagbane's command, though no doorkeeper could be seen. Joshua shuddered. He had little time to take in his surroundings. His captors marched him swiftly across an open courtyard and into a large bare room, where he was flung to the floor like a rag doll.

Slowly, he lifted his eyes. He could taste blood where he had bitten his lip. The evil Crone towered above him and her presence filled him with dread. Worse, she was not quite solid, like a huge dark and brooding ghost, constantly changing shape before his eyes.

'So, what strange creature do we have here!' she grated. 'Who are you? What is your name, man-child? Answer me now, or I'll make life very uncomfortable for you.'

'Please, my name is Joshua Brown,' he replied, thinking that it would be best to tell her the truth. 'I don't really know what I'm doing here, except that I came in through a passage and down some steps.'

At this the Crone's eyes gleamed. 'The old Passway, eh? I have heard tell of this, and I do not like it one little bit. Nor do I believe you are telling me all you know. Who sent you? Why have you come to the Great Forest – into my domain? Eh? Answer me now!'

'Well, nobody sent us, as far as I know...' began Joshua, feeling afraid, for he knew his answer would displease the Crone.

'Us? There are more of you?' she demanded.

'Me. I mean, me,' Peter replied hastily.

'Liar!' she spat, and she kicked him hard in the ribs with her pointed shoe. Joshua gasped with the pain and tears came to his eyes.

'Please, it's the truth. I don't know how I got into this. All I know is what Trotter has...has told me.' His mouth dropped in dismay as he realised that he had said too much.

'So there is more? I thought so,' she grimaced. 'What has that meddling old fool of a badger been up to this time?'

But Joshua had made up his mind. He would not betray his friends, let alone his brother and sister. He closed his mouth firmly and stared at the floor.

'Stubborn, eh?' the Crone snarled. 'Well, if you want to do it the hard way, that's fine by me. I can wait.' She snapped her fingers. 'Guards, take him away! A night in the dungeons will loosen your tongue – and if it doesn't, I have other, more painful ways. Think about it carefully, Joshua Brown. You will be chained up without food or water until you decide to speak.'

67

The Grogs dragged him down a steep flight of stone stairs into an underground dungeon. One of them lit a lantern, and then they propelled him along a foul-smelling corridor. In the flickering light he saw many wretched animals caged up and some groaned as he passed.

His guards pushed him into a grimy cell and tied his wrists tightly to an iron ring set in the wall above his head so that he was stretched up on tiptoe. The door slammed shut with a dull clang and Joshua was left alone in the darkness. His arms were already beginning to ache as the first wave of despair swept over him.

* * *

'Get out of my way, you great drip!'

The speaker was Grumble and that was how everyone knew that the three mice had arrived in the Trotter's front room. Grumble was addressing Fumble who had just trodden on his foot and poked an elbow in his ribs while trying to get through the door – though nobody could see why this should have been a particularly difficult task.

'Was a marrow wiv you? Hollow, every one.' The third member of the trio was the incoherent Mumble.

'These three are aptly named,' laughed Trotter as he rose to greet his guests. 'And I don't think I need to tell you who is who. Fumble, Mumble and Grumble, I want you to meet Sophie and Andrew Brown. Alas, I would have liked to be able to introduce Joshua as well, but…well, more of that in a minute.'

Fumble reached out a paw to shake Sophie's hand, but somehow his arms and legs got mixed up and he finished up in a tangled heap at her feet. 'Hello,' he grinned. 'Sorry about that. It must be the uneven floor.'

Sophie laughed, and liked him at once.

'Gooey ning, nice termiter,' mumbled Mumble to Andrew.

'Why don't you speak up, you dimwit?' bellowed Grumble. 'Good evening, both of you. Although I don't think it is at all good at the moment. A fine to-do this is, getting me out of bed with these two idiots. It had better be something important, that's all I can say. Anyway, here we are!'

Andrew glanced at Aldred who gave him one of those 'don't-say-I-didn't-warn-you' shrugs. The children were beginning to see his point, for these really were the most unlikely spies imaginable. Even saying hello seemed to cause a minor catastrophe. Trotter, however, was quite unmoved by all of it.

He took his seat and addressed the three mice, who stood in a row in front of him.

'Now, you three, I have a very important and dangerous mission that I wish you to undertake for us and for which, Elmesh only knows why, you are the only ones suitable.

'We're all ears,' said Fumble.

'More like all arms and legs!' Aldred muttered.

Unperturbed, Trotter continued. 'These two children, Sophie and Andrew, have a brother named Joshua. Unfortunately, Hagbane has captured him and locked him up in her castle. What we want you three to do is to find your way in and to discover his whereabouts.'

Fumble nodded his head so hard that he fell on his face. With considerable fuss Mumble and Grumble helped him up. Trotter had to wait until order was restored.

'Assuming you can do this,' he said – at which point

Aldred gave a snort – 'I want you to pass on the message that he is to be ready for a rescue attempt. Many die for lack of hope in that accursed place, so it is extremely important that you encourage him to hold on. Is that understood?'

Mumble muttered, 'Paw Joe Shah, emus felt table. Wee and stand.'

'Once you have found Joshua,' Trotter continued, 'I want you to spy out the land and find the easiest way for us to get to him, if there is one. You must return to us with that information as soon as possible. We will then plan our rescue attempt.'

'Fat lot of hope I've got of even reaching the castle with these two, let alone returning,' complained Grumble. 'But we'll do it for you, Trotter, if you say so. Though I don't like it one little bit,' he added.

Fumble, presumably intending to make a speech, stretched out his paw. Unfortunately, he succeeded only in knocking over a vase of dried grasses that stood on the table. Mrs Trotter shrieked as it crashed to the floor.

'My best vase!'

Trotter groaned and Aldred lifted his paws in despair.

'Go now,' he exclaimed. 'Before you do any more damage. And good luck, because you certainly look as though you're going to need it!'

* * *

The three mice crouched outside the castle walls. In spite of Fumble falling into a stream on the way and tripping over countless tree roots, and Grumble's continual complaints at fate for having given him such useless companions, nobody had noticed their approach. Not surprisingly, Mumble was the quietest of all.

'Now we need to find a way in,' whispered Fumble.

'Brilliant,' replied Grumble. 'Go to the top of the class!'

Mumble murmured something.

'What's that! Speak clearly for once, can't you?' yelled Grumble.

'Shush.'

They saw then that Mumble was pointing to a large water waste outlet emerging from the castle wall at ground level.

'That'll do. Well done, Mumble,' said Fumble. 'Well, what are we waiting for? Come on. Shall I lead?'

'Oh no,' Grumble replied firmly. 'You'll come last. It's safer that way!'

One by one they ran across to the wall – although stumbled and staggered is probably a better way of describing Fumble's progress.

'Let's get on with it, then,' Grumble growled.

Without further ado, the three mice scampered up the outlet to see where it would lead. They discovered that it drained the floor of the castle washroom. Luckily, nobody had decided to pour any water away while they were inside it.

'So this is where she lives,' said Fumble, looking around the dimly lit room. It smelt of old soap, damp stone and stale water. He twitched his whiskers. There was a deeper and more evil smell as well.

'Hobble,' said Mumble.

Very quietly (even Fumble was careful) they began to explore, creeping along the draughty corridors and peering into cold dingy rooms looking for any sign of Joshua. All the time their nerves were on edge in case any guards or even Hagbane herself should discover they were there. For a long time they found nothing and it was just as they were beginning to despair of ever finding Joshua that Fumble had his lucky accident.

The three mice were passing a floor-level opening protected by a set of iron bars when Fumble slipped on some candle grease, or maybe he tripped over a flagstone (afterwards nobody was sure which). Either way, he fell through the bars into the room below.

Grumble was leading at the time and didn't notice. Mumble, who saw what had happened, muttered something like, 'He's filing through the bus.'

Grumble was just about to shout at Mumble when they heard Fumble call out in a loud whisper from down below.

'I think I've found him. Down here.'

Sure enough, Fumble was right. They had stumbled upon the basement dungeon where Joshua was imprisoned. Without further delay the other two mice jumped down to join Fumble. They saw a dark figure tied to the wall.

'Psst. Are you Joshua?' asked Grumble.

'Y...y...yes. Wh...wh...who are you?' Joshua answered through chattering teeth, for by now he was numb with cold.

'Never mind that for now. We're from Trotter, and that's all you need to know. We've been sent to find you and to tell you that help is on its way. So don't be afraid, because you'll soon be out of here.'

Joshua was overjoyed. All he had been thinking about these past hours was what a mess he had made of everything and how stupid he had been to want the bike. He decided that he never wanted to see another bike, and vowed that he would never be so silly again. 'If I ever get out of here alive,' he said to himself.

But now there was hope.

'Is there anything we can do?' Fumble asked.

'Y...y...yes. Th...there is. C-c-can you untie my wrists? I don't think I can last out much longer.'

The three mice scrabbled over each other to gnaw at Joshua's bonds. It seemed to take ages and ages, especially as Fumble kept losing his balance and sending them all sprawling on the ground. However, at last it was done. The ropes gave and Joshua slumped to the floor in an exhausted heap.

'Thank you, thank you so much,' he gasped and, to his shame, he began to cry.

Actually, as it usually does, crying made him feel much better, and he soon pulled himself together.

'Sorry about that,' he said. 'But I've made such a mess of things. Are they really going to be able to rescue me? I honestly thought I'd be left here to die.'

'Yes, of course they'll get you out,' declared Grumble with somewhat more confidence than he actually felt. 'Trotter can do most things. Why, you know, he once saved my life when a Grog was chasing me and had me in a corner. So I'm sure he'll help you. Don't worry. We'll be back soon, so be ready.'

Mumble muttered, 'Trusses, an truss Trotta.'

Joshua looked puzzled.

'Oh, don't worry about him,' explained Fumble. 'He never speaks clearly, but then, he never says anything very important, anyway.'

Before a hurt-looking Mumble could protest, Grumble dragged them away.

'Come on, you two, we've still got to find a way for the others to get in. That drainway won't do. Look after yourself, Joshua. We'll be back as soon as possible.'

With that they were off, leaving Joshua feeling very much better.

As they left, Fumble tripped several times and brought the other two tumbling down on top of him at least once. For the first time that day, Joshua laughed. Then he winced as pins and needles set into his hands.

6
To the Rescue!

Andrew had given up trying to keep awake and was slumped fast asleep in an armchair. Sophie, for her part, could barely keep her eyes open; she kept on yawning in spite of trying not to.

Trotter smiled. 'There is nothing we can do until the three mice return, and that could take all night,' he said. 'We might as well get some sleep while we can.'

'Well, we've plenty of spare beds,' said Mrs Trotter, bustling to her feet. 'Come on, Sophie. I'll show you yours, though it looks like your brother has already found his! It seems a shame to wake him.'

'Oh, knowing Andrew, he'll be fine,' Sophie yawned. 'He can sleep anywhere. I should leave him.'

A few minutes later found Sophie snuggling down into a sweet-smelling bed of hay and sheep's wool. She gave a deep sigh. It had been an exciting and disturbing day, and a very long one. Exhausted by events, she soon fell fast asleep. For a while she slept deeply, but then, she began to dream....

She was climbing a great tree that seemed to go up and up for ever. Her legs ached as she clambered into the night sky – up towards a white star that glowed in the distance. Yet, however long she climbed, it was always too far away. Wearied by the effort she slipped, and began to fall.

Down and down she tumbled until she hit a long flight of dark steps. Rolling and bouncing, she glimpsed faces flashing past her as she continued to tumble – Trotter, Aldred, Andrew, Joshua, Hagbane – each shattered into a thousand pieces before her gaze, like the smashed reflection of a broken mirror.

Still she fell and the darkness seemed never to end.

Suddenly, she landed with an abrupt bump and found herself in the Enchanted Glade. The pool seemed to beckon her and she ran towards it. Reaching the pool she gazed deep into its waters, expecting to see her own reflection. With a shock that made her catch her breath she saw, not herself, but the face of a man staring blankly back at her.

Before she could recover from the fright, flames consumed the entire image. Then the glade was on fire, and the forest. Fire ran along the branches of the trees until everything was a sheet of flames. Sophie screamed and saw Sam Squirrel writhing in Hagbane's grip. Then she saw Joshua's face – and awoke with a start.

She lay for a while breathing rapidly in the pale light of early morning. A piece of straw tickled her nose and she brushed it away.

'Thank goodness it's only a dream,' she said to herself. 'But what if it's trying to tell me something?'

Quietly, she got up and crept from the house. Andrew was still curled up in the armchair and fast asleep.

The grey dawn made the forest look even more mournful and she shivered with the cold. Somehow she seemed to know which way to go – a turn to the right here, left there, under this branch, across these rocks; without faltering, she followed her instincts until she came once again to the mysterious splendour of the Enchanted Glade.

She hesitated now, the dream still vivid in her mind. Fear and doubt possessed her and she felt no desire to gaze into Elmere.

'Come on, Sophie,' she said to herself. 'You've got to do it.'

Reluctantly, she made herself approach the bowl, her heart thudding uncomfortably. Steeling herself, she peered into the shining water and saw – just her own reflection.

A mixture of relief mingled with disappointment flooded over her. Then she looked more closely. Lying in the bottom of the shallow pool and, as far as she could tell, perfectly whole was the mirror, Gilmere.

Gingerly, she reached her hand into the cold water and slowly withdrew it.

'Ah, so you have found it, have you?'

The deep voice from behind made her jump with fright, so much so that she almost dropped the precious mirror back into the water. The back of her neck tingled and her shoulders hunched as slowly she turned to face whoever it was.

'Trotter!' She gasped his name with relief, 'Oh, you frightened me! I didn't hear you coming.'

The badger smiled his apologies. 'Forgive me, my dear, but I followed you here. It is as well to be on the safe side in these days.' He glanced at the object in her hand. 'I see that Gilmere is made well again. That truly is good news for us, for I do not doubt that we shall need its power today. Now come quickly, child, for if I am not very much mistaken, those brave mice should be back with news by now.'

'More toast anyone?'

'Pass the marmalade, will you?'

Trotter and Sophie arrived back to find breakfast in full swing with Mrs Trotter busily supplying pots of nettle tea and platefuls of hot toast and marmalade to hungry mouths. The three mice began eagerly to report their good news as soon as Trotter and Sophie had joined them at the table.

'We found a way into the castle through a drainway,' said Grumble. 'Though it was a miracle that we found our way to the castle in the first place with these two idiots.'

'Now, now, Grumble,' Trotter cautioned. 'Enough of your complaining if you please. We want to know how Joshua is.'

'He's all right,' said Fumble. 'Well, better for seeing us, I think.' Fumble told them how they had found Joshua tied to the wall and chewed through his bonds.

Sophie was furious. 'The evil old bat!' she exclaimed. 'Just wait till I get a chance...'

But before Sophie could say what she would do, Mumble tried to explain how Fumble had found Joshua's dungeon. It sounded like 'Funnels lips and handles geese and eases dun gin.'

Grumble took a deep breath but then let it out again when he caught Trotter's warning eye.

'Could you repeat that, please?' Sophie asked Mumble.

'Um, perhaps it would be better if Fumble told us how we can get into the castle,' Aldred suggested hurriedly.

Fumble obliged. 'There's a side entrance,' he said. 'It's up a small sloping tunnel and barred with a couple of gates, but it's the best way in that we could see.'

'Excellent,' said Trotter. 'And we have Gilmere restored to us as well. A good night's work all round, I think.' He glanced in Mrs Trotter's direction. 'Is there any more toast, my dear?' he asked.

Everyone was very excited and cheered by the news and by the fact that the mirror was repaired. So, as soon as breakfast was over and the crockery cleared away, they prepared to launch Operation Breakout, as Andrew called it.

'I don't think we should send too many,' said Trotter. 'There's no sense in drawing attention to ourselves more than we have to.'

'I want to go,' said Sophie firmly.

'So do I,' Andrew added.

Trotter nodded his agreement.

After further discussion, it was agreed that the mice, the children and Stiggle would make up the rescue party, while Trotter and Aldred would station themselves outside the castle to deal with any pursuers once Joshua was out.

They all agreed that Mumble was the quietest, so he led the way. Within the hour, he had brought the party to within sight of the Crone's castle. The fortress stood in a broad clearing but gorse bushes grew quite thickly to a distance of about seventy-five metres from the wall on the eastern side and this provided good cover for the two children and their companions.

Sophie and Andrew stared at the high turrets and battlemented stone walls with their dark and watchful windows.

'I don't like this place,' Andrew whispered.

'Me neither,' Sophie replied. 'I bet it's even worse inside.'

'Quietly now,' cautioned Stiggle. 'There are bound to be guards about.'

They crept through the undergrowth until Mumble raised a hand for them to stop.

'There's the entrance,' whispered Grumble, pointing to an arched doorway that was obviously the opening to an upward sloping corridor. 'We'll have to break through the two gates once we're inside but at least we'll be under cover.'

Stiggle eyed up their situation. 'We'll have to take a chance and run across that open space,' he said. 'If you're ready, I'll go first.'

They all nodded and he shot out from the undergrowth, scampering towards the tunnel mouth as fast as he could. However, he had crossed no more than halfway when there was a loud roar and a huge and fearsome Grog stepped out from the shadow of the walls.

It was first time that Sophie and Andrew had seen a Grog and they were horrified. The creature looked like some two-legged prehistoric reptile. It had sallow green scaly skin and body armour made out of steel bands set with long, sharp spikes. He carried a long spear in his claw and ran towards the weasel.

'Stop where you are!' he commanded, aiming his spear at Stiggle's heart. 'One move and you're dead, vermin scum.'

Stiggle had no real choice but to obey. The Grog reached him and prodded him in the throat with the spear.

'What are you up to, you filth, and who else is with you?' he snarled.

Before Stiggle could attempt a reply, Sophie stepped boldly from the bushes, clutching Gilmere in her hand.

'Over here,' she cried.

The Grog spun round to face her.

'Well now, here's a pretty catch and no mistake. Mistress Hagbane will be interested.'

The Grog took a pace towards her.

At that very moment, Sophie flipped open the mirror

and pointed it towards him. A blinding beam of light blazed from the mirror, as triumphant and terrible as the sun in its full brilliance. She snapped the lid shut and blinked. The Grog was nowhere to be seen.

'Oh dear. I've killed him!' cried Sophie. 'I didn't mean to do that.'

She felt suddenly very sick.

'No you haven't,' laughed Stiggle. 'Look, he's turned into a frog!'

Indeed, they could see a very frightened frog hopping away into the bushes just as fast as his legs could carry him.

'Grogs into frogs,' Andrew chortled. 'Whatever next? That's some flashlight.'

With no further opposition, they quickly gained the shadowy entrance to the tunnel that led into the castle. Their next obstacle was an iron gate about ten metres along the corridor. It resisted all their efforts to open it in spite of there being no obvious lock.

'Here, let me have a go with that mirror,' demanded Andrew, and he snatched it from Sophie's hands. 'I'll melt it down or turn it into a metal frog, perhaps. You watch!'

He opened the mirror but, although the same radiance blazed out, the door remained completely unaffected.

'Huh, that's not much good is it? Looks like it can only do one trick a day.'

It was Stiggle who spoke to Andrew. 'I think it's not Gilmere that is at fault, but you. Nobody shows off with Elmesh's gifts: it's not given for you to do tricks with but to serve the cause of good. Now, Sophie, I think you have more idea. Take the mirror, will you?'

Sophie took Gilmere from Andrew's hands and directed the blazing light at the gate. She called out words that just came into her head.

'*Gate fast closed by Hagbane's might,*
Open up to Gilmere's light.'

At once the door flew open and they passed through unhindered. Andrew looked suitably shamefaced and had the grace to say sorry to Stiggle.

'That was a bit silly of me, I suppose. Trust Sophie to get it right!'

Nothing more was said about the matter and the second gate opened just as easily at Sophie's command. They came across no further obstacles until they reached an iron-studded wooden door.

'This is the door to the dungeons,' Fumble whispered.

Stiggle drew his sword in case there was anyone waiting for them on the other side. Sophie used the mirror for a third time and the door swung noiselessly open. It took a few moments for everyone's eyes to adjust to the gloom after the brilliance of Gilmere's light.

Before them lay a dark corridor lit by just one smoking torch set in a wall bracket halfway down. Steel-barred cell doors stretched along both sides of the corridor and inside they could make out animals cowering in the corners of their prisons. The stench was awful.

'This way,' said Grumble, and they followed him until they came to a cell that housed Joshua.

Thinking it might be the guards coming for him, he leapt to his feet and pretended that he was still tied to the ring on the wall.

'Josh, it's us,' said Andrew.

At once, Joshua rushed to the gate and clutched the bars.

'Andrew, Sophie! You've made it!' he gasped. 'Thank

goodness. And the mice. Fantastic!'

There was little time to lose.

'Stand back,' Sophie commanded as she angled the mirror and flicked it open.

Moments later Joshua was out of his cell and giving his brother and sister a big, thankful hug.

'Nice to see you, Josh. This is Operation Breakout,' said Andrew. 'Are you all right?'

'Yes, thanks to these mice, otherwise I'd have been very uncomfortable by now. She tied me up to that ring on the wall, you know.'

'Wicked old rat bag,' declared Sophie. 'Just wait till we get her.'

'Well not just yet,' said Stiggle. 'We must get out first.' He quickly introduced himself. 'Hello, Joshua, my name's Stiggle. I'm Aldred's second-in-command.'

Joshua clasped his paw. 'Thanks for coming, Stiggle. And you're dead right, I don't want to hang around here. Can we go?'

'What about the other prisoners here – the forest-folk?' asked Andrew. 'Can't we get some of them out?'

Grumble was just about to say that he wondered if there would be enough time when their questions were answered for them. A key grated in the lock of the main door at the top of the stairs.

'Quick, run for it! Run for your lives!' shouted Stiggle.

*   *   *

Hagbane had not slept that night. All through the dark hours she had paced to and fro in her den, muttering to herself, planning and plotting. This strange creature in her dungeon was a difficult problem; he was obviously from *outside*. True, she had worked out that something was up and very cleverly she had caught him. The question was, what to do now?

'Do I kill him? But then, he'll die with his secrets. Well, I'll get those out of him in the morning. Then I'll kill him!'

But that still left the possibility of others. And would they be the only ones? Muttering that there was more to this than met the eye, she brooded over the matter for many long hours. As soon as it was light, she hurried to her spell-room.

The place smelt evil, but it was Hagbane's favourite room. She cast her eye over the many jars that contained mysterious and horrible substances, many of them looking like bits of living creatures. Shelf upon shelf was lined with dusty, brown books of magic. But none of this concerned her at this moment.

In the far corner stood a table upon which lay an object covered with a purple velvet cloth. Gloating like a miser with his gold, Hagbane strode across and removed the covering. It revealed the object of her desire – the fabulous Merestone of the Great Forest of Alamore. The splendid, many faced jewel glowed faintly in the gloom of the den as Hagbane's greedy eyes took in its beauty and power.

'While this is mine I have nothing to fear,' she murmured to herself. '…and it is mine, all mine… with this I shall rule for ever. No one can touch me! I shall be the greatest queen in all the universe.' Her voice rose to a screech as she stretched out her gnarled hands in a gesture of defiance against the whole world and everybody in it. 'Mine! It is all mine!' she shrieked.

She covered the jewel once more with the purple cloth, her eyes still burning with desire. Then, with a swirl of her cloak she turned to the bookshelves and removed an old volume. Hastily turning the pages, she came across an ancient script:

Dark the eyes that look too deep
Heed the watcher's words, for we never sleep
A prince will rise from the setting sun
And children too – they shall act as one
The age-old stone to its place return
And break a curse by a judgement stern...

Hagbane spat and screeched. 'I must question the prisoner. He must know about this. I'll get it out of him. Guards!'

A sleepy Grog came running at her cry. He stood shakily to attention.

'Fetch the prisoner at once,' she ordered. 'And be quick about it or I shall turn you into a toad and boil you alive!'

She paced up and down waiting his return, twisting her fingers and smacking the palm of her hand with a clenched fist. At length the guard returned and burst breathlessly through the door.

''E's gone, yer 'ighness. Escaped down the tunnel. I don't know 'ow it could 'ave 'appened.'

'What!'

'I think they've only just gone, ma'am. Shall we get after them?'

Hagbane was beside herself with rage and her shape wavered menacingly before the guard.

'No, you fool. I shall handle this myself!'

She strode grim-faced from the room and began to climb the steps that led to the top of a tower from where she could view the surrounding forest.

The rescue squad and Joshua had fled for the tunnel in the wall. Stiggle was fastest away and he raced from the castle, darting for the undergrowth as fast as his legs could carry him. Sophie and Andrew had to go more slowly because Joshua was weak and his muscles were cramped and stiff from his ordeal. The three mice further hampered their progress, or rather Fumble did. He somehow managed to trip everyone up, causing absolute chaos as they scrambled for the exit and stumbled into the daylight.

'You stupid twit!' exclaimed Grumble. 'I've never seen anyone...'

He was interrupted by a shrill screech from high on the castle walls. They turned to see Hagbane standing on a towering battlement with her arms stretched out to the sky. She was a terrifying sight, rising up into the sky like a dark, brooding storm cloud and swaying in the breeze like belching smoke. In her hands she held two long, black wands.

'Run for it,' shouted Joshua. 'Never mind me. Run!'

Sophie and Andrew grabbed his hands and dragged him along with them.

'Come on, Josh, you can make it,' Andrew yelled.

A chilling blast hit them before they even reached the undergrowth. Thunder crashed and black lightning crackled from Hagbane's wands. Snow began to fall heavily; the wind blew up and moments later the children and the three mice were caught in the midst of a fierce blizzard that numbed them to the bone. It was as though they had been plunged into an instant Arctic winter.

Struggling knee-deep through the snow and half blinded, they lost all sense of direction and grew wearier and wearier, until it was almost impossible to lift their leaden limbs through the biting cold.

'I don't think I can go on,' gasped Joshua. 'You must keep moving. Save yourselves.'

'No, we've got to stick together,' Andrew cried above the howl of the wind. 'Look after those mice, Sophie, or they'll be buried alive.'

'That's what'll happen to us all,' she groaned. 'I feel so sleepy…so sleepy…must rest…'

With that, Sophie collapsed in a heap in the driving snow. The last thing she heard was a shrill shriek of maddened laughter echoing across the snow from the castle tower. Then everything went black.

7

The Wizards' Sacrifice

'We've got to find shelter,' gasped Joshua as he and his brother tried to lift Sophie out of the snow. 'Over there. There's something over there. Looks like a tree. Come on. Lift!' he yelled.

The force of the blizzard hampered every step as the boys struggled to half carry and half drag Sophie to safety. Their task was made harder because the only way Fumble, Mumble and Grumble could keep alive was by clinging to the boys' legs. To make matters worse, the driving snow crusted their faces and made it almost impossible to see. The tree that Joshua had spotted completely disappeared in a blur of white and they just hoped they were going in the right direction.

It took a terrific effort but with much puffing and panting at last they managed to drag Sophie to the shelter of what appeared to be a spruce tree that had snow-laden branches right to the ground.

'Round this side, Josh. It's out of the wind and there's no snow,' Andrew shouted.

They made it into the lee of the spruce and discovered to their relief that there was a hollow under its branches.

'Made it!' Joshua gasped as they dragged Sophie into the shelter and on to bare earth.

Andrew shook the snow from his body and wiped it from his face. 'I thought we were done for then,' he puffed.

The spruce made a wonderful shelter from the wind and the snow and it felt almost warm compared to outside. The three mice, who by now looked like three snowballs on legs, shook themselves free of snow and fluffed up their fur. Then they gathered anxiously around Sophie.

She began to stir.

'Where am I?' she groaned. 'What's happening? Oh, my head!'

'It's all right now, Sophie. You're safe,' Joshua reassured her as he brushed the snow from her and sat her up. 'I think we've beaten that old Crone's magic. Anyway, I'd sooner be here than stuck in that old dungeon of hers.' He looked round at the others. 'Thanks for getting me out, everyone.'

Sophie levered herself up onto her elbows. 'Hello, you three,' she said to the mice. 'You look all right. Sorry I made it hard for everyone. I just couldn't go on.'

Mumble said something that sounded like, 'Arfur keeps a swarm.'

'Oh, er, yes. Fur. I suppose it would be easier if you've got fur,' she said. She looked around. 'Where are we anyway? And where's Stiggle? He is all right, isn't he?'

We're sheltering under the branches of a tree,' said Joshua. He peered at the bark 'I think it might be a type of spruce. Anyway, we think Stiggle got away. He shot off like a rocket.'

'I expect he'll fetch Trotter and Aldred to help us back,' said Sophie and she smiled with relief at the thought.

'I hope that smelly Hagbane has got icicles stuck right up her nose!' Andrew exclaimed. 'She'll look like a warty walrus!' The idea struck him as funny and he started to laugh, and then he couldn't stop. Joshua joined in, then Sophie and the mice, until they were all rolling about in absolute fits of laughter.

'Oo, it hurts! Stop,' Sophie chuckled. 'It's making my ribs ache!'

'I can't!' Joshua gasped. He had tears streaming down his face. 'It's just so funny!'

'What is?'

'Hee, hee, I don't know!'

Andrew leapt to his feet and began to prance about, chanting at the top of his voice.

'Snotty grotty Hagbane! Potty, dotty Hagbane! Knotty botty Hagba...'

He never finished. At that moment, without any warning, everything went topsy-turvy. The ground beneath them gave way and all six found themselves tumbling in a crazy tangle of earth, roots and helpless bodies. Down and down they slithered until finally they landed in a mixed up heap at the bottom of a deep pit.

'Ooo! Ouch! Ow! What's happened?'

'Is everyone all right?'

'Whose leg is this?'

'It's mine!'

'Oh, sorry!'

'Get your foot out of my ear.'

'I can't. I'm stuck under somebody's bottom.'

'Yeuk! I've just got a mouthful of dirt.'

After much struggling and groaning, the six of them managed to disentangle themselves and take stock of their situation. It didn't seem to be too bright. They had fallen about three metres down a narrow hole and even if the mice might scramble up there seemed to be no way the children could climb out.

Glumly, Joshua shook the earth from his clothes and peered upwards. 'That's done it,' he said. 'We're stuck.

Now what are we going to do?'

'Sorry,' said Andrew, who thought it was all his doing.

'It's not your fault,' Sophie reassured him. She picked a piece of root out of her hair. 'None of us could know the ground was weak.'

'Do you think it's another of Hagbane's tricks?' Andrew asked.

'Dunno,' said Joshua. He shrugged his shoulders. Right now he was beginning to wish he had never suggested walking through the Passway in the first place. It seemed that nothing had gone right ever since they had arrived in this strange world.

Sophie knew how he was feeling and she put her hand on his arm. 'It'll be all right, Josh,' she said. 'We'll find a way out.'

'Here, wait a minute, everyone,' Andrew called with sudden excitement. 'Look, there's a tunnel here. It got half covered in by the earth when we fell.'

They turned and saw Andrew vanish into a small hole.

'Hey, you can stand up in here,' his voice boomed. 'It must lead somewhere.'

'Probably back to Hagbane's castle,' moaned Grumble.

'No..no, it's going in the opposite direction, I'm sure,' said Joshua, brightening up. 'Let's try it. It might just lead us out.' He held out his hands. 'Let's face it, we've got to do something.'

What he said made sense so – very cautiously – the others squeezed through the gap and began to follow Andrew along the underground passage.

It was so dark that he had to feel his way along the earth walls and to keep checking his steps to make sure there wasn't another hole. He had read about ventilation shafts in mines and didn't want to fall into one. But it made the going very slow.

'Why don't you let one of us lead?' suggested Fumble after a while. 'We're more used to tunnels.'

'So long as it's not you,' said Grumble with feeling. 'Here, I'll do it.'

'Good idea,' Joshua agreed.

Andrew didn't mind. In fact he was relieved as they sorted themselves out so that Grumble took the lead with Joshua holding his tail, followed by Andrew who held Mumble's tail, while Sophie brought up the rear holding Fumble's tail.

Soon they were on their way again.

'It's a bit scary, isn't it?' Sophie whispered.

'Yes, but at least it's warm and dry.'

'And away from Hagbane.'

'We hope.'

'Oh, don't say that.'

'Sh, there's a light ahead.'

Everyone stopped dead – except for Fumble, of course, who somehow tripped on Andrew's foot and wrapped himself around Mumble's legs, leaving Sophie wondering where his tail had gone.

'Gerrof. A forth year wear a spida!' cried Mumble.

'Quiet, you two,' ordered Joshua. 'This could be dangerous. Let's go carefully.'

The pale yellow glow was still a long way off and it took them quite a time to reach it.

Sophie could hear her heart beating loudly. She had lost track of how long they had been underground but her stomach told her that it was well past lunch-time.

At last, they reached a left turn in the tunnel and it was from round this corner that the light came. By now all their hearts were thumping. Full of trepidation, first Grumble, then Joshua, and then the others peered around the corner to see what awaited them.

What they actually saw was not very much. Just a fairly large underground chamber lit by burning torches set in brackets on the walls. The flickering light cast long shadows behind them as they emerged into the room.

'I wonder what this place is?' Joshua asked. He was just beginning to think he might have been wrong about the direction. Perhaps this was part of Hagbane's castle after all.

'Well, it must belong to somebody,' answered Sophie. 'The question is, who?'

'Good afternoon.'

The voice was smooth and low and it almost made them jump out of their skins. Sophie stifled a scream.

Huddling together, they turned to face its owner.

Before them stood two of the most bizarre characters any of them had ever seen. The taller one was a gaunt figure with hard features and a leering mouth. Andrew noticed at once the straggly black beard and moustache. It reminded him of a pirate captain – except that the figure before them wore a long silken scarlet robe covered with a mysterious yellow design that included lots of planets and signs of the zodiac.

His partner, who was very short, made Andrew think of an egg, for he was a fat, round creature, totally bald, and with apparently no neck. His robe of green silk was covered in a curious pattern of maths symbols and snakes.

The short one was the speaker. He smiled a bland, oily smile and continued in his smooth low voice.

'Good afternoon. Did we startle you? I am most sorry. Welcome to our humble abode.' He raised an eyebrow.

'And may I ask to whom we owe this pleasure?'

For a moment, nobody spoke. It was, unfortunately, Mumble who recovered his voice first.

'Good half nun. Wee fours fork annies cape from a bins car sale.'

Their hosts looked puzzled.

'Oh, shut up, cloth-head,' snapped Grumble. 'Why do you even bother?' He turned with a sigh to address the strange creatures. 'I'm sorry about that,' he said. 'What he's trying to say is that we are forest-folk and we have just escaped from Hagbane's castle. We accidentally fell into your tunnel trying to hide from a snowstorm. We're very sorry about that and don't want to inconvenience you, so – if you will kindly show us the way out – we'll be off.'

'Not so fast,' the taller one spoke for the first time. His voice grated hard and Sophie gave a slight shiver. 'How do we know this is true?' he continued. 'How do we know you are not friends of Hagbane come to spy on us? Who are these strange beings, anyway?' He indicated the children.

Joshua spoke up. 'Please, sirs, my name is Joshua Brown and this is my brother, Andrew, and my sister, Sophie. We've come from a long way away and all we really want to do is to get back to our friends. So, if you don't mind, we would be ever so grateful if you could show us the way out.'

'Quite, quite,' said the short one. He glanced at his partner. 'Only it is a fair journey to the exit and you all look very tired and dirty. And, I should think, hungry and thirsty as well. Won't you stay and have a small meal before you go?'

The mention of food and drink made them all aware of their stomachs, especially Joshua, who, of course, had not eaten or drunk since they first arrived at Trotter's cottage.

It was difficult to know what to do. He turned to Sophie.

'What do you think?' he asked.

'I suppose so,' she answered hesitantly.

Joshua nodded.

'Well, OK. Um, thank you very much,' he said. 'Only you will let us go soon, won't you?'

'But of course,' replied the short one smoothly. 'Now we must introduce ourselves. My name is Sorda, and this is my colleague, Terras. We are, um, what you might call explorers, delving into the realms of knowledge, trying to understand the secrets of the earth and the heavens.'

'Oh, we call those scientists,' interjected Andrew.

'Scientists? Why, yes. Yes indeed. Scientists. Now come this way, please.'

They were led through a door into another much larger underground chamber. Joshua glanced round trying to take everything in. Drawings and strange instruments littered a bench in the middle of the room, and rolls of yellowed parchments and books lined shelves on three of the walls. A sour smell of chemicals and decay hung in the atmosphere.

Almost at once Joshua wished he had not accepted the invitation. It reminded him too much of Hagbane's castle.

Fumble tripped over a flagstone and saw something lying under the table. He gasped with horror when he saw that it was a dead mouse. Lying on his back he glanced up to see a whole string of mice hanging by their tails under the bench. He shivered at such a terrifying sight, but – frightened for his own safety – he knew he had to stay there, well out of the way, to keep an eye on things.

'Come and sit by the fire.' Terras' invitation was more like an order, and the children obeyed with reluctance. They sat before the fire rigid with tension, their hands pressed together between their knees and their shoulders hunched, and said nothing.

A few moments later, the shorter of the two, Sorda, returned with a jug of steaming liquid and several metal goblets.

'Comfrey tea,' he beamed. 'Very thirst-quenching and refreshing.'

The children watched with suspicion as he filled the goblets and they waited until Terras and Sorda began to drink before savouring the brew themselves. Except that Sophie just pretended to drink hers by holding it to her mouth without taking any in.

Andrew and Joshua both stared into the fire – and then the room began to spin. They tried to stand but found their legs wouldn't hold them. Faster and faster the room span until first Joshua and then Andrew slumped unconscious to the floor.

'What have you done?' Sophie shrieked as she saw her brothers pass out. 'You've drugged them, haven't you?'

She was furious and rose to her feet to face the two wizards (for that is what they surely were) with her fists clenched and her jaw set. Grumble and Mumble dashed to her side.

With their eyes gleaming, the wizards advanced towards her.

'Gilmere. Use Gilmere,' Grumble hissed from the side of his mouth.

'Oh! I've given it back to Joshua.'

Sophie made a dash for her brother but before she could reach him Terras pounced on her and pinned her to the floor.

'Let me go!' she gasped. 'Let me go!'

Sophie kicked and punched and scratched for all she was worth but it was no use. The tall wizard was too strong for her. Grumble and Mumble leapt in to help but Sorda grabbed them both and banged their heads together so hard that they were instantly knocked out. He dropped their limp bodies to the ground and turned to his colleague.

'Tie those two up,' ordered Terras from where he held the still struggling Sophie captive. 'Don't worry about the boys. They'll be out for a good while yet.' His face took on an evil leer. 'We'll use them for experiments later. Meanwhile,' he hissed, 'this girl will make a nice sacrifice for tonight. What a stroke of luck, eh?'

Sorda gave a sinister laugh as he bound Grumble and Mumble with cord. 'Yes, this should get us nicely into Hagbane's favour, and please her Grims.' He looked around him. 'By the way, weren't there three mice?'

'Yes. The other one must be somewhere about. But no matter. We'll get him later. Let's deal with this one first.'

Sophie struggled and screamed as they hauled her to her feet and twisted her arms into a painful hammerlock behind her back.

'Why are you doing this?' she sobbed. 'Please let us go. We haven't done you any harm.'

Sorda smiled. 'Foolish child. Did you really think we would let such an opportunity pass? We told you we experimented in…shall we say…strange matters, and here you are, creatures we have never seen before. Those boys will make excellent subjects for our studies, and the mice, too.' He sniggered. 'But you, my dear, you will be offered as a sacrifice to Hagbane's Grims. That way we shall keep her happy as well.'

'No, No! Let me go!' Sophie struggled in their iron grip as the two wizards dragged her across the room and up a short flight of stairs to a wooden door. Opening it, they forced her outside and on to a stone threshold.

Straight in front of them there rose a long stone staircase cut into the rock. Each step was covered in strange symbols that had been cut by an ancient hand. The wizards forced her to the foot of the stairs.

'Start climbing or I'll break your arm,' Terras grated.

Sophie dug in her heels and tried to resist but it was no use. As the late afternoon sun began to set, the two wizards forced her protesting form up the steps. A cold breeze blew across the darkening forest.

At length, and in spite of Sophie's struggles, they reached a high stone platform at the summit of the stairway. There they lashed ropes tightly to her wrists and tied her arms outstretched above her head to two pillars on either side. Sorda drew a slender wand from the folds of his cloak and touched torches affixed to each post. Instantly they burst into flames and the two wizards chuckled as they watched their victim writhe in the flickering light.

'Heh, heh. The more she struggles, the more appetising she will be!' gloated Terras.

Hearing this, Sophie ceased struggling at once. She would give no pleasure to her wicked captors, she decided.

The stone stairway stretched like a grey corrugated ribbon below them down to the yellow glare of the open doorway. The wizards turned and began to descend the steps leaving Sophie in the gathering gloom under the flitting light of the blazing torches.

She cried. She shouted. But nobody came. The door below closed with a dull *thunk* and, alone and helpless, Sophie awaited her fate.

Fumble had seen what was happening from his hiding place under the table. He had not been idle. His first task had been to gnaw through the cords that bound his fellow-mice. They were just coming round.

'They're going to sacrifice Sophie to the Grims.' He spoke urgently to his dazed companions. 'We must get Joshua and Andrew awake.'

Still dazed, Grumble and Mumble staggered across to where the boys lay unconscious.

'Water. We'd better try water, I suppose,' said Grumble, rubbing his head.

They found a low trough of water and grabbing the goblets began to splash the boys' faces.

'Wassamarra,' groaned Andrew. 'Ugh!'

'Wake up,' urged Fumble. 'They're going to kill Sophie.'

'What?' It was Joshua who spoke first. 'Kill Sophie?'

Both boys retched and were violently sick on the floor.

'Ugh! Disgusting!' Andrew spluttered.

What happened?' gasped Joshua, wiping his mouth. 'The last thing I remember was having a drink. Then everything started spinning…'

'You were drugged,' interrupted Fumble. 'Listen, Sophie's in great danger. We must stop those wizards.'

'Too late!'

All five whirled round to see the two wizards standing at the doorway. They heard the bolt slide into place as Sorda locked the heavy door. Then together he and Terras strode down the staircase to where the boys and the mice cowered.

'You are too late,' continued Terras with a triumphant leer. 'She will die and so will you.'

His cold-blooded words cleared Joshua's head more effectively than the cold water.

'We'll see about that,' he yelled and, leaping aside, he drew Gilmere from his pocket.

With a press of the clasp the mirror sprang open and living light gushed forth like a jet of golden water from a powerful hose.

Saturated with such intense light, books and parchments burst into flames under its glare. A crystal ball exploded into a thousand fragments. Apparatus began to melt into smouldering heaps. Jars cracked and chemicals crackled and hissed into flame.

'Taste Elmesh's fire!' Joshua shouted.

The wizards screeched with rage and lunged towards him. But there would be no stopping Joshua. One look at the fury on his face was enough. With cries of fear and rage they fled for the tunnel.

'Now for Sophie,' Joshua cried.

He, Andrew and the mice rushed the flight of stairs and reached the locked door.

'This time I'll do it right,' muttered Joshua. 'Stand back everyone. By the light of Elmesh, let this door be broken. Let this door be broken!' he cried.

At once, to the sound of splintering wood, the oak door shattered into firewood before the blazing light. In moments they were outside. Ahead of them stretched the long stone staircase where they could see the distant figure of Sophie in the flickering torch light.

'Come on!' cried Joshua.

They rushed up the stairs as fast as their still shaking legs could carry them.

'Don't worry, we're coming, Sophie,' Andrew called breathlessly.

At that very moment a shrill screech pierced the night sky. All their eyes turned in the direction from which it had come. They saw a black dot high in the sky that even as they watched grew rapidly in size as it plummeted towards them.

Down it shot at unbelievable speed, a mighty bird with powerful wings and outstretched talons that glinted in the flames from the wizards' den. Eyes glaring, it streaked straight towards the helpless Sophie.

Before anyone could react to this horror, three other cries rent the air. They turned in dismay to see other dark shapes speeding on great black wings towards the sacrificial victim. They were coming from the direction of Hagbane's castle.

'Quickly, quickly!' screamed Sophie. 'Help me. Please, please help me!'

8
Battle in the Sky

Joshua and Andrew were halfway up the steep steps in their race to save Sophie. The mice scurried at their heels, but already they knew it was too late. By the smoky light of the flickering torches they could see her struggling hopelessly against her bonds. They would never reach her in time. Already the outspread wings of the giant bird seemed to fill the twilight sky above Sophie's head.

Hovering like some prehistoric and terrifying bird of prey, a monstrous white eagle was ready to pounce. Tears of frustration and defeat choked Joshua. His own sister was about to be torn to pieces!

'No!' he gasped. 'No!!'

Desperately, he reached into his pocket for Gilmere.

Yet, instead of clutching Sophie in his fearsome talons or hacking her flesh with his hooked beak, the giant white eagle landed beside her and began to tear at her bonds until her hands were loosed from the pillars. Nearly faint with terror and unable to hold herself up any longer, the exhausted girl collapsed to the ground.

Joshua was almost at the top of the stairs by now, and though his legs were trembling, he seized his chance and flicked Gilmere open. In desperation he pointed it at the bird. A blaze of light seared through the twilight and struck the creature full on.

'Take that!' Joshua gasped.

However, to his dismay, far from destroying the creature, the eagle seemed to grow larger and brighter in Gilmere's glare. From the tips of his half-opened wings to the crown of his head his feathers shimmered with a dazzling silvery sheen until he looked as though he were made of shiny metal gleaming in bright sunlight. Yet nothing further happened; he wasn't burned, and he wasn't destroyed.

The panting would-be-rescuers stood amazed at the sight, and they felt utterly defeated. Sophie gazed up at her attacker and then bowed her head in despair.

Then the bird spoke.

His voice was harsh and cawing and full of authority. 'I am Arca, the envoy of Elmesh. I see the glory of Gilmere is here, too. It is well – but you do not need to shine it upon one who shares its nature. Close it, Joshua Brown, for you reveal too much by its light.'

Dumbfounded, and after a moment's hesitation, Joshua obeyed. The light died away and, except for the eerie shadows cast by the flickering torches, everything else was cloaked in darkness. Slowly, Sophie raised her head and looked once more at the eagle. He hadn't killed her. Was he really on their side?

The eagle – Arca, he called himself – spoke once more.

'There is little time, for the enemy has smelt blood. It is Sophie they want, though you are all in great danger. I will take her to safety and deal with the foe, but you must flee for your lives,' he explained. 'Down the steps you will find a path to the left. It leads to the river where you will find a boat. Look now, the enemy comes!'

The children raised their eyes. Above them wheeled three bat-like creatures of such enormous size that they looked like giant shadows on the dark canvas of the twilit sky. At an unseen signal they swooped towards their target.

'On my back, Sophie,' Arca commanded as she struggled to her feet. 'Quickly now, the rest of you. Flee!'

Joshua pushed the mirror into Sophie's hands. 'Here, take this and use it,' he panted. 'And look after yourself.'

'Go on, Sophie!' Andrew cried.

Sophie clambered onto the eagle's neck as he bent low. As soon as she was astride his back Arca's mighty wings swished the air. With Sophie clinging on in fear for her life he soared aloft and wheeled sharply towards the right. For a moment, the boys and the three mice stood in awe gazing after the eagle, but the sight of a Grim diving towards them jerked each one back to reality.

'Come on,' yelled Joshua. 'Run!'

Down the steps they raced, feeling a cold rush of wind as the Grim, with its talons bared, swooped low over their heads. For once, Fumble was a help because he tripped over the other two mice and they tumbled together to the bottom of the steps in record time. Not that Grumble was very impressed.

'You stupid mouse,' he cried. 'Why can't you ever look where you're going?'

'Mmmggh,' agreed Mumble.

'Oh, shut up!'

Before a row could develop, Joshua and Andrew leapt down the last few steps to join them.

'Come on, you lot, there's no time for arguing now,' Joshua cried breathlessly. 'Look he's coming back again. Where's that path? Quickly!'

Fire still poured from the doorway of the wizards' lair and by its light Andrew made out a dark hole in the undergrowth just to their right.

'This must be it,' he cried. 'Come on.'

In no mood to hang about, the mice and the boys scrambled through the hole. They discovered that they were in a low tunnel that disappeared steeply through a dense thicket of holly bushes.

'Whew. Let's hope we're safe in here,' puffed Fumble.

They looked back at the sight of a monstrous bird flapping outside and screeching in fury. Its sour stench assaulted their nostrils.

'Ugh, what a stink!' gasped Andrew.

'Let's keep moving,' said Joshua, coughing. 'This is too close for comfort.'

'I hope Sophie's all right. I suppose that bird was telling the truth?' said Andrew.

'We can't do anything about it now, can we?' Joshua replied.

' I think he's OK,' Fumble said. 'After all, Gilmere seemed to make him glow.'

'Wrecking weaken trusses honour sighed,' offered Mumble.

Joshua nodded. 'Well, come on then. Let's find that boat.'

'If there's a boat,' Grumble muttered. 'And if there is, it'll probably be miles away.'

Boat or not, they had no choice but to follow the tunnel as it dropped away through the holly.

*   *   *

Sophie had never experienced anything like it in all her life – the feeling of immense power as Arca's tremendous wing-thrusts lifted them upwards; the rushing sound of the wind past her ears, its force tearing at her clothes; the dizzy view of the forest below as they whirled into the twilight sky. It was breathtaking and scary too. She clutched tightly at the eagle's neck.

Arca let out a wild spine-shivering screech that echoed across the treetops.

Sophie gasped. She could see the Grims now – three shadowy killers soared above them in the pale afterglow of early evening – and they were coming for her!

Full of menace, they circled closer. Then one of them swooped. Sophie could see the snapping fangs and the outstretched talons that would tear her from her feathery perch. She screamed and flinched, and for one awful moment she thought she would fall. But Arca was swift and strong; with a few powerful wing beats he outmanoeuvred the enemy and rose in the sky.

The other two Grims wheeled and screeched. One after the other they attacked but they were no match for the tireless eagle. Sophie's confidence grew as Arca swooped and swerved through the sky. The eagle's back felt warm and secure and the thrill of battle began to stir in her. She remembered then that Joshua had given her Gilmere and, gripping tight with her knees, she took it from her jacket pocket.

'Enough of this,' screeched Arca. He soared upwards in a steep climb, then turned in mid-flight and plummeted like a stone towards his enemy below. Sophie clung to his neck and flipped open the lid of Gilmere. Light streamed forth as intense as a laser beam and before Arca's claws could strike, the Grim beneath them shrivelled to a cinder and vanished in a puff of smoke. Arca blinked.

'You strike at the speed of light, Sophie Brown!' he exclaimed. 'I am impressed, and you are no coward.'

The two remaining Grims began their attack, one from above and one from below. Arca streaked across the sky as they homed in on their target and Sophie gritted her teeth for the moment of impact. Then, with astonishing skill and enormous strength, Arca threw open his wings and stopped in mid-flight.

The move was too much for the Grims and they hurtled headlong into one another, colliding with a mighty clatter of leathery skin and bone. Sophie saw one drop like a stone into the trees far below, mortally wounded. The other, sensing defeat, recovered quickly and flew hard and low back towards the sanctuary of Hagbane's castle.

'We shall not let this one escape,' cried Arca as he set off in rapid pursuit. 'Death to the enemies of Elmesh!'

Although fear propelled the Grim at great speed, the eagle was faster and the gap closed rapidly. Sophie opened the mirror and tried to focus the beam on her target but found it impossible. It looked as if he would make it to the castle. They were right over the ramparts when Arca struck. His talons sank deep into the Grim's neck. With a horrifying screech the creature writhed and fought to shake off its attacker. Sophie clung on in desperation as the giants fought. It didn't last long. Arca executed a deathblow with his sharp beak and the Grim fell mangled to the courtyard beneath.

At once, Arca began to climb, but hardly a moment too soon. A crackle of fire leapt from the wand of a furious Hagbane who had followed the action from her castle ramparts. Sophie heard the Crone scream with rage as the fiery bolt merely singed Arca's tail feathers. Hagbane's face contorted in hatred, and her clenched fists shook with anger as they made their escape.

'Whew, that was close,' Sophie gasped.

'Yes, but we are safe now,' the eagle replied as he climbed away into the night. 'I shall take you to a place of rest and refreshment so that you may renew your strength.'

107

The excitement over, Sophie suddenly felt very weak and sick. She closed her eyes and, nestling against the eagle's back, sank into the oblivion of sleep.

*   *   *

Joshua and Andrew and the three mice struggled down the steep secret path in pitch darkness. It turned out to be an extremely muddy and twisting route through a tangle of prickly holly, hawthorn and gorse bushes, and the two boys had to scramble bent double most of the time.

'It's getting worse,' said Joshua as he slithered on the mud. 'Ouch! Watch out for the prickles here, Andy.'

'What prickles? It's all prickles!' Andrew gasped. 'Aahh! I see what you mean. Worse prickles!'

At last, after much slithering and sliding, exhausted and miserable, and covered in mud and scratches, they emerged into the clear and found themselves by the river.

'Yeuk, I thought that would never end!' exclaimed Andrew as he tried to wipe the mud and blood off his hands. 'I wonder where we are now.'

'Anywhere's better than back there,' Joshua answered, peering through the gloom. 'Did you hear those screeches? I just hope Sophie's all right, that's all.'

'I expect so,' said Andrew. 'It's all gone quiet now so I reckon they got away all right.'

'It's a good job that bird turned up when he did,' said Joshua. 'What did he call himself – Archway, or something.'

'No, Arca. Hey, he's pretty good though, isn't he?' Andrew laughed. 'Who would've imagined we'd be saved by a giant white eagle?'

'We wouldn't have stood a chance against those bat things without him, that's for sure,' Joshua agreed. He hesitated. 'I wonder where those two disgusting wizards have got to?'

'Well, not back to their lair, that's for sure. You certainly put an end to that,' laughed Andrew.

'We were stupid to be taken in by them. Just think what might have happened to us!' Joshua shivered at the thought.

A call from Fumble interrupted their conversation. 'Hey, we think we've found the boat. Over here.'

They followed the direction of his voice until Andrew tripped over Fumble and fell on the muddy ground with a loud *splat*.

'Ouch, who was that?' he exclaimed. 'As if I couldn't guess!'

'Where are you, Andrew?' Joshua called.

'Over here. With Fumble.'

In the darkness they could just make out the shape of a small rowing boat hauled up on the bank. They crowded round it. At that moment, a pale glow lit the scene as the rising moon peeked over the treetops.

'Do you know where we are?' Joshua asked

'We know this river. It's the Wendle,' answered Fumble. 'It should be possible to get back to Trotter.'

'Yes, but at night-time everything looks so different. We're bound to get lost,' Grumble protested.

'We can't afford to make a mistake. The river runs too close to Hagbane's castle,' added Fumble, nodding. 'I for one don't want to go back there.'

'Nor me,' said Joshua with feeling. 'That settles it then; wizards or no wizards, Grims or no Grims, we're staying here tonight. I'm too tired to go on, anyway. Does anyone think different?'

Nobody did and so the three mice and the two boys clambered into the boat. Fortunately it was dry, and the two boys and three mice were soon snuggled up together for warmth as best they could.

'I wonder when we'll see Sophie again – and Arca?' Joshua yawned as he settled down.

'Dunno,' Andrew murmured. 'Soon, I hope.'

In next to no time, the drama and exhaustion of the day overtook them and they fell fast asleep. Nothing stirred as they slept, and the dark river flowed silently on beneath the cold light of the moon and the stars.

9

The Honeycomb Queen

The bleak moor known as the Waste Plains stretched in front of Prince Oswain. Behind him lay the inhospitable mountains of Cadaelin, their peaks already shrouded in cloud as if to bar his way back. Further ahead eastwards, out of sight across the rolling moor with its scrubby grass and heather, lay the Great Forest of Alamore and the reason for his journey.

'Onwards, ever onwards...,' he said to himself as he shouldered his pack.

The keen wind and dull sky matched his mood as he tramped through the long hours. The days to come would test him and though he hoped to win through, he could not be certain. Oswain suspected that the battles would be fierce but as yet he had little inkling of what those battles might be. Strong and well-trained though he was, he would have to muster all his courage, wisdom and skill to face the challenge when it came.

In a sombre frame of mind he marched all day until, at length, he came within sight of a dark expanse of wintry trees stretching from one end of the horizon to the other. He had reached the edge of the Great Forest itself and before it in the fading light of evening glinted the serpentine silver thread of the River Wendle.

'Tomorrow, I shall enter the forest and find out why I have made this journey,' he breathed. Somewhere in the distance he heard the wild screeching of birds.

*   *   *

A cold, pale dawn awoke the occupants of the boat; the trees rose stark and grey through the mist that lay over the river.

'Brr, it's cold,' shivered Andrew. His teeth chattered as eased himself up.

'Oof! Ouch! Oh, my leg, it's stuck,' Joshua grunted.

Slowly and lazily the three mice uncurled themselves from where they had huddled together.

'Reckon they slept better than us,' Andrew laughed ruefully. 'Ow, my neck doesn't half hurt. I wonder what time it is?'

'No idea, but we'd better get back to Trotter as soon as possible. They'll be worried sick about us. Come on, you mice, wakey wakey!'

'Go away,' groaned Grumble. 'Give us some peace and quiet.'

'Grummffn,' added Mumble.

'Breakfast time,' Andrew called – and in an instant all three mice were awake. 'Egg, chips, baked beans and bacon. Cereal, anyone?'

'Oh, shut up, you're only making me feel even hungrier,' Joshua complained. 'Come on everyone. If we want breakfast we'll have to get a move on or there'll be none left. Plenty of water, though!' he added, nodding towards the river.

'I wonder what sort of night Sophie's had. She's probably tucking into loads of food by now.' said Andrew.

'Well, let's hope so,' Joshua answered. 'Anyway, keep an eye open for those two wizards. I don't think we've seen the last of them.' He heaved a sigh. 'I still can't get

112

over how we let them take us in like that.'

'We must be stupid,' Andrew yawned. 'I felt something was wrong the moment we met them, but I didn't take any notice of it.'

'Perhaps that's the trouble; none of us did,' said his brother. 'Anyway, the quicker we get moving, the further away we'll be from them. Come on, let's get this boat into the water.'

Joshua clambered out of the boat and onto the bank, followed by Andrew.

'Wait for us, then. We'll give you a hand,' said Fumble.

So, the boys and the mice together heaved and shoved until the boat slid with a slight splash into the water.

'Look out, hold on to her or she'll float away,' cried Andrew. 'Grab that rope, quick!'

He pointed to a mooring rope from the prow. Fumble, who was nearest, leapt for it and caught the end.

'Hey, well done, Fumble,' Andrew cried.

Unfortunately, Fumble caught not only the rope but his feet as well. He found himself being dragged along the bank in a complete tangle as the boat drifted downstream.

'Ow! Help! Ouch!' he cried.

The others chased after him and just managed to prevent him being dragged into the water.

'Stupid cheesehead!' exclaimed Grumble. 'That nearly cost us the boat. Then where would we have been?'

'Walking, I suppose,' retorted Fumble. He rubbed his head. 'Oh, I must have banged my head on something. It hurts.'

'Perhaps it'll have knocked some sense into you,' Grumble retorted.

'Hey,' laughed Joshua. 'Come on, you two. We've got

the boat, so it's all right. Hop in now and let's be on our way.'

Everyone clambered aboard and Joshua pushed away from the bank with a broken branch.

Soon they were drifting along in a pleasant light current. The mist lifted as the sun rose above the trees and the air felt surprisingly warm, almost like spring. For a little while, they could forget their worries and cares and could bask in the sunshine while the water lapped and gurgled around the boat and the banks slid by.

'Hey, this is pretty good isn't it?' said Joshua.

Andrew leaned back and trailed his fingers in the water, pretending that they were miniature water skiers racing each other.

For most of their journey the trees came right down to the water's edge, but every so often a small grassy clearing broke the monotony.

'Watch out for a small boulder on the bank when we come to a clearing,' said Fumble. That's where we'll pick up the path back to Trotter's house.'

Everyone agreed to keep their eyes open for the landmark.

'Lock icy pretty floors.'

Mumble tugged at Joshua's sleeve. He was pointing to a clearing that lay ahead on the left bank. Joshua heaved himself up from the bottom of the boat where he had been lazing and everyone crowded to see what Mumble was pointing at. Nobody, of course, had understood what he had said.

'Look at that!' cried Joshua in amazement. 'Those are flowers, I'm sure.'

'We've not had flowers in the forest for years,' said Fumble. 'How unusual.'

'We had better stop and look,' said Grumble.

'Yes,' Fumble agreed. 'I wonder what it means.'

The patch of bright yellow that had caught Mumble's attention drew closer. Compared to the drab and bare forest all around, it looked simply brilliant in the morning sun. But as they drew closer it became apparent that the flowers were not flowers at all but something even more amazing.

'They're alive,' exclaimed Joshua in wonder. 'They're moving!

'Moving? They can't be,' said Andrew.

'They are,' Joshua replied. 'I don't believe it! I..I think they're...they look like..like fairies!'

'Fairies? Don't be daft,' said Andrew. 'There's no such thing.'

'What do you think they are, then?'

They were close enough now to see that there were dozens of little yellow figures prancing about on the grass in the sunshine. The light glistened off their gossamer wings and happy laughter accompanied their dancing. Andrew shrugged his shoulders and had to agree with his brother.

A sweet, heady scent wafted over the entranced onlookers. It seemed to come from large yellow puffballs that the little creatures were tossing to each other in a game of catch. Every so often a puffball would burst in a shower of scented pollen dust that the light breeze carried towards them over the water.

Joshua pushed the tiller over until the boat ran lightly aground on the bank side.

As soon as they came to rest, one fairy emerged from the dance. She was taller and of greater splendour then the rest, wearing a magnificent daffodil-yellow robe edged with gold braid. Her blond hair fell across her shoulders in long tresses and she wore a bejewelled crown of fine spun gold. Smiling, she approached them with grace and poise in every movement.

'She must be the queen of the fairies, or something,' whispered Andrew, who was by now thoroughly convinced.

'Hail, travellers,' she cried in a sweet, musical voice. 'Welcome to you on this fine morning!'

'Er, um, hello,' stammered Joshua, unsure of how to addressed a fairy queen. 'Er, excuse me, but you...you are fairies, aren't you?'

The queen replied with a laugh. 'Why, yes, indeed we are. And I am their queen. And yourselves? Pray tell me who are you?'

'Well, we're travellers, actually, though we're not going very far. We're looking for the path that will lead us to Trotter the badger. Do you know where it is?'

'Why, yes, of course. It's around the next two bends in the river. But what brings you this way in the first place, dare I ask?'

Andrew spoke. 'Well, er..ma'am, we've just escaped from two wizards and a great eagle rescued our sister. That was last night. Now we're trying to meet up with her again.'

'Then you have not eaten?' the queen enquired.

'No, not a thing, your highness,' replied Grumble, who could feel his stomach grumbling.

The queen clapped her hands. At once, two fairies came forward bearing a golden plate piled with pieces of honeycomb.

'Eat this,' she invited. 'It is magic honeycomb that will refresh you and give you strength for the rest of your journey.'

Joshua remembered his mistake of the night before

and hesitated. Seeing this, the queen smiled.

'Ah, you think it may be poisoned, do you? I assure you, by Elmesh himself, that it is not. See for yourself.'

So saying she took a piece from the plate and ate it before their eyes.

Seeing that it had no ill effects, Grumble agreed to have a bite and, to their relief, pronounced it very good.

Almost drooling with hunger the others began to stuff pieces of honeycomb into their mouths. Within a few minutes they had completely emptied the plate of the delicious food and, as the fairy queen had promised, they each were feeling much better. The events of the previous day and the uncomfortable night in the boat began to fade like a nasty dream and life seemed suddenly pleasant again.

Joshua pushed the boat back into the current and, waving cheerfully to the fairies, they began once more to drift down the river.

'Farewell, brave travellers,' the queen called after them as she waved goodbye. 'On your way. Byee.'

'Bye, bye, dear fairies, thank you,' sighed Joshua, who now felt so warm and relaxed that he flopped down in the boat and closed his eyes. 'Keep an eye open for the second bend, won't you?' he said to nobody in particular.

Fumble had never felt so confident in his life. He leapt onto the gunwale of the boat and began to prance about like an acrobat.

'I can walk, I can dance, I can balance. Watch me!' he cried.

He ran to the prow of the boat and balanced on one of his fore paws.

'Fumble the fantastic!' cried Andrew.

Everyone cheered and shouted as the mouse did a

117

twirl on the end of his tail.

Joshua lay back grinning to himself.

'Utterly brilliant, my dear friend.'

'Who said that?' Grumble murmured. He looked around him. Everyone was staring at Mumble with their mouths open.

Mumble rose and addressed the crew with perfect diction: 'My dear fellow-mice, yeomen among the forest-folk, and Joshua, and Andrew, Children of Time Beyond Time and noble visitors to our realm – welcome. What a grand company is gathered here! The wizards are defeated, and the Grims, too. Soon the Crone herself will fall. Nothing will stop us. Of that you may be confident, gentlemen.'

For a moment everyone listened in stunned silence. Then Grumble began to clap and cheer and stamp his paws, and finally he burst out laughing. The effect was catching and soon all five lay doubled up in the bottom of the boat, hooting with laughter until their sides ached and the tears streamed down their faces.

Which is why none of them looked back.

If they had, the sight would have sobered them up in an instant. Where the bright fairies had danced there remained nothing but a black, stinking patch of rotting weeds, and the fairy queen was no more than a bent slimy stalk. The whole thing had been a clever illusion, a projection created by Hagbane herself.

Back in her castle she gloated over her crystal ball by which she had seen and controlled the whole business.

'Meddling brats! It worked even better than I expected. I shall destroy them now, once and for all. Heh, heh, heh!' she cackled.

Her laughter echoed through the castle corridors as the sun passed behind the clouds.

Still quite intoxicated by the magic food, the company in the boat failed to notice that the river was beginning to flow faster and that the water was becoming rougher. They also missed the landmark that indicated the path back to Trotter's house.

The little boat began to bob and buck in the quickening current. It rounded the two bends in the river and sped into a straight stretch strewn with boulders that jutted from the hissing water like fossilised teeth. Soon it was racing out of control. A muted roar filled the air, its sound drowning out the noisy rush of the water. To anyone looking the river appeared to end in mid-air, but the occupants of the boat were not looking. Instead, they lay in a tangled heap in the bottom of the boat, still laughing helplessly and with no idea of the danger they faced. Bobbing like a cork and trapped in the surging current the boat sped straight towards a raging waterfall.

Suddenly, there was a sickening crunch as the boat crashed into one of the jagged rocks jutting from the river bed. Water poured over the bows, dowsing everyone on board, while the current hurled the boat forward once again.

The effect of this sudden cold soaking was to bring the mice and the boys to their senses. Joshua scrambled up and peered over the gunwale. He gasped with fright as he saw the menacing rapids through which they were rushing, and the way the river just dropped away to nothing right ahead of them.

'Quick, everyone,' he yelled. 'We're heading straight for a waterfall!'

The boat crashed and ricocheted off the rocks one more time and then shot towards the brink.

Everyone clung grimly to whatever they could and

prepared for the worst. Andrew gritted his teeth and Joshua braced his legs against the seat. With a bone-jarring crash their craft slammed into more rocks and then jammed fast between two boulders right on the very edge of the falls.

The force of the impact was so great that Fumble was thrown overboard and would have been swept to his death if his leg had not once more caught in the mooring rope. Gurgling and spluttering, choking in the foam and spray, he struggled to stay alive in the swirling current. Just in time, Joshua seized the rope and hauled the poor mouse back on board.

'Thanks,' Fumble gasped. He was coughing and shaking with fright as he tumbled into the boat to join the others.

Together, the boys and the mice cowered in the bottom of the boat. The deafening roar of the waterfall numbed their minds and for a moment nobody dared move.

Then Joshua slowly inched himself up and peered over the gunwale.

The sight that met his eyes was awesome. It took his breath away. They were trapped on the very edge of the waterfall. Through the spray he could see the trees and the distant mountainous horizon. Somewhere below them he knew the river must continue, but on the edge of this precipice all he was aware of was the sheer drop into thin air.

The boat creaked and groaned and the sound snapped him back to their predicament. Some of the planks had sprung and the hull was rapidly filling with water. Joshua knew that they had only minutes before it broke up and they were swept over the brink to their deaths. Aghast, he turned to his companions. They all looked utterly terror-struck.

The thundering rush of the waterfall made speech impossible. Desperately, Joshua made signs to say that they could do nothing except shout together for all they were worth.

'Help! Help!' they cried, 'Somebody please help us!'

10
Safe and Sound

The warmth of the morning sun woke Sophie from an untroubled sleep. Lazily, she opened her eyes and squinted against the sun's glare. She gave a dreamy smile and her hand felt the softness of the sheepskin rug on which she lay. For a long moment she imagined she was in her own bedroom back home.

Then it all began to come back to her – the flight from Hagbane's castle, the awful wizards, the terror she had felt when Arca swooped towards her, that fearsome battle against the Grims – and then, her mind was a blank. She didn't know what had taken place after that. She sat up with a jolt and gazed around her.

'Where am I?' she said.

To her astonishment she was lying near the entrance of a small, sunlit cave high up on a rocky precipice. A breathtaking view of Alamore stretched before her – an immense ocean of treetops, with silvery rivers and purple mountains in the hazy distance. The air smelt fresh and invigorating and she breathed it in deeply.

'Arca must have brought me here,' she thought to herself. 'I wonder where he's got to?'

She rose and made her way to the cave entrance.

The sight made her gasp. The rock fell sheer away to a dizzy depth beyond her imaginings. She stepped back quickly, realising that she was very high up a mountain and that only Arca could take her back down.

She looked around the cave and noticed with surprise a bowl of clear liquid and a lump of bread. Arca must have brought it, she thought. It reminded her that she had not eaten or drunk for a long time. Thankful to Arca for his thoughtfulness, she sat down cross-legged and began to eat hungrily. The bread was deliciously fresh and the liquid tasted sweet and tangy. Whatever it was, it made her feel full of life and energy.

Having eaten her fill, she flopped back on her bed in the warm sunshine to wait for Arca's return. The air about her seemed wonderfully good and clean and for the first time since she and her brothers had arrived in Caris Meriac she felt not a care in the world.

'I think I'll call the drink 'Arca-ade',' she said aloud. 'Hm, Arca-ade, like lemonade, and Arca-ade because it aids you.' Smiling, and satisfied with that she closed her eyes and snoozed in the sun.

* * *

Far, far below and on the opposite side of the Great Forest, Prince Oswain came to the banks of the River Wendle. There he found the ford and crossed from the Waste Plains into the shadows of the tall barren trees. No one noticed his arrival except the trees, some of which seemed to tremble at his coming as though they were expecting him.

'My journey is almost ended and my destiny about to begin,' he announced to the silent woods. So saying, he plunged into the depths of the Forest.

* * *

'Help! Somebody rescue us,' cried Joshua. 'Help!'

The water continued to crash into the doomed boat. Another plank snapped off with a sharp splintering noise and was carried over the roaring falls to the rocks below. By now, what with the spray and the water that more than half-filled their disintegrating boat, the boys and the mice were soaked to the skin.

Andrew wondered how much longer they could last out. Already he was growing numb with cold and his teeth were chattering. Joshua reckoned the boat had only minutes to survive before the force of the water smashed it to match wood. He called out even more earnestly.

They were just beginning to lose hope when a faint voice called from the bank.

'Hold on. We'll soon have you out of there. Don't worry. Just hold on.'

'It's Trotter!' Andrew shouted. 'And look, there are lots of other animals with him.'

They spotted a large crowd of forest-folk waving to them from the riverside. In desperation they waved back.

'But how are they going to rescue us?' bellowed Joshua above the roar of the falls.

'I don't know, but Trotter seems pretty sure he can do it,' his brother shouted. 'Look, he's sorting out something or other.'

The next moment, they saw a fluttering of black wings, and to their surprise several blackbirds began to fly across the intervening water. Dangling from their claws was a length of rope. The other end was being firmly grasped by the animals gathered on the river bank.

Joshua laughed. 'Fantastic! Look at that. It's a lifeline.'

The rescue was a marvellous piece of teamwork. The

blackbirds dropped their line into the eager hands of the boat crew and Trotter called out instructions from the bank.

The plan was to haul the mice across together but Mumble and Grumble refused to go with Fumble in case he messed it up.

'And I'm not going with you, either,' Grumble said to Mumble. 'I won't have a clue what you're talking about.'

Joshua stepped in quickly. 'We haven't much time,' he yelled. 'You all go together, and no more arguing.'

Swiftly, and before they could protest further, he tied the rope around the three mice with a bowline and pushed them into the water. At once, those on the bank began to pull on the rope for all they were worth.

Stiggle the stoat was in charge of the rescue party. 'Heave!' he cried. 'Heave!'

Fumble struggled to stay afloat in the rushing current. Water filled his mouth and ran up his snout. He began to choke. Terrified for his life, he thought he would drown before his friends could pull him and his companions from the raging torrent.

But after what seemed an age, the three mice were pulled into calm water and with much cheering their rescuers dragged their bedraggled bodies onto dry land. As soon as the mice were safely beached the blackbirds flew back with the rope and dropped it into Joshua's waiting hands.

'Our turn now,' Joshua shouted. 'You go next, Andrew. No, don't argue; this thing's going to break up any minute. Go on!'

After the briefest hesitation, Andrew plunged into the icy current. The chill took his breath away. For one awful moment it looked as if the forest-folk wouldn't have the strength to pull him out and he would be swept over the falls. However, they never lost their determination and after a lot of heaving and blowing they managed to pull him safely to the shore.

'Get the rope to Joshua. Quick!' he gasped as he staggered ashore, the water streaming off his clothes.

They were only just in time; with a final sickening crunch, the boat broke into pieces and disappeared over the falls. Joshua clutched in desperation at the rock and only just managed to grab hold of the rope. Thankful that they had left his knot intact, he squeezed through the loop and plunged into the foam.

His journey through the raging torrent was a little easier than Andrew's because Andrew was able to pull the rope as well, but it was still hard work and everyone was much relieved when he finally climbed out of the water to rejoin his friends.

'Thank you, thank you, Trotter,' Joshua panted. 'And everyone. You turned up just in time.'

'Wee fought weir gun ass,' said Mumble.

'Huh, that fancy talking of yours didn't last long,' Grumble sneered.

Andrew turned to Trotter.

'But how did you know where we were?' he asked. 'Did you hear us calling?'

'All in good time,' replied Trotter with a smile. 'The first thing to do is to get you home and dry with something hot to eat. You have done very well, all of you. I feel extremely proud of you. But we must go. No more questions until we've had some of Mrs T's cooking, eh, Andrew?'

Three-quarters of an hour later they were gathered around a blazing fire in Trotter's home and drinking tea after eating a splendid meal. The boys and the mice were feeling much better and had more or less dried out.

'Now then, Trotter, please tell us what's been happening and how you found us,' Joshua insisted.

'Very well,' replied the badger. 'Aldred and I waited for a long time after you went into the castle, but nothing happened. We began to fear the worst and think you had fallen into a trap. Then we saw Hagbane in her tower conjuring up that snowstorm. We knew then that you must have escaped from the castle.'

Aldred the weasel took up the tale. 'We tried to find you, but the storm was too bad. I've never seen anything like it. Anyway, we searched for ages until it was almost dark but even our best trackers couldn't find you,' he explained. 'The snow around her castle made it difficult. We couldn't pick up even the trace of a scent, let alone a footprint.'

'That's because we were underground by then,' interrupted Andrew. He went on to tell them all about Terras and Sorda.

'Ah, that's how it happened, is it?' Trotter nodded. 'No wonder we couldn't find you.'

'Did you know about those wizards?' asked Joshua.

'No, that is an unexpected development, and a bad one,' said Trotter.

'Rumours have reached us of some mischief afoot.' It was Aldred who spoke. 'Forest-folk have been disappearing without trace, and those Grims have been seen flying at dusk,' he said. 'We hadn't realised the connection until now.' His face was grim. ' It's utterly awful.'

'I agree,' added Stiggle. 'If I ever get my claws on those two....'

'Well, to continue,' Trotter interrupted. 'We kept searching for you, hoping to find a clue and then the great eagle, Arca, met us. He told us what had happened.'

'Yes, he advised us to get some rest' Stiggle explained, 'and then he came back this morning to help us meet up with you. He had seen what happened to you and he directed us to the waterfall.'

'Why didn't Arca rescue us, then?' Andrew asked.

'I don't know, but he told me that he had other very important matters to deal with,' Trotter explained. 'He felt we could manage by ourselves.'

'Well, he was right about that,' said Joshua. 'You did brilliantly.'

Andrew looked mystified. 'I still don't quite understand what really did happen on the river,' he said. 'All I know is, we met some fairies and the next thing I remember is the waterfall.'

'That is not too difficult to explain,' Trotter answered. 'You were the victims of one of Hagbane's tricks. There are no fairies in the forest but she created an illusion that fooled you and took away your control of the boat. As far as she is concerned it was as good a way as any to destroy you.'

'And she very nearly did,' said Joshua with feeling. 'What a fool I was to be taken in twice.'

'You weren't the only one,' his brother consoled him. 'We were all tricked this time. Just thank goodness for Arca's help.'

'Evil has often copied good,' said Trotter seriously. 'Do not trust appearances or words, particularly smooth and flattering words.' He looked Joshua seriously in the eye. 'Remember too, Joshua, that a thing of great evil can also be a thing of beauty; nor are ugly things necessarily bad. You must learn to see the inner nature of things, and especially of people, if you want to be wise.'

Joshua wasn't sure that he understood, so Aldred tried to explain. 'Arca is a good example of what Trotter means. He frightens me, to tell you the truth, and he's a strange creature, living in a high and lonely world, where he keeps his own secrets. But he's altogether good and he is a true messenger of Elmesh.'

'Sophie! Is Sophie all right? Did Arca save her?'

Joshua felt guilty for not asking after his sister sooner.

'She's fine,' Aldred laughed. 'Arca will return her to us very shortly. He may be scary but he's scary on our side, if you know what I mean.'

Joshua and Andrew were delighted to know that their sister was safe and were thrilled to hear about the aerial battle against the Grims and the part Sophie had played in it.

'I wish we'd stayed behind to watch,' said Andrew.

'No you don't,' Joshua answered. 'Just remember that Grim!'

Andrew grimaced in agreement. Then he noticed the mice and realised that nobody had heard a squeak out of them for a while.

'Ah, look,' he said. 'They're fast asleep.'

The three mice were curled up together in front of the fire.

'They were marvellous,' laughed Joshua. 'You were right, Stiggle, they were the ideal choice to rescue me.'

Stiggle grinned at Aldred, who grudgingly agreed.

Trotter suddenly became serious again.

'Listen,' he said. 'All this worries me. I do not pretend to know all that Elmesh is doing. Doubtless, he has good reason for sending you children here, but it is obvious to me that even with Gilmere you are no match for Hagbane.'

'I agree,' said Joshua. He faced the badger squarely. 'Can I be honest? Ever since we arrived here I've felt completely out of my depth. I mean, it's really no use asking kids like us to help you fight Hagbane. Then there's Terras and Sorda as well. I don't know even where to start.'

'We do have Arca on our side,' his brother reminded him.

Joshua shrugged.

'He is a great fighter,' said Aldred. 'But I'm not sure if even he could beat Hagbane single-handed. The trouble is, so many of our best troops are locked up in her castle. If only we could rescue them things would be much easier.'

'I know,' said Joshua with feeling. 'I saw some of them. They looked in a bad way and I just wish we could have set some of them free. There must be a way to get them out.'

'We need help,' Trotter declared. 'and I don't know where it is to come from. I shall seek Elmesh's wisdom tonight but I cannot risk your lives again.'

'But you said we were sent here to help you fight Hagbane,' Andrew protested.

Trotter shook his head. 'Things are too unevenly matched at present and until matters change I think we must simply lie low and keep out of harm's way as best we can. Though, goodness knows, she will be out hunting us soon enough,' he added.

They sat brooding over the problem. Nobody really knew what to say and the longer they sat the more oppressive the enemy seemed. A dark despair settled over their spirits like a low winter cloud.

Suddenly there were noises outside; a heavy footstep, a cracking twig. Everyone jumped as the sounds broke their silence.

Then with a light creak of the hinges the door swung slowly open, and a long black shadow fell across

130

the floor. Horrified, Mrs Trotter screamed aloud, and her teacup crashed to the floor.

11
Oswain Takes Charge

Fear and dismay paralysed everyone in the room as they stared at the long shadow darkening the threshold. Only one thought went through each of their heads: Hagbane had come in person to wreak her vengeance!

Not an eye blinked as the shadow advanced. Joshua could barely breathe. Andrew gripped the arm of his chair. His face was taut with fear.

Yet it was no evil-looking Hagbane who stepped into the room. Instead, they found themselves confronted by a tall stranger dressed in a hooded, green travelling cloak, the hood of which completely hid his face.

For a moment, nobody moved; then Aldred whipped out his sword and leapt forward. All his doubts about the children came flooding back. If this wasn't Hagbane, then he could only be one of the wizards or some other enemy.

'Show yourself,' growled the stoat, 'before I run you through.'

There was a moment of tense silence. Then the stranger laughed and threw back his hood. A clean-shaven young man stood before them. To Joshua he seemed both noble and kindly, yet his dark eyes flashed with an inner fire.

'There will be no need for that, Aldred,' he said. His voice was rich and deep. 'Please permit me to introduce myself. I am Prince Oswain, the son of Argil, High King

132

of Castelfion, and of all the lands westwards.'

He smiled and bowed slightly. There was an authority in his manner, and a fearlessness that made Aldred lower his sword. Joshua relaxed a little.

The stranger looked about him.

'You must be Joshua and you, Andrew – two of the Brown children. Yes, and you are Trotter, the lore-master of the forest-folk, if I am not mistaken. To you, I offer my apologies for having entered your house unannounced, but I felt it wise to be discreet.'

Andrew, looking incredulous, whispered to Joshua, 'How does he know who we are?'

Joshua shook his head, looking equally bemused.

The prince turned to Mrs Trotter. 'Dear lady of the house, my apologies for causing you such a fright. Please forgive me.'

'Well, I...I'm sure I do, sir,' replied a flustered Mrs Trotter. 'You are welcome to our home.'

Aldred coughed loudly at this point. 'Um, with due respect,' he said, 'could you explain yourself to us? Why are you here?'

'And how do you know so much about us?' Trotter asked.

The tall stranger smiled. 'You are quite right. First, let me put you at ease by saying that I have been sent to the Great Forest of Alamore by Elmesh himself.'

'If that is so, you are truly welcome,' said Trotter. 'But you will understand our caution when I tell you that our enemy is highly skilled at deception. We have been fooled in the past and will not make that mistake again.' He looked keenly at Oswain. 'To say you are from Elmesh is a strong statement, my friend. What proof do you bring?'

Oswain glanced at them each in turn and nodded.

'First, I give you my oath which I make by the fire of the Merestone and the light of Elrilion. Furthermore, I bring a token that will demonstrate the truth of my words.'

Joshua and Andrew watched as he removed his glove to reveal a ring upon the second finger of his right hand. The gold ring was large and intricately fashioned, but what caught everyone's attention was the jewel set within it. This was no ordinary diamond or emerald; it did not catch light and reflect it. This jewel smouldered and flashed with its own fire. It was like nothing that any of them had ever seen. Joshua swallowed as he felt the hair tingle on the nape of his neck.

Trotter shuffled forwards and took Oswain's hand in his paw. He peered closely at the fiery stone and then raised his eyes to meet Oswain's, his gaze filled with awe and wonder.

'Yes, you judge correctly,' said the stranger, without waiting for Trotter to speak. 'It is a fragment of the Merestone itself.'

'Sit down, please,' whispered the old badger. 'I need no further proof. For one who has gazed upon the Merestone, it is enough. You are welcome among us.'

At this point the three mice stirred and woke. Seeing Aldred with his sword drawn, Grumble leapt to his feet and confronted the stranger.

'Don't move a muscle or I'll have you by the throat!' he cried up at Oswain.

Fumble and Mumble joined him and prepared to do battle. Mumble grabbed the poker from the fireside and brandished it at Oswain while Fumble bared his teeth and tried to look menacing.

'It's all right,' Trotter reassured them. 'This one is a friend. His name is Prince Oswain.'

He motioned Aldred to put his sword away and as

everyone settled down he ushered Oswain to the best seat in the room. Even Aldred seemed to relax.

Once they were all seated Oswain began to speak.

'My mother is Queen Talisanna and she gave me this ring several years ago. She would not say how she obtained it, but I remember feeling that it had cost her much suffering to do so.' He twisted the ring with his other hand. 'It has never been removed from my finger and nor could it be now, as you can see. Yet one day it will be removed, for it is said that this jewel will be reunited with the Merestone – although I do not know how.'

'The prophecy!' cried Joshua looking eagerly at Trotter. 'The one you showed us.'

'Yes,' Trotter nodded. 'You are quite right, Joshua. Then you, Oswain, are the promised ruler, the coming one who will set the Great Forest free.'

'You were right about the signs, and the coming of the children. I knew it!' cried Mrs Trotter, beaming at her husband. 'Elmesh be praised!'

Trotter pushed himself out of his seat and bowed low before Prince Oswain.

'Sire, I am your servant and at your command,' he said.

Aldred and Stiggle took their cue from Trotter and did likewise. Aldred motioned the three mice to follow them. Mrs Trotter, still beaming, curtsied.

Joshua glanced across to his brother. 'Us, too?' he asked.

Andrew nodded enthusiastically and both boys bowed awkwardly.

Oswain held up his hand.

'I am honoured to lead you,' he said, 'but enough of this bowing and scraping. We must work together, for

135

we all have a part to play in defeating this tyranny.' His eye caught Mrs Trotter's. 'So, perhaps this is a good moment for some refreshment.'

'I'll put the kettle on,' said Mrs Trotter. 'It's not every day we have royalty in our home.'

Oswain smiled at her. 'If you knew the truth, Mrs Trotter, you would realise that you are of royal blood yourselves. True nobility has little to do with birth but much to do with how you handle pain and adversity.'

Mrs Trotter's fur bristled with embarrassment.

'Well, I'm not sure about that, sir, but I can see you're a good sort, and all that.' Slightly flustered she hurried out to make the tea.

Oswain faced the others once more. 'I know your plight. My destiny involves the Merestone. I am also aware of the dark force that oppresses you and I am determined to break it. It will be a hard battle, of course, but one that we must win.'

Andrew put his hand up uncertainly. 'Um, did Elmesh tell you all our names, too?' he asked.

Oswain laughed. 'No. There is a very simple answer to that question, Andrew. I have spoken with Arca already. That is why I know so much about what is going on.'

'Arca! Of course. And Sophie – is Sophie all right?'

'She is very well, as you will see for yourselves quite soon.'

With that, Oswain led them outside and, gazing up into the sky, he gave a long shrill whistle. For a moment nothing happened. Then Andrew spotted a small dot high among the clouds.

'Look, there!' he cried.

The dot grew rapidly and moments later they could see the unmistakable shape of the great white eagle as he plunged towards the earth. Joshua and Andrew shaded their eyes as they tried to spot their sister.

With his great wings outspread, Arca swooped down to make a graceful landing just a few metres from where everyone stood waiting.

'There she is!' cried Joshua.

He ran forward as Sophie, with her hair flying all over the place, tumbled from the eagle's back.

'Sophie!'

'Joshua! Andrew!' she squealed breathlessly. 'Thank goodness you're safe. Oh, I'm so glad to see you again!'

She threw her arms around her brothers and for a few moments they just hugged and squeezed one another for all they were worth. None of them were able to find words to express their relief at being together again.

The silence didn't last long and soon they were swapping stories eagerly and asking all the who, what, when and where questions they could think of.

'I've been to the most awesome place – a cave in the mountains...and you should have seen the view!' Sophie enthused, spreading her arms. 'And I've had this amazing drink that I've called Arca-ade....'

'But what's it like riding on Arca's back?' Joshua interrupted.

'Awesome. Really awesome.'

'Did you really kill a Grim yourself?' Andrew wanted to know.

'Yes, but let's not talk about that. Tell me what happened to you two. Arca told me about the waterfall. That must have been so scary.'

'It was,' said Joshua.

'And wet,' Andrew added.

'So, how did you get rescued?'

Joshua explained about the lifeline.

137

'Tell us about the battle with the Grims,' said Andrew. 'I want details, all the gory details.'

'Are Fumble, Mumble and Grumble ok?'

'They're fine. Don't worry. So, what about these Grims?' Andrew persisted.

'I bet you were scared out of your brains when you first saw Arca,' said Joshua.

'I was terrified,' Sophie answered. 'I thought he was going to rip me to pieces.'

'But the Grims?' cried Andrew.

Joshua saw Oswain coming across to join them. He motioned to his brother and sister and they turned to face the prince.

Oswain was smiling. He looked directly at Sophie and suddenly she felt very special.

'Hello,' he said. 'You must be Sophie.'

She gazed up into his dark eyes and caught the flash of a deeper fire. Sophie knew there and then that she and Oswain would have a special understanding between them. For a brief moment it made her skin tingle strangely and she wondered what this meeting would mean for the future.

'Hello,' she said quietly.

At that moment Mrs Trotter came to the door with a tray of steaming mugs.

'What a to-do,' she exclaimed. 'I come into the front room and you've all gone. And there I am standing here with all these cups of nettle tea and nobody to drink them.' She spotted Sophie. 'Sophie! You're back, my dear. Here, somebody take this while I give her a kiss.'

Mrs Trotter handed the tray to Andrew while Joshua went across to where Arca stood preening his feathers.

'Um, sir, I want to say thank you for saving Sophie's life and, well, all of us really. You've been...brilliant.' It was the best Joshua could manage, overawed as he was by the might of the eagle.

Arca looked up from his preening and held Joshua's gaze for a moment.

'Elmesh has sent me to play my part in the destruction of evil. He has sent you too. It is right that we have met,' the eagle replied.

'Yes, well, thank you, anyway,' Joshua replied slightly nonplussed by the eagle's manner.

'You must not mind Arca's ways,' said Oswain joining them. 'He does not feel as we do. He is a creature who inhabits harsh and lonely places, but to do the will of Elmesh is his one desire.' He smiled. 'Now I must speak with him out here for a little while, since he will not enter a house. We have to make plans before nightfall.'

*   *   *

'So, how are we going to defeat Hagbane?' Joshua asked.

A council of war was taking place in Trotter's front room.

Everyone felt more confident and determined now that Oswain was with them. He was the type of person that made you feel that you mattered and that together you could win the game. No one questioned his right to leadership in the campaign, and he led their discussions.

'We need to be wise,' he said. 'It would be no victory if Hagbane escaped with the Merestone. We must recapture that at all costs.'

This rather put paid to Andrew's suggestion that they should simply blow her up in her castle, assuming that they possessed explosives – which they didn't. They needed a more subtle plan.

Aldred spoke up. 'It seems to me that we must rescue the prisoners before we do anything else. Some of my finest troops are in her dungeons and she will certainly kill them if she suspects an attack. In fact, recent events may have already put their lives at great risk.'

'Yes, and she can always blackmail us while she has them. Their lives for her terms,' added Stiggle.

'I agree,' answered Oswain. 'Then that must be our first priority.' His eyes scanned the group. 'Now, we need to find a way of drawing her and her guards away from the castle. We must find her weak spot. Does anyone have ideas?'

'Oh, that's easy enough,' said Trotter with a laugh. 'She is vain. The most conceited creature you could ever imagine.'

'She might be open to a bit of flattery then,' said Oswain.

'In that case, I think I have a plan.' It was Stiggle who spoke. Carefully, he explained to them his ideas.

'It might work. It might just work!' cried Oswain. 'Yes, Let's give it a go!'

*   *   *

That night there was a flurry of activity on the part of the forest-folk. Animals scurried to and fro in the darkness and there was much whispering of instructions and passing on of progress reports. The younger animals, like Mavis the rabbit and her friends, found it especially exciting to be part of such a secret plan.

It was not until the cold dark hour before the dawn that most fell tired but satisfied into their beds. Indeed, if it had not been for sheer exhaustion many would have stayed awake with excitement. However, Trotter was stern. 'Everyone needs their rest so that we are all alert enough to get away with this. So off to your beds!'

Stage two of Stiggle's plan began quite early the next morning when Fumble, Mumble and Grumble – who to the relief of many had been excused the night's work – set off once more towards Hagbane's castle. Only this time they made no attempt to conceal their coming.

'Ouch, that hurt my toe,' groaned Fumble as he picked himself up after tripping on a tree root.

'Huh, if you carry on at this rate we'll never even reach the place,' Grumble complained. 'Not that I think that would be a bad thing, if you ask me. Why is it always us who get landed with the dangerous jobs, that's what I want to know?' He shrugged his shoulders. 'I mean, she's likely to kill us on the spot after the trouble we've caused her.'

'Hows top man in.'

'What's that you say, Mumble? Eh? Speak up then, you daft cheesehead!' Grumble was feeling very moody indeed.

'Leave him alone,' said Fumble. 'I'm sure it'll be all right. Oswain thinks it will.'

'I just hope you're right, that's all I can say.'

At last they came in sight of the castle.

'Here we go then,' said Grumble.

With hearts thumping, in full view, the three mice approached the dark and forbidding main door. Dead bats hung from trees on either side of them, the sight of which made the mice shiver with disgust. These were, after all, their cousins.

The moment they came under the castle's shadow a Grog guard stepped out to bar their way. He held a spear at the ready.

141

HAGBANE'S DOOM

'Halt! What's yer business 'ere? Don't yer know yer trespassin'?' He grinned wickedly, showing his broken yellow teeth, and brandished his spear in their faces. 'Yer can git yer froat cut fer that.'

'Please, sir, your honour,' began Fumble. 'We have come to beg an audience with the great Queen Hagbane. We bring an important message for her and we come in peace.'

At this point Grumble produced a white flag, and waved it before the guard.

'News, eh? And yer want ter see 'er majesty do yer? Wait 'ere, an' I'll go an' ask 'er if she wants ter see yer. An' if she don't, I'll slit yer froats,' he added as an afterthought before vanishing inside.

'Do you think it's going to work?' whispered Grumble.

'I hope so. Anyway, so far so good. Look out, here she comes!'

The Crone appeared before them as though she were made of wavering grey smoke. She fixed them with a baleful glare.

'You! Yes, I've seen you before, haven't I?' she snarled. 'With those meddling children, were you not? And you have thwarted me twice. Vermin!' she screamed. 'For that you shall die – and very slowly.'

The mice trembled but somehow managed to keep their nerve.

'Please, your majesty,' said Fumble, who had been appointed spokesmouse. 'Before you kill us, please hear what we've come to say. We come in peace with a message from the forest-folk.'

'Message? What message?' she snapped. 'Speak, vermin scum. Your life depends on whether I like what I hear.' She moved menacingly towards Fumble and

142

towered over him.

Fumble stood humbly before the Crone and recited the speech he had practised earlier. Taking a deep breath, he said:

'O Mighty Queen of the Great Forest and Holder of the Merestone, Ruler of Grogs and Grims, Fearsome Majesty – if it pleases you, your highness, we bring a humble petition,' he quavered. 'We have regretfully fought your Majesty over many years but we believe that now is the time for surrender.' He held out his paws, imploring. 'We have had enough, and we wish a speedy end to the fighting. So, O Mighty One, our petition is this: To give you the honour due to you, your Majesty, the forest-folk crave an open-air audience with you today. They wish to acknowledge and celebrate your true worth and greatness.'

The Crone glared suspiciously at the mouse but then, as Trotter had correctly judged, her vanity got the better of her. She interpreted Fumble's speech as praise.

'Really?' Her eyes gleamed. 'So you have seen sense at last, have you?'

'I believe we have, your majesty,' Fumble replied solemnly.

'Very well, I shall grant you your request, though you are hardly worthy of it,' she smirked. 'Where will it be?'

'If it pleases your highness, we would like you to come to the old clearing at noon. It is an ancient place of honour, fitting for such an occasion as this,' he answered.

'And you will demonstrate your loyalty to me?'

'Your majesty, we are prepared to demonstrate everything that we owe you.'

Hagbane eyed the three mice closely and pondered for a moment.

'Then this is how I shall want it shown,' she commanded. 'You will hand over to my care those Children of Time Beyond Time. Do you understand? They do not belong to the forest and I must deal with them as I see fit. Is that clear?'

'B…b…but, your majesty…'

'Silence! You speak of owing me something. Very well, we shall see!'

'If you say so, ma'am,' said Fumble.

'I do say so, and I shall bring my guards too. So no tricks,' she threatened. 'If you fail, I shall take my vengeance on all of you. There will be no mercy.'

'We understand, your majesty,' Fumble replied.

'Then go, before I lose patience with you. No, wait! You!' She pointed at Fumble. 'You almost questioned my will. I shall keep you as a gesture of good faith.' She turned to Fumble's companions. 'If you are deceiving me, then he will be the first to die. Guard, take him!'

Before the others could protest, the guard seized the hapless mouse in his scaly grip. Mumble and Grumble watched helplessly as he was marched away, followed by the shadowy figure of Hagbane.

'Hm, that didn't work out too well. Poor old Fumble, and he made such a good job of that speech. I would have lost my temper. And as for you, well, she wouldn't have a clue what you were talking about,' said Grumble. 'Anyway, I just hope he'll be all right.'

'O coarse wheel, down wherry,' said Mumble.

'What? Oh, never mind. Well, all I can say is, the plan's got to work now, for Fumble's sake.' Grumble spoke fiercely and his whiskers twitched. He straightened his shoulders. 'Come on, we'd better report back to the others. I dread to think what's going to happen next.'

12

Hagbane Trips Up

'What is this place?'

Joshua asked Stiggle the question later that morning as they reached an open grassy area surrounded by gorse bushes. They were no more than about one kilometre from Hagbane's castle.

'We call this the old clearing,' Stiggle explained. 'The forest-folk have used this place as a gathering point for many years. It's where we announce important news and hold talks about matters that affect all of us. At least, where we used to.'

'Did Hagbane stop all that?'

'Oh, yes. She has banned any kind of free speech,' Stiggle replied with feeling. 'It's one of the first things tyrants do. In any case, most folk feel the clearing is too close to the castle to risk meeting here any more.'

Joshua looked about him. He could see animals of all kinds – foxes, stoats, badgers, weasels, voles, rabbits, field mice, hares, squirrels, and many more – slowly gathering in the clearing. Most of them appeared very uneasy and he could sense the tension in the air.

'You and Andrew must stay out of sight, remember,' Stiggle cautioned. 'Keep behind the gorse. I must go and take my place with the others.'

'Sooner them than us,' said Andrew as he watched Stiggle join the rest of the animals.

'Trotter told me that most of them wanted to stay out

of the way,' said Joshua. 'He and Aldred had to work hard persuading them that they'd be all right.'

Trotter had said to Joshua that – scary though she was – most animals had a picture of Hagbane in their minds that was far worse than the truth. It was this that helped keep them in fear of her.

He thought about this as he watched the animals that, in spite of their fears, gathered in the clearing. Trotter had tried to explain to him that evil thrives when people make too little of it. But evil also thrives when people make too much of it because then they lose the courage they need to break its grip.

'Only those can win who respect the power of evil and yet believe firmly in the greater power of good,' the badger had said.

Joshua wasn't sure that he completely understood, but when he saw Trotter standing alone and unafraid at the head of the uneasy band of animals he knew that the badger had a very special kind of courage.

A weak sun filtered through the silvery-grey sky, giving small comfort as the hour of meeting drew near. Everyone waited in silence. Then Aldred called out that the Crone was on her way, and she had with her a large company of Grogs.

Each animal nervously checked their position and waited. Soon they could see the gaunt, shadowy shape striding towards them, her hair and cloak swirling in the breeze. The gang of Grogs marching raggedly behind her.

High in the sky and so as not to be seen, Arca hovered between the clearing and the sun. From her perch on his back Sophie looked down on the forest. She could make out the dark specks of the animals huddled together in the grassy clearing. A little further away she could see the castle and the paths that led from it.

'Now is our chance,' cried Arca, whose eyes had taken in every fine detail. 'We must be swift. There will not be much time.'

So saying, he soared in a wide sweeping arc and then swooped low over the tree tops out of Hagbane's line of vision and over the castle walls. Gritting her teeth, Sophie braced herself and prepared to use the mirror.

It was as well that she did because the remaining guards rushed them the very moment that they landed. From her feathery perch on Arca's back she wielded the mirror and Gilmere shot forth its fearsome light, striking one Grog after another.

Sophie lost count of how many she hit but each one turned into a frightened frog that fled for its life. The opposition collapsed with scarcely a croak.

'So far so good,' panted Sophie, closing the mirror. 'Now what?'

Glancing around the courtyard they saw a number of iron-barred gates from which all sorts of animals stared in wide-eyed wonder.

'Don't be afraid,' called Sophie. 'We've come to rescue you.'

She slipped from Arca's back and ran from gate to gate, focusing the mirror on the locks. In an instant the doors sprang open and the prisoners were free. Many could hardly believe it and walked out stunned and blinking in the sunlight; others leapt free with great joy; some who were very weak had to be carried from their cells. However, in a short time a great crowd of amazed stoats, foxes, weasels, squirrels, moles, voles and badgers had assembled in the courtyard.

Sophie, meanwhile, had run downstairs to the basement cells where Joshua had been held. There she found many more animals and soon busied herself releasing them.

It was here, too, that she found Fumble who was so overjoyed to see her that he flung himself against her and brought them both crashing to the ground in fits of laughter.

'Come on, stop being silly,' Sophie laughed. 'We really don't have time to mess about. Let's just get everyone out of here.'

Arca, meanwhile, was using his talons to airlift the weakest of the animals over the castle walls so that they could escape into the shelter of the trees as soon as possible.

Sophie came panting up the stairs followed by a jubilant host of creatures.

'This way,' she cried as she ran towards the heavily barred main gate.

Swiftly, she trained Gilmere's light on to the lock, muttering a prayer to Elmesh that it would work. The bars began to slide back and slowly the great oak doors swung open.

Freedom beckoned.

It was then that misfortune struck. Even as the gates opened, a loud, raucous trumpet sounded from high in the castle turret. No one could fail to hear it, including Hagbane.

'It must be some kind of alarm,' Sophie gasped in dismay. 'Quick, all of you, run! Run for your lives!'

*   *   *

Hagbane strode purposefully into the clearing. She was plainly in a no-nonsense mood.

Her eyes scanned the assembled animals.

148

'Halt,' she commanded her guards. They shambled to a standstill.

Folding her arms, she fixed the forest-folk with a contemptuous gaze.

'Well?' she demanded, her voice imperious. 'Here I am. Your queen! Do you have someone worthy of my presence that can speak?'

The Crone had seen Trotter standing at the head of the forest-folk but she deliberately ignored him. However, the old badger was not to be outdone.

'Yes, your majesty,' he said boldly and with dignity. 'As lore-master of the forest-folk, I will address you.'

Hagbane frowned in annoyance and sneered. 'Lore-master? I do not recognise positions I have not appointed but, very well...speak, and make it good – or I'll make it bad.' She cackled at her own wit.

Trotter unfurled a scroll and cleared his throat.

'Ahem. If it pleases your majesty I, Trotter, offspring of Rufus the Strong, member of the forest elders of the noble days of the Great Forest of Alamore in Caris Meriac – The Land Beyond the Far Places – I who am appointed lore-master of the forest-folk by the command of Elmesh, address you on a matter of great importance.

Hagbane began to tut and to arch her eyebrows. But Trotter carried on.

'For a long while, indeed many years, your majesty, you have held power in this forest because you possess the Merestone. Many of us have fought against you during these years and there has been much suffering for our people, many deaths, many imprisonments. The forest has grown weary and is dying.

'The time has come for this to end, your majesty; the days of war must cease and peace return to the Great Forest of Alamore. Now, we would like to express some feelings of loyalty if we could – but first you must show your true queenliness before us, not by violence but be returning the Merestone to its rightful place and….'

'What is this insolent nonsense?' Hagbane screeched. She had been growing more and more irritated by Trotter's speech. Now, she could contain herself no longer.

'How dare you speak to me like this, you impudent filth!' she cried. 'Trying to tell me what to do! Me? Hagbane, the mighty queen of all this land! You bring me out for *this*? I will have no more of it.' Her voice was hard and angry, cold as steel, and she spoke through gritted teeth. 'But I will have your loyalty. Bring me those children. Bring them at once before I destroy every one of you.'

Trotter had known all along that he would have little time to keep Hagbane occupied but he had hoped to delay her for as long as possible. He tried to stall her.

'I am sorry my words displease you, your majesty. Please accept my… '

'Enough! Where are those Children of Time Beyond Time?'

'I…er…they are not actually quite here, if you see what I mean.'

'No, I do not,' she snapped 'Bring them this instant.'

'But, your majesty…'

Trotter's words were interrupted by a loud trumpeting sound that echoed across the forest. It came without doubt from the direction of the Crone's castle.

A sudden flash of realisation crossed the Hagbane's face as she heard the alarm call.

'Stop!' she cried out. Her face contorted with rage and her body shook with sudden fury. 'I've been tricked. Tricked!'

She turned to her guards. 'Do you hear that? It's the alarm.' Her fists clenched, and with a face like thunder she cried out her orders. 'Kill them! Kill every one of them. I want no mercy. Tear them limb from limb. Rip them apart!' she screamed. 'And you can start with him.'

The Crone turned back and pointed at Trotter.

Only Trotter was no longer there. Nor indeed were any other of the animals. Every one of them had vanished as though into thin air.

Hagbane stared wildly about her, her eyes popping with amazement.

'What's the meaning of this? What trickery is going on?' she spat.

Full of rage, she strode forwards – and at once fell flat on her face.

The Crone's foot had caught itself in a deep hole that was barely covered by grass.

For a moment Hagbane lay where she had fallen; then slowly she rose to her feet. Realisation dawned on her face as she saw the size and depth of the hole.

'So that's how they escaped, is it?' she hissed.

'There's another one 'ere, yer 'ighness,' called a Grog. 'And another.'

'It's a plot,' the Crone screamed.

She jumped up and down in a frightful rage, cursing everyone and everything she could think of. 'Why? What are they up to? I'll make the scum pay for this,' she vowed.

The holes were too small for her guards to venture down and so all they could do was run around searching in the gorse. But though they found other holes there was not a single sign of the forest-folk.

'Come here, you fools,' the Crone called. 'Back to the castle. And run! Something's up and I don't like it.'

So saying, she gathered up her skirts and began to run after her guards as fast as her legs could carry her.

Deep in the forest, Joshua tried to catch his breath as he spoke.

'Whew, that was close. I thought Trotter had misjudged it for a moment,' he puffed.

'Yes,' Oswain agreed. He had watched everything from a distance. 'Yet it worked. A brilliant idea of Stiggle's, even if it was a gamble.'

'What was that trumpet sound?' Andrew asked.

'I suspect it was an alarm of some kind,' Oswain said. 'Let's go and see if everything is well. Though I have few fears where Arca is concerned,' he added.

Stiggle's plan had been hard work and risky but it was actually quite simple. The previous night dozens of animals, especially moles and rabbits, had dug long tunnels from behind the gorse bushes and into the centre of the old clearing. From these long tunnels came shorter ones, and from these, shorter ones still, until the whole area was laced with a network of tunnels. After this, they had dug many holes to the surface and covered them carefully with grass.

The next morning when the forest-folk assembled in the clearing, each one had stood just in front of a hole or as near to one as possible. Trotter's instructions had been clear:

'You must all wait until I give the signal,' he told them. 'However afraid you feel, you must stand your ground until then.'

Trotter's chance came, as he had guessed, the moment Hagbane turned to address her guards. Hurriedly, he rolled up the scroll and waved it twice. At his signal each animal simply stepped backwards

152

and bolted into their tunnel.

After that it was easy. The forest-folk scuttled through the network of tunnels until they emerged in the thick of the gorse bushes. It was then simply a matter of scampering away into the depths of the forest just as fast as their legs could carry them.

The plan had been a most successful way of luring Hagbane and her guards from the castle long enough for Sophie and Arca to rescue the prisoners – and those who had taken part in the operation had got away without a scratch.

Deep in the woods that afternoon many meetings took place among the forest-folk. The children wandered from one group to another. They saw loved ones, long separated, being tearfully reunited. Prisoners who had given up hope walked around in a daze, greeting old friends and acquaintances. Parents and youngsters met again, sometimes hardly recognising one another.

Some, whose loved ones had not returned, wept openly and were comforted by others; but then there were the tales being exchanged, tales of brave exploits, of courage in the face of suffering, and of noble deaths.

'We've won a victory, at last,' Andrew exclaimed. 'Isn't this brilliant?'

'Yes,' replied Sophie, who was crying a little herself. 'Yes, it's really wonderful. I feel, well, just so happy.' She wiped her eyes with the back of her hand. 'I feel like... full, if you know what I mean. Letting those prisoners free was the most fantastic thing I've ever done in my life. Just look at them.'

'You were only just in time, though,' said Joshua.

Sophie nodded. 'Mmm. It was close. You know, I nearly died when that alarm sounded. We just ran for it.'

'You should have seen Hagbane when she heard it,'

said Andrew. 'She went ballistic!'

'The best bit was when she stepped into that hole and fell flat on her face,' Joshua laughed.

'Yeah, and then she started running back to the castle with her guards and she looked really stupid,' Andrew chortled. 'Did you see how knobbly her knees were?'

'We had only just got to the shelter of the trees when we saw her guards coming,' said Sophie. 'Like I said, it was close. But we did it!'

'Yes, you did it, and a happy day it is for all of us. Elmesh be praised!' Trotter joined them, beaming through his spectacles. 'You know, I haven't seen such rejoicing in many a year. Not since, well, I can't even remember.' He laughed, 'This is the first real victory we've had over that Crone. She's always thwarted us before – so maybe things are changing at last.'

'You were great, Trotter,' Joshua declared. 'I thought you were so brave to face her like that.'

'Not really, Joshua. I did only what was necessary.'

'And that speech,' Andrew said. 'What were you going to say next?'

Trotter smiled modestly. 'Yes, it was a bit of a mouthful, wasn't it? But I was trying to take as long as possible, you see.' He chuckled. 'If I had continued, I would have told her how evil she was and how Elmesh was angry with her – and that she had better change. That would have made her really angry. Then we would have done our vanishing trick.'

Aldred joined them at that moment. 'I owe you an apology,' he said, addressing Joshua, Sophie and Andrew. 'I should have trusted you. I'm sorry.'

'It's all right,' said Joshua. 'We can't really blame you. After all, we did make a mess of everything at first.'

'We're just glad that it's all turned out so well,' Sophie

added. 'But thank you, anyway. It's nice to be trusted.'

The only person not joining in the festivities was Oswain.

Sophie, who noticed such things, caught the faraway look in his eyes. She could sense a deep sadness, a longing, a heartache too great to be expressed. Wondering what it meant she decided that she must ask him when she got the chance.

'Hey, look everyone!'

Andrew sounded very excited and those nearby turned to see him pointing at the ground. Filled with curiosity they gathered around him and stared at what he had found.

There, growing proudly from the dark soil, was a bright mauve crocus. It was the first to be seen in many a long year.

'A sign of spring,' breathed Trotter. 'The power of Hagbane is beginning to break.'

13
Oswain Finds Out

'And then there was the time when I stumbled across a Grog. Right in my path, he was…'

'I was picked up by a Grim. If I hadn't punched him between the eyes…'

'My dad crept right up to the castle gate…'

'That's nothing. Mine climbed right over the wall!'

It was a night for laughter and for telling tall tales of brave exploits, some of which might even have been true. The forest-folk were in fine spirits and nobody was in a rush to go to bed.

As the light faded and the shadows grew to dusk, the story of the meeting in the old clearing was told and retold with much gusto and imagination. So much so that anyone would have thought Trotter had chased the Crone away single-handedly, while the rest of the animals beat the Grogs to a pulp!

'And you should have seen Arca and Sophie. The Grogs were grovelling even before they landed!'

'Do you remember that one called Slurrit? Well, when Sophie turned him into a frog I squashed him!'

'Really?'

'Yeah.'

'How many Grogs do you think she destroyed. then?'

'Hundreds!'

At length, things began to quieten down and those staying at Trotter's house made their weary but happy way to bed.

Sleep came surprisingly easy for Sophie and for a long while she slept deeply. Then, once again, she began to dream.

She was a feather floating in the warm up-current of a summer's day.

Suddenly, great bats began to swoop and whirl around her and she tumbled crazily through the air. Desperately, she called for help, and in the distance she heard an angry screech as Arca dived to her rescue. Flashes of white fire shot from his eyes and frizzled the bats to smoking cinders that dropped harmlessly to the ground.

Feeling safe once more Sophie grew drowsy and drifted higher and higher in the balmy air.

Bang!

With a shock Sophie found herself in Hagbane's lair. The Crone was feeding a wild fire with parchments and cackling with glee as she did so. A bright jewel – the Merestone – pulsed with light in the centre of the room. Madness showed in the Crone's face.

Then, to her horror, Sophie saw Oswain being dragged into the fire by Hagbane.

She ran to save him, shouting and screaming as she went, but however hard she ran she could get no nearer. Anguish gripped her heart as the flames rose higher and higher until she could no longer see either the Crone or Oswain. The heat and noise of the roaring sheet of fire was too much for her. Everything went black.

Sophie woke, shivering with cold, not sure for a moment whether she was truly awake or still dreaming. She was lying on the floor with a blanket tangled around her arms and legs and her body bathed in sweat. For a while she lay still, trying to understand her dream.

'What's going on with me?' she said to herself under

her breath. 'I never used to dream like this, not back at home.'

Thoughts of home made her wonder about this strange adventure and how they had ever got into it. What a story she would have to tell her friends at school when they got back! If they got back. She reminded herself that she had no way of knowing whether they could or not.

Just then she heard a faint click that broke her thoughts. Curious, she rose and crept to the door. Opening it without a sound, she was just in time to see Oswain's shadowy form disappearing through the front door of the cottage. Sophie hesitated only for a moment before deciding to follow him.

It was cool outside, but fear and excitement made her insensitive to the cold. Although it was dark, the stars and the moonlight bathed the forest in a pale glow that enabled her to see her way. Stealthily, she crept from tree to tree, always keeping a good distance behind Oswain, afraid that he might turn round and spot her. She soon realised that he was heading for the Enchanted Glade.

Sophie relaxed a little. She knew the way and no longer needed to trail Oswain so closely. He would not see her if she hung back and she would reach the glade only minutes after him.

Passing through the great sentinel stones that marked the entrance to the Enchanted Glade, Sophie made straight for the Star Pool. There she found Oswain. Unaware of her presence he was staring intently into the silvery water. Something made Sophie hesitate and instead of rushing up to him she approached softly from one side.

The pool lit Oswain's face with a soft glow, allowing

her to see lines of deep sadness etched into his features. He shook his head slowly, his mouth forming soundless words. The powerful shoulders heaved a great sigh and his whole body shook with unspoken sorrow. Sophie gazed in wonder as silent tears fell from his eyes into the waiting pool. Like the drops of water that fell from the rock above, his tears seemed to catch the shimmering light of Elrilion before mingling with the clear water beneath.

It was all too much for Sophie. A wave of pity swept over her and she began to weep without even understanding why. Forgetting her secrecy she ran to his side and flung her arms around him.

'Oswain, it's me, Sophie,' she sobbed. 'Please don't be cross.'

The prince lifted his head with a start and spun round, seizing her shoulders and holding her at arm's length.

'Sophie! What are you doing here,' he gasped.

Her tear-filled eyes searched his features.

'Please, Oswain, what is it? Why are you so sad?' she asked.

'Why are you here, Sophie?' he repeated, ignoring her questions. 'Did you follow me?'

The words tumbled out. 'I'm sorry, really I am, but I had this terrible dream and when I woke up I heard someone leaving the cottage. I looked out of my room and saw that it was you and I wondered why, because my dream had been about you, and I knew you were sad. So I followed you. I'm awfully sorry if I did wrong.'

His smile when it came was tender, and as he looked into her tear-streaked face she felt both safe and a little afraid all at once. She imagined the stars in those deep, dark eyes of his.

'No, you did not do wrong, Sophie. Not really. Elmesh knows, perhaps it is altogether right for you to be here tonight.' He took her hand and they sat down on a fallen log beside the pool. 'Now tell me about your dream.'

Sophie wiped her eyes and recounted all that she could remember. Oswain listened intently until she had finished.

He gave a sigh. 'Sadly, I believe you have had a true vision of the future, Sophie. I'm afraid something like this will come to pass. Though it is little comfort to know it beforehand,' he added.

'What do you mean?' Sophie exclaimed. 'I don't want anything awful to happen to you. I don't understand all this.'

'No, I do not expect you to. You have fallen into something far bigger than you could possibly understand,' he replied. Then, seeing the sadness in her eyes, he smiled. 'I will try to tell you a little bit about it. It's the least you deserve.'

He rose and walked a short way from her before turning to speak.

'All my life I have known that one day I would be sent to the Great Forest,' he began. 'There was a prophecy, a revelation, many years ago. It spoke of a prince who would journey alone to undo evil and put matters to rights throughout Alamore. The wise said this was the will of Elmesh and taught me that I would know for myself when to begin my journey.'

'How did it happen?' Sophie asked.

Oswain smiled. 'You would understand this, I think. I had a dream. Amazing as it seems, I saw your faces, you and Joshua and Andrew – and the face of Hagbane. That's when I knew my destiny was calling me.'

'So we're part of *your* prophecy as well as Trotter's,'

160

said Sophie wonderingly. 'It's just amazing.'

'Amazing or not, we are all here together – Arca, too, of course – to defeat Hagbane and restore the Merestone,' Oswain answered.

'So have you come from a long way away?'

'Not as far as you and your brothers. At least I come from the same world,' he answered. 'My city, Castelfion, lies across the Waste Plains and beyond the Cadaelin mountains. It is several days away – a hard journey – and there were times when I felt opposed at every step.'

'Are you going to rule the forest in place of Hagbane?' Sophie asked.

'That is so,' he replied solemnly. 'It is Elmesh's decree.'

Sophie looked puzzled.

'Then why are you so sad? I don't understand. After all, we've already begun to beat her. Yet you were sad this afternoon and now you've seen something in the pool that's made you even more unhappy.'

He nodded.

'When I set out I knew that there would be suffering and pain. I wasn't afraid of that and in any case I trusted that Elmesh would protect me. What I didn't understand was why I should be chosen for this destiny. Even the sages in my father's household were unable to tell me that.'

'Is that what you've found out tonight?' whispered Sophie.

'Yes,' Oswain spoke with a great effort. 'Tonight, the pool has spoken and told me why it is I, and I alone, who must walk this path – and I am saddened by the knowledge.'

He turned and walked away. Sophie ran after him and pulled at his sleeve.

161

'Oswain, why? What is it?' she pleaded. 'Please tell me!'

He hesitated and gazed into her earnest face. He almost spoke but nothing came.

'I am sorry, Sophie,' he answered at length. 'But I cannot speak of it. It is too much for me and I must think.'

'Oh, Oswain, this is awful. Whatever must it be? And my dream. Oh…my dream! Does it mean you'll die?'

He was silent and Sophie felt quite helpless. She began to sob.

'No…no…please don't let it happen. There must be another way.'

He put his hands on her shoulders and spoke quietly.

'Sophie, if it is the will of Elmesh…'

'But isn't there anything we can do? Is there no other way?'

He shook his head slowly.

'Oh, why does it have to be like this?' she cried.

'You ask questions too deep for you to understand the answers. You must await the outcome – and there may yet be some surprises. After all, you and your brothers have a part to play in all this.'

'Fat lot of use we've been,' Sophie sniffed. 'All we've done so far is get in the way.'

'That is not true,' he reassured her. 'Tonight you have done something precious. You have brought me comfort in the loneliness of my destiny. I shall not forget that. Now come, we must be back before daylight. And, please, not a word of this to anyone.'

She nodded and tucked her arm into his.

'Look, up there. See how bright Elrilion shines tonight.'

The star's light was strangely comforting and Sophie

felt a little better.

They returned swiftly to Trotter's house where they found that they had not been missed, and Sophie slept soundly for the rest of the night.

*   *   *

Hagbane, however, was not sleeping. She was burning with fury. When she discovered the loss of her prisoners she went into such a rage that her guards fled from her presence and cowered in the empty dungeons. For the rest of the day she stormed and stamped around the castle, screeching out her hatred and vowing terrible destruction on her enemies.

Eventually her rage eased and she lapsed into a gloomy, brooding silence. One by one her troops crept out of the dungeons and quietly went about their business. No one dared to disturb her and for many hours she neither ate nor drank.

Then her mood changed. The anger returned but this time it was not an explosive rage but a cold calculating fury. Her eyes gleamed with hatred as she thought about the forest-folk.

'I shall destroy them all this time,' she muttered. 'There will be no mercy. I've been far too soft on them in the past. But not any longer!' She rose to her feet. 'They will all die, and then I will extend my power until I conquer the world. No one will ever make a fool of me like this again. How dare they think they can do this to me and get away with it? To me! Hagbane the mighty!'

She began to pile together strange powders and vile looking objects on her table – sliced slugs, boiled worms, jellified spiders, and all kinds of other nasty things. Swiftly, she moved to and fro, glancing from time to time at books of magic and all the while muttering dire threats against her foes.

When the foul mixture was complete she mixed it up with her hands and placed the whole disgusting mess in an iron bowl that she then set on a tripod in the middle of the room. After wiping her hands she drew out her wand and pointed it at the floor beneath the tripod. At once, a fire began to burn, heating the contents of the bowl. Hagbane watched as the mixture began to simmer. Her eyes glowed yellow in the firelight and dark shadows flickered about the room.

'Now for the next bit,' she gloated.

She fetched the Merestone and placed it, covered by its velvet cloth, on a stool to the far side of the tripod. With her eyes gleaming, she slowly removed the cover to reveal the jewel. It glowed dully with its own hidden fire.

Hagbane chuckled to herself.

'Now, let's see what we can do with this, shall we?'

The Crone sat down on another stool, this time on the opposite side of the tripod so that the simmering mixture was between herself and the Merestone.

Her eyes fixed on the iron bowl and its steaming contents. It smelt foul but that didn't trouble her. Slowly, rhythmically, she began to sway from side to side. A low moan escaped her lips. In spite of the fire and muted light of the Merestone a terrible darkness descended upon the room. Hagbane began to chant an incantation.

At first nothing else happened.

Her chant grew stronger; her words were fierce and intense, her voice droning like the threatening sound of an angry wasp's nest. A blue flame began to hiss above the iron bowl, lighting her gnarled features with a ghostly hue. Her eyes opened, unseeing, and she grew paler and paler until she was no more than a transparent wraith.

The flame hissed higher and an icy wind filled the air. Doors slammed and things clattered. The room seemed to tilt. Formless shapes whirled about the Crone and throughout the castle her soldiers cowered in nameless dread as she summoned to her aid every dark force she could imagine.

The wind rose to a howl and the room shook so violently that shelves collapsed and cupboards fell crashing all around her. Hagbane breathed a long ragged cry that came from deep inside her.

'Aaaahhhhhhhhhh!'

Suddenly, the Merestone flashed a terrible flame. It shattered the tripod and the bowl with its steaming contents. In their place a ball of radiant blue fire hovered just above the floor. The Crone, now barely visible, fell from her stool and for a long time lay silent and unmoving.

Slowly, Hagbane rose to her hands and knees.

A gleam came into her eye and her mouth twisted into a smirk of pleasure as she saw what lay before her on the floor. She stretched out a hand and grasped a grey rod. It was about a forearm's length and as thick as a broomstick, pointed at each end. Possessed as it was with a strange and terrible power, the rod tingled to the touch.

She gripped it greedily.

'I've done it,' she breathed. 'With this sceptre I shall rule the world. Absolute power will be mine. All will despair before me!'

14
What Sorda Overheard

After the daring raid on Hagbane's castle and the rescue of the prisoners, the morning saw the forest alive with activity. The reason was very simple. Everyone was afraid of what Hagbane would do in return.

'It's all very well, rescuing everyone,' said Grumble, 'But she's going to be after us before you know it. Mark my words!'

With this in mind, many of the forest-folk began to move house altogether, especially those who lived nearest to Hagbane's castle. Quite a few felt that they would be safer if they were near to the Enchanted Glade. Others dug deep burrows and moved their meagre food supplies and scanty possessions as far underground as possible.

'Aren't you going to move house, too, Trotter?' asked Joshua as they stood outside Trotter's cottage.

'Not me,' the old badger replied with a laugh. 'I have lived here too long to leave it now. And Mrs Trotter would never dream of doing so, in any case. No, we will stay and leave our fate in Elmesh's hands.'

'All the same,' Andrew interrupted. 'You ought to have some protection. I mean, I reckon you're the one she's most likely to be after.'

'Well,' smiled Trotter. 'I've got Aldred and Stiggle. They're afraid of very little, you know.'

'Yes, but…'

'Trotter is right.' The speaker was Oswain, who had just joined them. 'This moving is unnecessary. Things will not go as many of the forest-folk fear.'

Seeing the look of surprise on their faces, he added, 'The days of Hagbane are numbered.'

'What do you mean?' Andrew asked in the silence that followed. 'Is there something you know that we don't?' He gave a sidelong glance at Joshua.

"Cos if there is, haven't we got a right to know?' said Joshua. 'I mean, we're part of this as well...'

Sophie said nothing but she watched Oswain closely. Like her, he said nothing.

'You went to the Star Pool in the night.' Trotter said. 'Did you find out your destiny?'

Oswain nodded, his face betraying just a flicker of emotion.

'Joshua is quite right,' he said. 'I should tell you more about why we are all here.'

So Trotter, Mrs Trotter, the children, Aldred and Stiggle, found a grassy bank and sat down with Oswain to hear what he had to say.

'Long ago,' he began, 'as far back in the mists of time as you can imagine, the Great Forest of Alamore was appointed by Elmesh to be a very special place. It was given a certain magic. Indeed, there are those who say that Elmesh himself walked these paths and it was his presence that enchanted the forest. As you well know, the glade still retains that enchantment. It is untouched by Hagbane's curse.'

The others nodded their agreement.

'Legend has it,' Oswain continued, 'that a small meteorite from Elrilion plunged into the forest and its impact carved out the pool. That is why it is called Elmere, the Star Pool.'

'And that is why there is a link between the starlight and the water. I too have heard of the meteorite. Some say it is the origin of the Merestone,' Trotter added.

'Then it's from outer space,' Andrew cried excitedly.

'If that is what it should be called,' replied Oswain with a smile. 'One day you may find it is less 'outer' than you imagine.'

Ignoring Andrew's puzzled frown, Oswain continued.

'Be that as it may, the Merestone is no ordinary jewel. It possesses a power of its own and while it lay in the Enchanted Glade it brought well-being to the whole of the Great Forest. The trees that you see around you grew tall and fair, and birds of every kind and colour rested in their branches. Flowers bloomed in colours and scents that could take your breath away.' He paused. 'Trotter, you know more of this because you were born at the latter end of those days.'

The badger nodded. 'Yes, they were wonderful times. I remember them well; I was just a cub in those days.'

'Me, too,' cut in Mrs Trotter. 'Though, from what my parents told me, it was back in those days, long before there was any trouble, that Gilmere was formed in the pool. Strange that, almost as if trouble was expected.'

'The revelations were delivered by the wise at the same time,' Trotter added, stroking his whiskers. 'Elmesh knew, you see.'

'And then Hagbane came?' Joshua asked.

'Then Hagbane came,' Trotter nodded.

'But why?' Sophie wanted to know.

'I think I can answer that, at least in part,' said Oswain. 'It has to do with the world outside of the Great Forest. I mean the world over which my father rules.'

The prince had their full attention.

'Nobody can fully explain it but everything became unsettled. It was as though there had been a deep earthquake or...or a change in the climate. Nothing was quite as it used to be any more,' said Oswain. 'People felt uncertain about the future and about their safety. In the Westward lands, where I come from, there was much fear and unrest. It seemed that people were always on the move but didn't know where they were going. Bands of outlaws began to appear around our towns and many evil deeds were done. It was as though we had lost control of our lives. Even the air we breathed seemed somehow threatening.'

'How horrible,' said Sophie. She shuddered at the thought.

'Nothing changed here in the forest because of its special enchantment, of course,' Oswain continued. 'That is, until one dark night.' He hesitated. 'A young woman appeared from outside the forest. She came as a pilgrim to Elmere. The woman was still in her teenage years but a bitter evil had already poisoned her heart. She looked upon the Merestone and was hungry to possess it.'

'Hagbane!' they breathed in unison.

Sophie regarded him curiously.

'She came from your country, didn't she? And...'

'Yes,' he cut in before she could continue, 'and on a certain night she entered the glade again and, by some terrible magic, wrenched the Merestone from the Star Pool. Clutching her glittering prize, she fled from the forest and back to her own land. From that moment on the Great Forest began to die. The trees shed their leaves, flowers drooped, and most of the birds perished or fled.'

'For a while we couldn't understand what was

happening,' said Trotter. 'Then we discovered that the Merestone had vanished. Despair filled our hearts, because we did not know what had become of the jewel. All we heard was a rumour of a young woman visiting the glade some time before. It was not until a year later that the full and awful truth dawned on us.'

'Was that when Hagbane came back?' asked Joshua.

'Yes,' said Oswain. 'She came with Grogs and Grims – evil creatures that she herself had a part in producing. She built her castle and began to dominate the forest-folk. Many died who tried to oppose her and many were taken captive to be used in her evil experiments.'

'The wicked creature! I really hate her!' exclaimed Sophie angrily.

Oswain held up his hand.

'All was not lost, however. The Enchanted Glade closed itself off from Hagbane so that she has not been able to find it again to this day. Whenever she tries, she loses her direction and comes back to where she started. That is why the glade still has something of the former life of the forest.'

'Aldred took up the tale. 'Only those who are unpolluted by her evil can venture there. The wise, such as Trotter and his father before him, found wisdom at Elmere and learned to recognise the voice of Elmesh – which is why Trotter knew of your coming.'

'When my father was dying,' said Trotter, 'he gave Gilmere to me, along with the prophecy that I read to you when you arrived.'

'So Elmesh chose to send us?' prompted Joshua.

'Yes, and then Oswain himself. The promised ruler. There was no mistaking the token that he carried.'

'What token?' Andrew asked.

170

'I think he means the ring,' Sophie whispered.

'Oh, right. Where did you get it?' Andrew asked Oswain.

'It came from my mother,' he said, twisting the ring so that they could see its stone. 'This stone is part of the Merestone itself.' He hesitated. 'You see, I discovered last night when I looked into the Star Pool that my mother had battled with Hagbane to seize the Merestone from her. This fragment broke off in the struggle.'

Everyone gasped on hearing this.

Stiggle was the first to find his voice. 'Then your mother has met Hagbane?' he exclaimed.

Oswain looked pained.

'More than that,' he replied heavily. 'I also have known Hagbane before.'

There was a stunned silence at this news. Then everyone gabbled at once.

'Who is she, Oswain?'

'How do you know her?'

'Where did you meet her?'

Before Oswain could respond to the barrage of questions, there was the sharp crack of a twig snapping in the bushes behind them.

Aldred held up his paw.

'Quiet everyone,' he urged. 'There's somebody there.'

Everyone leapt to their feet, tense and alert. They stared at the unmoving shrubs.

Carefully, with Stiggle leading in one direction and Aldred in the other, they encircled the bushes. Then, hearts thumping, they rushed in from both sides.

There was nobody to be seen.

'Perhaps we were imagining it,' said Joshua.

'I don't think so,' Aldred replied, pointing at a broken twig. 'Look, it's not safe to talk for too long outside like this. We should have set a guard. Spies are nothing new to the forest.'

'Yes, yes, you are quite right, Aldred,' agreed Trotter, looking concerned. 'We must warn everyone to be alert to the dangers. In fact, we should do that right away. If anyone was listening I just hope not too much was overheard.'

The sun passed behind a cloud and it was suddenly chilly.

'Let's pair off and pass the message around,' Stiggle suggested.

Everyone agreed and set off to warn folk to be on their guard.

Nobody, for the moment, remembered the unanswered questions; except Sophie, who thought that she might know the answers.

* * *

Not far away, a beady-eyed Sorda watched with an oily smile on his round face.

'Very interesting,' he said to himself. 'Very interesting indeed!'

The treacherous wizard had overheard every word of the conversation and already his mind was hard at work. Glancing about him quickly, he hurried back to their underground lair to speak with Terras.

'Where on earth have you been?' snapped Terras. 'Can't you see there's work to be done? Here am I working my fingers to the bone and all you can do is wander off. I thought we were supposed to be partners. What do you think she's going to say if we don't start up again soon? Eh?'

Terras was in a bad mood when Sorda arrived. He

was till trying to put together what was left out of the mess created by the children's onslaught three days before. Worse, they had been on the receiving end of Hagbane's wrath for having failed to provide a sacrifice for her Grims. She had refused to listen to their explanation and warned them that if they did not improve quickly they had better leave the forest, or die. The news of Hagbane's recent defeats only made them more afraid of displeasing her.

'Far from doing nothing, I've been finding out things of great value to us,' Sorda replied.

'Here, give me a hand with this table, will you? Or at least, what's left of it. If only I could get my hands on those children again – and those meddling mice. What've you been finding out, anyway?'

'Stop messing about with all this and I'll tell you. By the time we've finished, my friend, we shall have our own suite of rooms in the castle itself. Now listen.'

Sorda recounted all that he had seen and heard. When he had finished, Terras' eyes gleamed.

He rubbed his bony fingers together with glee.

'Heh, heh. Not only will this get us back into her good books, but it'll also destroy those children. Play this one right and we've got it made.'

'Just think, a proper spell-room and real power. Perhaps even the use of the Merestone.' Sorda's eyes glittered at the thought.

'We must go to Hagbane tonight and share our news. I'm sure she will be most interested to hear what we've found out.'

'What I've found out,' corrected Sorda.

* * *

That night, dark counsels took place in Hagbane's lair. The air hung heavy, thick with evil, as the trio plotted the doom of Oswain and the children.

Hagbane had received the two wizards with impatience at first and kept them standing while they spoke. But, at the mention of Oswain's name her attitude changed. She sat them down, eager to know more.

'Oswain. Oswain?' A strange look passed across her eyes as she mouthed the name. 'So it's him, is it? After all this time.'

'They spoke about prophecies,' said Sorda. 'Something about him being a ruler.'

'Pah! The prophecies are the vain hopes of fools. Don't you know that I hold the Merestone and nobody can defeat me? Nobody, do you hear?'

'Yes. Yes, your highness,' Terras replied hastily.

The truth was that Hagbane had been disturbed by the mention of Oswain's name. Although she didn't accept the prophecies, she couldn't deny the fact that both he and the children had come as predicted.

The only way to deal with her unease was to act as soon as possible, but with cunning. To achieve her ends she was quite prepared to form an alliance with the wizards. They could be dealt with at a later date.

'We must work together,' she hissed. 'This Oswain must be destroyed and I want to do it myself. None of us is safe while he lives, do you understand?'

They nodded.

'Good. Then we will set a trap between us and lure all of them to their doom. This is what I suggest….'

Three pairs of eyes gleamed in the darkness as they hatched their plot.

Hagbane thought of another use for her newly forged

weapon and smiled as she pictured the scene in her mind. The old score would be settled at last.

15

The Trap is Sprung

'You're not going out by yourself and that's final.'

'Aw, mum! Why not? I only want to see the flowers.'

Mavis the rabbit, like many of the younger animals, was fed up with being cooped in the family burrow. She had ten brothers and sisters but they were all younger than she was and as the eldest she felt she at least should be allowed to go out and play – and especially now. Something really exciting was happening. Life was returning to the Great Forest. Buds were swelling and leaves had started to unfold on the branches like little green butterflies. The lone crocus had been the herald of many others and the clearings and undergrowth glowed with fresh splashes of bright colour. A new, and more powerful magic was at work. Mavis had never seen anything like it in her life.

But her mother would have none of it.

'It's not safe,' she said. 'There's no knowing who might be watching in all this new greenery. And you know we've all been told to keep our eyes open for spies.'

'But I'll be careful, mum. Really I will,' Mavis insisted. 'I won't go far.'

'Anywhere is too far at the moment,' her mother answered. 'As it is, folk are moving away from here to be near the Enchanted Glade. It's getting too dangerous.'

What Mavis' mother said was true. To make matters

worse, although Hagbane had been ominously quiet for the past three days, flashes of light had been seen coming from the castle at night and black smoke by day. Something was going on.

Mavis wasn't the only one feeling frustrated. Those gathered in Trotter's house could only sit and wait for the next move since clearly there was little else they could do. Oswain seemed unwilling to talk any further about how he and his mother had come to know Hagbane and was in a brooding mood that not even Sophie dared intrude upon. By the third day of being cooped up indoors, Joshua, Sophie and Andrew were feeling thoroughly irritable. Trotter and Aldred had set out early to attend to various matters among the forest-folk, and nobody knew where Oswain had gone.

'I'm fed up with this!' exclaimed Joshua. 'I'll go loopy if we have to sit here much longer.'

'Well, what shall we do?' asked Sophie.

'I don't know, but I've got to get out of this house. Anyone want to come for a walk?'

'Yeah, I do,' said Andrew. 'I'm fed up with being stuck here, too.'

'Just mind you're careful, my dears,' said Mrs Trotter, who had overheard them. 'And don't be too long now.'

'Thank you, Mrs T. We'll watch out, don't you worry. We've got Gilmere with us just in case,' Andrew answered.

The weather was beautiful outside, bright sunshine, blue sky and fresh, clear air. Joshua took a deep breath and laughed.

'It does smell good, doesn't it?' said Sophie. 'There's less of that dead smell than when we first arrived. Come on, which way shall we go?'

'Let's follow this path,' Andrew suggested, pointing

to the left.

Before long, the pleasant stroll along the meandering woodland path had them all feeling much happier. Life wasn't so bad after all and forgetting the threat of Hagbane they began to laugh and joke and chase one another with bits of twig.

They had been playing around like this for about twenty minutes when, all of a sudden, there was a movement in the bushes bordering the path just ahead. They each froze. The next instant, none other than Sorda the wizard stepped out in front of them. Sophie stifled a scream and Joshua's hand dived into his pocket for the mirror.

He was about to open it when Sorda spoke. His voice was smooth and soft.

'I wouldn't do that if I were you, young man. At least, not if you wish to see your friend Trotter alive and well again.'

'What do you mean?' Joshua demanded. 'What have you done with him?'

'Not me. I haven't touched him,' Sorda sneered. 'No, Hagbane has. Or rather her Grogs have. They've caught him.'

'Oh, no!' gasped Sophie. 'Not Trotter. What are we going to do?'

'Rescue him, of course,' snapped Joshua, rather more sharply than he had intended. His eye gleamed. 'That is, if he's really been captured.' He addressed the wizard. 'Why are you telling us this? After all, you're on Hagbane's side and you tried to kill us. It's got to be a trap!'

Sorda smiled.

'What's in it for me? Why, I'm changing sides, that's what. I want to bring Hagbane down, the same as you.

And you have the power.' He indicated Gilmere.

'And you expect us to believe you? Just like that?' Joshua answered.

'Why would you want to change sides, anyway?' Sophie demanded.

Sorda shrugged his shoulders and held out his palms. 'We are no longer in her favour,' he replied. 'Things keep going wrong for her since you came on the scene, and she's blaming it on us. I figured that if we're to be blamed anyway, I might as well join the better side.'

'What about your pal?' Andrew asked.

'Terras, I am afraid to say, hasn't yet seen sense,' Sorda replied. 'I expect he'll come round, but I'm getting out while the going is good.'

Joshua was far from convinced. He remembered that this was one of the men who had offered his sister as a human sacrifice.

'We don't make bargains with the likes of you,' he said. 'So forget it. We're not interested.'

'You overlook the fact that Trotter has been captured and is not far from here. They'll be marching him off to Hagbane and you know what that'll mean,' the wizard replied. 'I know where you can stop them.'

'I don't believe you,' Joshua replied.

'Hey, listen, Josh,' Andrew interjected. 'Look, I'm not sure I believe him either, but we've got to take a chance, just in case. It'd be awful if Trotter really is caught.'

'Yes, Joshua, please let's check it, just to be sure,' Sophie added.

Joshua hesitated before turning to the wizard again.

'You'll have to prove yourself to us. Take us to Trotter and if he's rescued we'll think about what you've said. If you try anything funny I'll fry you alive. Now move!' he gestured angrily with the mirror.

Sorda flinched and muttering to himself stumbled down the path in front of them. He seemed to be taking Joshua's threat seriously and kept casting nervous glances over his shoulder as he hurried along.

'Just keep your eyes open for a trap,' hissed Andrew. 'This path is leading us towards the old clearing, I reckon.'

'Well, we'll know soon enough if he's telling the truth, we're nearly there,' Joshua muttered.

Just as he spoke, Sorda gave a cry of fright and to their absolute astonishment fell crashing into a hole in the path and disappeared from their sight. The children stopped dead in their tracks.

'He's fallen into a trap!' exclaimed Andrew.

'Do you think it was meant for us?' Sophie asked.

Before anyone could answer her question, all three were thrown to the ground by the weight of a huge net that fell on them from the trees above. After that, everything happened so quickly that there was nothing they could do to save themselves. Six Grogs leapt to the ground and swiftly bundled up the children, whose struggles only entangled them further. To his dismay, Joshua felt the mirror slip from his fingers in the confusion.

The Grogs thrust a stout pole through the netting. Balancing it on their shoulders, they hoisted their load and carried the captive children at a swift march towards the clearing ahead. They were followed by a grinning Sorda who, having just clambered out of the pit, was brushing down his clothes.

Sophie looked back and saw his smirk. It was a trap after all.

'I'm so sorry, Josh. It's my fault for saying we should go with him,' she groaned.

'No, it's mine too,' said Andrew.

'Nobody's to blame, Joshua replied. 'Let's just hope they haven't got Trotter as well. If only I hadn't dropped Gilmere… Ouch!'

The Grogs had come to an abrupt halt and stood to attention in the clearing.

Hagbane was waiting for them. With her hand on her hip and a leer on her face she swaggered towards the helpless children.

'Stupid young fools,' she mocked. 'You fell right into my trap. I've caught you good and proper this time, haven't I?' She waggled a gnarled finger at them.

Sophie was furious. 'You're evil and horrible and nasty! I hate you!' she cried. 'Let us go. Just let me get at you, you wicked old bag!'

She struggled violently in the net.

'The Crone sneered. 'Your words mean nothing to me and in any case it's too late for you to interfere with my plans now. Guards, prepare the next part of the plan. You know what to do.'

At her command, the Grogs carried their struggling load across the clearing until they came to a pole shaped like an old-fashioned hangman's post. There they dropped the children in a heap and fixed a rope to the net. One of the Grogs threw the end over the crossbar. With much puffing, the Grogs hauled on the rope until the children were suspended in the net about two metres off the ground. They struggled to readjust their limbs as best they could.

'What are they doing?' gasped Andrew.

'I don't know,' his brother replied. 'I thought for one moment that we were going to be hanged.'

'I'm frightened,' Sophie whimpered. 'I don't like this at all. If only Oswain were here.'

Hagbane said nothing. She simply watched. Her guards went off into the bushes on the edge of the clearing.

They returned carrying bundles of dried gorse and at a nod from their mistress they began to pile it beneath the children.

The job was soon done and all the children could do was look on in silent trepidation.

'Is she going to drop us into it?' whispered Andrew. 'It looks ever so prickly.'

'No, I don't think so,' Joshua muttered grimly, as the truth dawned on him. Sophie also realised what was happening.

'She's going to burn us alive!' she shrieked.

Her dreams came rushing back with stark vividness, and she screamed with all her might.

The three children stared horror-struck as Hagbane advanced on them. In her gnarled hand she bore a burning branch and her face was twisted into an evil leer. One of her Grogs started a slow beat on a bass drum. Two others put trumpets to their lips and began to blow long, raucous blasts.

Joshua, Sophie and Andrew struggled desperately as the Crone came closer.

* * *

In the depths of the forest everyone heard the beat of the drum and the blare of the trumpets. They stopped what they were doing and began to ask one another what was going on.

Trotter and Oswain were together when it began.

'Something bad is going on,' said Trotter.

'I suspect Hagbane is making her move at last,'

Oswain replied.

Trotter frowned. 'I wonder where the children have got to? I haven't seen them for quite some time now.'

'Nor have I, and I don't like it. That sound is coming from the direction of the old clearing, if I'm not mistaken. Come on, Trotter, hurry!' Oswain sounded grim.

They raced out of the house together and found themselves along with many other of the forest-folk rushing towards the incessant beat of the drum and the insistent blast of the trumpet. It still took some time to reach the clearing and everyone arrived puffing and panting behind the gorse bushes that marked the edge.

As they began to creep through the gorse the forest folk quietened down. Everyone was on the watch for trouble, but they could never have been prepared for what they saw. There, hanging from the post were the three children, and Hagbane stood before them clutching in her hand a burning torch. Dozens of Grogs stood to attention in a semicircle behind them. The monotonous sound of the instruments continued.

'This is dreadful! Dreadful!' gasped Trotter.

'So this is how it is going to happen.' Oswain spoke almost to himself and his lean face looked taut.

'Surely she's not going to kill them,' cried the badger. 'I must try to stop her.'

He darted forward, heedless of his age or personal danger, and fearlessly approached the Crone.

'Hah! So you've arrived, have you?' she snapped, glaring at him with venom. 'All of you, I trust?' She emphasised the 'all'.

'Trotter, go back! Don't worry about us. Look after yourself.'

It was Sophie who shouted and the two boys joined

183

in, entreating Trotter to return to safety.

'Take no notice of them,' snarled the Crone. 'Now listen to me. I hold all the cards, so you had better….'

'No, you listen to me,' Trotter interrupted angrily. 'These children came as visitors to the forest. They mean nothing to you. Let them go. Let them go and take me instead. They can return to their own country and you will have me as your prisoner.'

Hagbane roared with laughter.

'You! Do you think I want you, you decrepit old ruin? You're nothing to me. You don't seem to understand, you old fool. I'm playing for higher stakes.' She bent forward and narrowed her eyes at the badger. 'I want Oswain. I know he's with you. Hand him over.'

'No, no,' called the children. 'Don't do it, Trotter. Leave us.'

'If we refuse?' the badger asked lamely, already knowing what the answer would be.

'If you refuse, I shall simply set fire to this gorse and burn your friends alive! In fact, I shall count to one hundred and if Oswain is not delivered by then, they die. Now go!'

'How can I trust you not to destroy the children anyway?'

'You can't, can you? Now hurry, I haven't got all day,' she snapped.

Trotter stood for a moment, trying to think of a reply.

'One, two, three…'

He ran back to the shelter of the gorse to speak with Oswain and the others. The Crone's voice rang out to the melancholy beat of the drum.

'Thirteen, fourteen, fifteen…'

'Well?' Aldred demanded when Trotter arrived. 'What does she want?'

It took Trotter just a moment to give the grim news. Aldred fumed with rage and frustration.

'She's outwitted us this time. What can we do? We lose both ways. Even a head-on charge wouldn't help now.'

'We haven't much time. We must speak with Oswain quickly.' Trotter replied. 'Where is he?'

The three children hung in dread and despair. Everything appeared to be lost. It was them or Oswain. If only it were a dream, thought Sophie, but she knew that this time it was happening to them for real.

'Seventy-five, seventy-six...' The beat went on relentlessly.

Nothing moved in the gorse. The air hung still and silent.

'Eighty-nine, ninety, ninety-one...'

Tension mounted to breaking point. Andrew's skin prickled.

'Ninety-six, ninety-seven, ninety-eight...'

Hagbane moved towards the pyre with the burning brand. Implacably, she lowered it towards the gorse.

'Ninety-nine, One hun....'

16
All Seems Lost

'Stop!'

The firm voice rang out across the clearing.

'It's Oswain!' cried Joshua.

Hagbane looked up suspiciously and grimaced. Oswain stood tall and noble in the sunlight, in vivid contrast to the crooked old Crone. He spoke again.

'Leave the children alone. I agree to your terms, Hagbane; I will deliver myself up to you in exchange for their lives. See, my hands are bound.'

He began to walk towards the Crone.

'Stay where you are,' she demanded. 'I want to be sure there's no trickery. You two!' she motioned to Terras and Sorda who by now had joined with the Grogs. 'Go and check his bonds, and be quick about it.'

The wily wizards slunk from behind the guards and made their way across the clearing towards Oswain, all the while looking about them for signs of a trap. There was none. Oswain stood his ground while they checked his ropes. At Hagbane's command a Grog came running with a hank of stout rope. The wizards made doubly sure of Oswain's captivity by winding the rope several times around his body and legs, pinning his arms to his sides and making it impossible for him to walk.

'Heh, heh, try getting out of that,' Sorda sniggered.

'It's all right,' Terras called out to Hagbane. 'He can't escape from us now.'

'Very well,' snarled the Crone, hiding her relief. 'Guards, go, fetch him!'

At a signal from their captain, half of the Grogs advanced on the bound man. The children watched in silent dismay as Oswain was lifted from his feet and carried across to the Crone.

Back in the gorse bushes, where the forest-folk looked on with horror, Aldred and Stiggle fumed.

'This is ridiculous! Here we are absolutely powerless while that scheming Crone gets away with it. It makes me sick. I mean, it's stupid! She's got them all now. Why on earth did we give up Oswain as well?' Aldred demanded.

'We had no choice really, did we?' Stiggle replied. 'He was so insistent that it was the right thing to do that we couldn't have stopped him if we'd tried. What Elmesh would wish, he told us.'

'Well, I don't know about that,' said Aldred. 'I don't trust that Crone as far as I could throw her. Stiggle, get the troops ready. I want action, not negotiations. We can't just sit here and do nothing.'

Stiggle ran off obediently.

The Grogs reached Hagbane with their burden and dumped Oswain on his feet in front of her. For a long time there was silence as the two stared at each other. At length the Crone spoke.

'So. We meet again at last, Oswain, son of the High King of Castelfion,' she sneered. 'It's been a long time. You have changed very little by the looks of you. Just a bit older.'

Oswain's face betrayed his sense of horror. 'What has become of you, Dorinda?' he whispered.

Overhearing them from where they hung, the children looked puzzled. 'Dorinda? What does he

187

mean?' Andrew asked.

'You have changed so much since I first knew you.' Oswain shook his head sadly. 'What is this evil that has ruined you?'

'I am not ruined, Oswain. Fool! Do you think outward appearance is all that matters? My beauty lies in my power; power that will conquer the world. That is, when I've finished with you.' She laughed in triumph. 'Take him away!'

'Wait! You have my life in exchange for the children. That was the agreement. Release them!'

The Crone still held the flaming torch. She stared at it for a moment, considering. Reluctantly, she doused it on the ground.

'Your friends can get them down. Pah!' she spat. 'I don't need them now. Not when I've got you, Oswain. No, they can go back to where they came from.'

'Let him go, you rotten old rat-bag,' Andrew shouted. 'You've no right to make him a prisoner.'

The Crone spun round.

'Right? Did you question my right? I hold the Merestone, fool. I have the might – so I have the right!'

Hagbane thought this sounded rather clever so she repeated it. She marched away from the despairing children and back towards the castle, followed by her guards, who carried the captive Oswain slung across their shoulders.

The moment he saw that the Crone and her crew were well clear of the children, Aldred spoke to Stiggle.

'It's now or never. Do you agree?'

Stiggle nodded. He glanced round at the animals assembled behind them. They had armed themselves with sticks and stones, catapults and slings, spears and swords and just about anything else that they could lay their hands on. It was time to engage the enemy.

'This is it then. *Charge!*' Aldred cried.

He led his troops at full tilt across the wide clearing. Heedless of danger now and full of pent-up fury, the animals surged towards the children and their retreating captors. They had almost reached Joshua, Sophie and Andrew when Hagbane heard the commotion behind them. She turned and her face flashed with anger.

'The cursed fools! Do they think to stop me now? I'll give 'em something to think about!'

So saying, she drew her wand from beneath the folds of her gown and pointed it with cold deliberation in the direction of the captive children. A blinding flash of fire shot from its tip, bright as the sun. In the next instant the pile of gorse beneath them burst into flame.

'Meddling fools. That'll teach them not to cross me,' she snarled.

Oswain struggled vainly in his bonds as he realised what had happened.

'Put it out, Dorinda. Please,' he begged. 'They haven't harmed you. What about our bargain?'

The Crone laughed with harsh indifference and turned on her heel. Oswain groaned in anguish for the children's lives. There was nothing he could do to help.

The gorse began to crackle into life as the fire took hold and smoke started pouring upwards, rapidly enveloping the children. Sophie screamed and the boys called hoarsely for help. Already they could feel the heat of the fire beneath them. Struggling in desperation, they began to cough and splutter and their eyes smarted in the smoke.

The forest-folk, led by Aldred, stopped short in their tracks when they saw what Hagbane had done. For an instant nobody moved, each creature paralysed by his natural fear of fire.

Then Aldred, heedless of the danger, leapt forward and plunged into the burning gorse. Frantically, he began scattering it as far apart as possible, pushing the whole mass away from the children. The other animals reacted swiftly to their leader's example and rushed to help. Trotter swiftly organised the remaining animals into a chain to pass along bark containers filled with water from a nearby stream. Vast hissing clouds of steam soon mingled with the acrid smoke and the desperate helpers were soon coughing and spluttering.

For a while total confusion reigned. Nobody could see a thing in the smoky fog and many of the animals found themselves pulling one another away by mistake rather than grabbing the gorse branches. Orders were lost in the noisy chaos of shouting, choking and crackling firebrands, so that nobody really knew what was going on. It looked like a complete disaster.

Yet, in spite of everything, the animals' work was rewarded. The flames eventually died down and the smoke began to clear.

Stiggle found the rope securing the children in the net and released it. With cries of relief, Joshua, Sophie and Andrew tumbled out one on top of the other in a confusion of arms and legs and soot-blackened clothes.

It had been a near thing and the children were shaken and exhausted by their terrible experience. For a moment they lay on the ground among the sodden cinders just clutching at one another. Andrew and Sophie were still shuddering as Joshua slowly opened his eyes and staggered upright. His eyes stung horribly and to the animals anxiously watching they stood out pink and bloodshot against the blackness of his face.

'Come on,' he said as he pulled his brother and sister

190

to their feet.

Together, they tottered across to Stiggle.

'I don't know what to say,' he gasped. 'Just thank you.'

Sophie was still shaking from her ordeal. 'I really th...thought we were g...going to d...die,' she shuddered. 'It was terrible.'

Andrew was trying to brush some of the soot off his clothes. 'Thanks for everything, Stiggle,' he said.

'It's Aldred whom you must thank rather then me,' the weasel replied. 'If it weren't for him none of us would have had the courage to tackle this by ourselves. He just charged straight in without any thought for his own safety. Incredible bravery, if you ask me. I've never seen anything like it.'

'Yes. You're right, Stiggle. But really all of you were fantastic. You saved our lives,' said Joshua.

'Where is Aldred?' Andrew asked. 'I can't see him anywhere.'

The smoke had more or less cleared by now and the animals were beginning to sort themselves out. Some stood back to admire their handiwork with satisfied smiles on their faces. Others, who bore singe marks here and there, were busy checking their tails and whiskers. Many were discussing the events in small groups.

'Aldred? Aldred?' Joshua called.

'Aldred, where are you?' cried Andrew.

In spite of their repeated calls there was no reply. Gradually, one by one, the animals stopped their chattering. An ominous hush fell over the crowd.

'Oh!' cried Sophie. 'Oh, no! Look!'

Everyone turned to see her pointing to a pile of scattered gorse. Her finger trembled as she did so and all eyes turned to see where she was pointing.

There, badly burned and quite still among the ashes lay the body of the brave Aldred.

Trotter hastened across and bent over the stoat while everyone waited with bated breath, watching. Then slowly he raised his head to face the crowd. The badger's old eyes were full of tears and he shook his head.

'I am afraid our noble captain is dead,' he said quietly. 'I'm sorry. This is a terrible loss for every one of us.'

A stunned silence greeted the news. Then, as it sunk in, a great howl of sorrow and anguish arose from the assembled forest-folk.

Sophie burst into tears. 'He was the bravest person I ever knew,' she sobbed. 'He gave his own life to save ours. Oh, I can't bear it! I can't bear it!'

She stumbled away from the dreadful scene with tears streaming down her smoke-grimed face.

Joshua just stared horror-struck at Aldred's body.

Andrew began to sob quietly and he clutched at his older brother's arm for comfort.

For a long while, nobody could do anything but weep and a cloud of utter despair seemed to settle over the clearing.

At length, Trotter pulled himself together. With a great effort he called for everyone's attention. When he spoke his voice was grave.

'Matters are very serious for us, friends. Our enemy has Oswain and we have lost our fighting leader. I know how hard it is, but we must not, we cannot, allow ourselves to go under.' He looked about him. 'Stiggle, you will assume Aldred's role. Joshua, Andrew, Sophie, we must talk without delay. The rest of you must return home and prepare for war.' He raised his paws. 'This is a dark day. Elmesh help us! Come, let us all get to the safety of our own homes and remove Aldred from this awful place.'

At Trotter's command, four young stoats bore away the body of their captain upon their shoulders. With slow and solemn steps they walked towards the trees and a place of burial. The sour stench of burnt and wet wood hung in the air. Small burns began to sting in the cool wind. With aching hearts and weary bodies the sad procession wound its way into the cold shadows of the silent trees.

17

Oswain Refuses to Bow

'So, my dear Prince Oswain, the so-called servant of
Elmesh – at last I have you!'

Hagbane stood before her prisoner, gloating over her
prize, her voice heavy with sarcasm. Strong chains
bound Oswain to the cold stone wall of her spell room
and his wrists were fixed to an iron ring above his head.
He made no attempt to free himself, but gazed at the
Crone with mixture of sadness and revulsion while she
rubbed her bony hands together with glee. She noticed
his look.

'Can't get used to it, eh? Not like your old Dorinda,
am I? What did you expect to find? Some beautiful
princess? Pah! You always were stupid.'

Oswain spoke with difficulty.

'I loved you, Dorinda. You were once the fairest
woman in the land and the most precious person in my
life. What caused this dreadful evil that has overtaken
you?'

'Evil? Hah! If you call power evil, then evil it is. But I
want power, Oswain. I desired it even when we were
younger but neither you nor your family would grant
me it. So I sought it for myself. And I found it!'

'We couldn't give you what you wanted because you
had already turned sour. Your heart was full of pride.
You would have brought nothing but pain and sadness
upon our people. That's why I couldn't marry you, even

though I loved you.'

'Love? Oh, yes, love,' Hagbane answered dreamily. 'How much you loved me! Enough to ditch me, that's how much. And for what?' she spat. 'For some noble concern for others? What rot!'

'It wasn't like that, Dorinda, and you know it,' Oswain answered.

'So what was it like, then? Tell me,' she demanded. 'No, I'll tell you. It was like this: I expected to marry the prince and to have all my dreams fulfilled. I would become queen and have honour and influence. People would know their place, and I would know mine....'

'But that's not what it's all about,' Oswain interrupted. 'My family doesn't rule like that. We are there to serve our people, not to humiliate them.'

'Serve the people? Do you really think that's what ruling is about?' Hagbane arched her eyebrows incredulously. 'People are there to serve their rulers. That's what. What's the point of being in charge if you can't order people about and take their money? Power to the powerful, I say! You and me together.'

Oswain shook his head sadly.

'You are wrong, Dorinda,' he said. 'I could never be married to someone who thought like that. I am sorry it had to end but you really gave us no choice. Rejecting you was as hard for me as...'

'Oh yes, you rejected me all right!' Hagbane cut in bitterly. 'And don't think I have forgotten it. The humiliation! You have no idea how I felt before my friends and advisors.'

'What advisors?'

'Well, never you mind. You wouldn't understand, anyway. Let's just say that you ruined our plans.'

If Oswain had ever had doubts he knew now for sure

195

that he had made the right decision in not marrying Dorinda. Even back in the days of their courtship a sinister plot had been hatching between Dorinda and her secret advisors.

Hagbane was speaking again.

'Strange how the wheels turn, isn't it? I vowed vengeance against you and your loathsome mother and sought other powers to help me. They have done well.' She grimaced. 'I have waited a long time for the chance to destroy you and your wretched family. And now, at last, you have come within my power.'

'I did not expect it to be you I would face,' Oswain replied. 'It was a deep shock when I discovered that in the Star Pool. I nearly turned back there and then.' His eyes pleaded with the Crone. 'Dorinda, I want you to give up this madness before the judgement of the prophecies falls on you and destroys you. Make no mistake; the time for their fulfilment has come.'

Oswain spoke earnestly but Hagbane only laughed in his face.

'Yes, they say you've come to fulfil the old prophecies. Revelations? Pah! I do not believe them. Delusion! Only fools listen to such old words – and you are a fool Oswain, and those meddling children. You think to scare me with your vague threats? It is you who should be afraid, not I!'

Oswain winced at the mention of the children.

'You broke your word, Dorinda. You killed them for no reason.'

'My word? Fool!' she screeched. 'You and your words. Words of prophecy. Words of honour. I care nothing for them. It's power that counts. Power, my dear Oswain, power that I shall soon unleash upon the world. No brats or stupid animals will stand in my way, and nor will you. Your pleas are wasted. I shall not change. Do you hear? I shall not change!'

'Then the vengeance of Elmesh will strike you, for it is from him you have stolen the Merestone,' Oswain replied. 'What you seek to use for your own ends will turn against you and kill you.'

'Stupid superstition! Why should I fear Elmesh?' she retorted. 'He has hardly helped you, has he? You threaten me with doom but it will be yours, not mine, because I have the power to do anything I want to you. This is the day of my revenge!'

Her wild eyes gleamed yellow as she spoke. She approached him until her face was only centimetres from his.

'Do not think these are mere words, Oswain. I have created a weapon that will make all people serve me – or die! In fact,' she sniggered, 'I've planned to try it out on you. Then we shall see the value of your worthless prophecies.'

With a dramatic swirl of her cloak, she turned from him and crossed to a cupboard. She reached in, giving Oswain a sly smirk as she did so. Then she drew out the strange rod that she had formed in league with the dark forces.

'With this,' she cried triumphantly, 'I shall rule the world!'

Oswain looked puzzled.

'What is it?' he asked.

'What is it? It is the power of light and darkness fused into one. It shall be terrible to behold, more powerful than even the Merestone itself, more dreadful than Grogs or Grims. With this, I shall sweep all before me.'

Madness filled the Crone's eyes as she spoke, and Oswain looked at her with horror.

'Dorinda, renounce this evil while you can.' he pleaded. 'Destroy this thing before it destroys you. I beg you.'

'Yes, you will beg, but not like this,' she answered. 'For it is not I who will change, but you. You must become as I am and serve me – or you will die. That will be my revenge.'

'Never!'

'We shall see. Watch!'

Hagbane pointed the rod at the floor and muttered a spell. Oswain stared as the rod glowed to a bright orange. There was a brilliant flash and a vast heap of bread – loaf upon loaf – appeared before Oswain's startled gaze. The Crone appeared pleased and she muttered again. Another flash, and the bread frizzled to cinders.

She turned to Oswain.

'The power to create and to destroy food. I can make plenty or I can cause famine. Who will dare challenge me with such a temptation – or with such a threat?'

She turned away and pointed the rod at the far wall. Projected there Oswain could see great multitudes of people thronging the city streets as they went about their daily business. Hagbane muttered a spell and, to his horror, fire began to consume one side of the vision. It spread rapidly, devouring everything before it. He heard the screams of terrified people, saw them fleeing madly, felt the heat of the merciless flame as it swallowed up people and property alike.

'Do you not think that it is a great power?' Hagbane demanded. 'I shall use it, make no mistake. Now watch this.'

She held the rod at arm's length, then pointed it at herself. Closing her eyes she murmured a third spell. As

Oswain watched, still helplessly bound, the Crone grew larger and larger until her menacing form towered above him. She swayed as though made of liquid smoke and then slowly evolved into a beautiful princess who gazed at him with soft melting eyes. Oswain started as he saw once again the love of his youth standing before him. He longed to reach out and touch her and his heart was filled with all the yearnings of lost love.

The vision changed again and she became a regal lady, cold, aloof, absolute in her power, looking down upon him with utter contempt. He felt totally despised. The figure doubled, trebled, multiplied until the room was full of Hagbane clones. One by one their faces twisted and aged until they became nightmarishly ugly, more ugly than Hagbane herself. Terror gripped Oswain as they approached him, their long, gnarled fingers outstretched like talons to tear out his throat. The next moment, she was a sweet little girl looking up at him with appealing eyes and offering him an apple.

Then she was Hagbane herself.

Oswain's heart jumped. He realised he was trembling, and sweat covered his forehead.

'Impressive, eh? What do you think? There's nothing I can't do with this.'

Oswain remained silent.

The Crone's eyes glinted. When she spoke, her words were cold and clear. 'The demonstration is over. You, Oswain, will bow to me and serve me. If you refuse, I shall kill you.'

'I shall never bow to your evil power!' he replied, as he recovered his composure. 'I will no longer call you Dorinda. You are Hagbane truly. You have tormented and killed the innocent. May Elmesh strike you!'

The Crone's face darkened with fury and her voice

rose to a wild scream.

'Fool, you dare to resist me? You will worship me and plead with me before I am finished with you! You will call me your queen. I will have my vengeance on you and your house.'

The wildness in her eyes mirrored the years of bitterness and resentment that filled her being. Slowly, deliberately, she lifted the rod and pointed it with an outstretched arm towards her captive. It glowed brightly in her hand and a bolt of lightning shot from its tip. Blue fire crackled all around Oswain and his face contorted as he struggled against the dark powers that sought to break him. He twisted and turned in his bonds but not a word passed his lips. Hagbane muttered a spell and more arrows of fire pounded into Oswain's body, yet still he resisted.

'Worship me!' she screeched. 'Call me your queen, curse you!'

Her hands shook with rage and the rod glowed to white heat in her grasp. Flurries of bright sparks sprayed over Oswain and with his eyes closed he called upon Elmesh for strength and remained unbroken.

At length, the Crone lowered the rod.

'So, you do have some power after all, do you,' she muttered. 'Very well, we shall see about that. Don't underestimate me, Oswain. I will break you – or you will surely perish.'

The Crone strode across the room and brought out her most prized possession – the Merestone itself. Carefully, she placed it on a table before him.

'Now we shall see what your power is worth,' she breathed.

She removed the cover and the stone glowed in the dark room. A humming noise filled the air and the jewel began to glow more brightly. Hagbane started to chant spells. The light increased and the hum became a roar.

'Acknowledge me, or die now!' she screamed above the noise. 'Even the Merestone will obey me now, for my rod was forged in its light.'

Oswain twisted in his bonds. His face set with concentration as Hagbane's darkness sought to overwhelm him.

'Never! Never will I bow to you, Hagbane. I reject you. By Elmesh, I refuse you,' he cried.

'Then die! Die Oswain, son of the High King!' she shrieked. 'Die!'

She pointed the rod at his chest and uttered a deep and powerful spell. The rod shone like polished silver and from the inner depths of the Merestone fire began to flash. The roar became a deafening thunder and the whole room began to shake. A single beam of blue light blazed from the Merestone and struck the ring on Oswain's finger. It dissolved the gold in an instant.

Immediately, the fragment of the jewel it had contained flew through the air to rejoin the stone. A thunderous crash marked the uniting of the Merestone, and the room streamed with dazzling, ricocheting light. At that very instant, Oswain's bonds fell from his body and his hands were loosed.

Hagbane was stunned and could only stare in amazement. Then, with a howl of rage, she lunged at Oswain with the white-hot rod. Light and fire spattered the walls in a storm of colours. Lightning flashed. The ground shook beneath their feet.

With a fierce twist of his body Oswain evaded her thrust and found himself locked in a desperate life and death struggle with the Crone. The whole room burst into flames and at that very instant a mighty earthquake shook the floor upon which they fought. With a deafening crack the floor tore apart to reveal a vast abyss of unimaginable depth. Fire burned a sullen red deep within the chasm.

Together, Oswain and Hagbane struggled on the brink of the pit while the Merestone wreaked its own terrible revenge. They fought grimly, oblivious to the havoc around them, gasping and panting as each sought to gain the advantage over the other.

By now they were teetering on the very edge of the chasm. Then Hagbane had him; the gleaming rod was under his throat. With a cry, she lunged upwards. In the nick of time Oswain twisted away and the Crone lost her balance. She clutched at Oswain's clothing as she struggled to regain her footing. He tried to free himself, but it was no good. She staggered back and fell, taking him with her. There was nothing he could do and together they plunged into the unspeakable depths of the pit.

A long piercing scream of despair echoed up from the flaming abyss. Fire and smoke billowed out until the room was filled with roaring flames and nothing else could be seen.

18
Into Battle

Stiggle paced restlessly up and down in Trotter's front room, his furry face furrowed with emotion. He was deeply grieved over the loss of his commander and the all too recent burial had been difficult for him to bear. Now Trotter had made him leader of the forces; Stiggle, who had always been second-in-command; Stiggle, who was good at carrying out the orders of others but who had never been one to make the decisions. And his first task was to do something about Oswain! It was a worrying business.

Joshua entered the room and stood for a moment watching the weasel. He sighed in sympathy.

'I know how you're feeling, Stiggle, and...well, I just want you to know that I feel the same.'

Stiggle stopped his pacing and turned to Joshua.

'Thanks, my friend. It helps to know that someone understands.'

'I think we all do,' Joshua replied. 'It must be a terrible responsibility for you.'

'What do you think we should do, Joshua?'

'I'm not sure. But we can't waste time,' Joshua answered. 'If she's going to kill Oswain I reckon she'll do it quite quickly. We'll have to get a move on before it's too late. Then again, I suppose, he may be dead already,' he finished miserably.

'If he is, or if we don't rescue him, then her power will

grow even more and we'll become utter slaves. I'd sooner die than serve her evil ways, and I think most of our folk feel the same.' He looked Joshua in the face. 'I don't know about you three. You're strangers here, not forest-folk. It's still a bit of a mystery to me how you ever came in the first place, but I suppose you can escape and go back to your own land.'

Joshua shrugged. 'Maybe…'

'I don't know why things have gone so wrong, either,' Stiggle continued. 'I've always trusted Trotter's word and he's always been right about the revelations but…well, maybe he's got it wrong this time. What are we going to do?'

'Listen, Stiggle,' Joshua said. 'I know we're visitors, a bit like people from another planet and all that, but we're in this with you. Look, Aldred gave his life to save us. We would have died if it wasn't for his courage, and I feel we owe a lot to him.'

Stiggle nodded. 'Everyone does.'

'Well then, I think he had the right idea in attacking even if it didn't work out as he wanted' said Joshua. 'At least it's better than sitting around doing nothing. Then there's Oswain. We can't just go away and forget he ever existed.' A lump rose in his throat. 'No, we're willing to die, too, if necessary,' he concluded.

'Yeah, let's get 'em!'

Andrew had slipped into the room unnoticed and now stood with his hands behind his back looking rather pleased with himself.

'I agree, Josh. We've got to attack that evil old bag together,' he said. 'And guess what? I've got something that will help us quite a lot,' he added.

They waited for him to show them what it was, but he just smiled.

'Well, come on. What is it?' Joshua demanded.

Slowly, Andrew drew from behind his back a small, round, flattish object.

'Gilmere!' gasped Joshua. 'Of course! Stupid! I thought the wizards had got it.'

Andrew grinned from ear to ear.

'Well, I wondered about that, but I thought I'd take a look just in case. It wasn't on the path, of course, and I was just about to give up when I saw it lying under a bush. I don't think I'd have found it if I hadn't been really looking.'

'Brilliant, Andy. At least we've got something on our side now.' Joshua was suddenly full of enthusiasm. 'Come on, Stiggle; things are looking up a bit. I think we should attack the castle and at least do as much damage as we can. Who knows, it might turn out better than we expect and old Trotter may be right about those prophecies after all.'

'Less of the old if you don't mind! Of course I'm right about the prophecies. Elmesh does not lie – even if it is all somewhat confusing.'

They jumped at the sound of Trotter's voice as he and Sophie slipped into the room through the study door. Both carried swords in their hands and were dressed in the old metal and leather battle uniforms that the fighting forest-folk used.

'Hey, what's all this?' Joshua asked.

'Quite simple,' his sister replied. 'Trotter and I are ready to fight Hagbane. We're also quite willing to go alone if you lot want to stay at home.'

'What?'

'Yes, we've decided it's gone too far to just sit around any more. We've nothing to lose, so we're going to fight. And we're ever so glad about the mirror, Andrew.'

She smiled at her younger brother but he could see the glint of determination in her eyes. It was a sure sign that Sophie meant business.

'Oh, er, yes…great. Yes, we've just come to the same conclusion – we fight. Glad you want to come along,' Joshua said awkwardly. He wondered why it was that old folk and girls always seemed to make their minds up quickly in a crisis.

'Right then,' cried Stiggle, feeling much happier now that a decision had been reached. 'To arms everyone. Let's prepare the troops!'

* * *

So it was that a large company of forest-folk swiftly rallied to Stiggle's call. This time they were in deadly earnest, ready to fight to the death, if needs be. Encouraged by Trotter's example, many of the older animals joined in, proudly bearing ancient swords and clubs, slings and staves.

Stiggle took command.

'Right, fall into ranks of six,' he ordered.

Everyone obeyed with much shuffling and good humour, particularly when Fumble managed to bring four others tumbling over with him as he tripped over his own staff.

'I give up!' groaned Grumble, who was one of those who had fallen.

Stiggle addressed his troops.

'We all know why we're here. If we don't defeat Hagbane we will be her slaves for the rest of our lives, which she may shorten, in any case. We either accept that or we fight and maybe die in the attempt. This will be a fierce battle, with no quarter given; so if anyone wants to drop out, let him do so now.'

Silence descended on the company as he waited. Nobody moved.

'All right, then, let's go!' he cried. 'Death to Hagbane and all her evil! Vengeance for Aldred!'

Everyone present took up the cry. Stiggle gave the command, 'Forward, *march*!' and the motley army set off for the castle and whatever fate was in store for them.

The company moved at a fast pace and before long was in sight of the grim stone walled fortress. Stiggle held up his hand and ordered a halt.

'Surprise is our best weapon, so we'll charge straight in,' he said. 'Those of you with ropes and grappling irons, use them. Those who can climb walls, get up there as quickly as possible. It's important that we get the main gates open for the rest as soon as we can.' He pointed to those on his right. 'Some of you, under Foxy's command, are to take the tunnel entrance through which Joshua escaped. I don't think they'll expect us, so there may not be many guards on duty. Even so, be ready for anything. Fight hard, and Elmesh go with you.'

He drew his sword and an eager murmur ran through the company. Nerves and sinews tightened as the thrill of battle gripped each of their hearts.

'*Charge!*' yelled Stiggle, and the army surged forwards as one. Brandishing their weapons, they flooded across the open ground before the castle, shouting and yelling as they ran. Most were about halfway across the intervening space when without warning the ground trembled beneath them. It was followed immediately by a great earthen wave that heaved with such violence that many were thrown to the ground.

Dismay and confusion replaced courage as the troops

scrabbled to their feet and tottered about. Hagbane must have been expecting them after all. The battle was lost before it had even started. Expecting to be swallowed up alive at any moment, many of the forest-folk dropped their weapons and just stood waiting their fate at the hands of the Crone.

Worse was to come; a great roar rose from within the castle walls. It was followed by an almighty crash, and then a vast sheet of billowing flame shot into the sky. Everyone stared awe-struck at the sight. Another crash followed, and the walls began to split. Fire and smoke poured from the windows.

'What's happening?' cried Joshua.

'The prophecies are coming to pass, I believe,' Trotter replied quietly as he lay beside the boy on the still shaking ground. 'I think the Merestone has been made whole at last.'

The walls continued to crash down and they saw dark Grogs fleeing for their lives.

'Get them!' Stiggle commanded as he regained some control over the situation. 'Attack now, while we have the chance.'

In spite of their fear, the animals rose to the order and streaked after the fleeing guards who had for so long held them in terror. At that very moment, a terrifying screech rent the air. They stared upwards.

'It's Arca!' cried Sophie. 'Hurrah! He's come to help us.'

The mighty eagle swooped low with his fearsome talons outstretched, his shadow racing across the ground like an avenging angel. Terrified Grogs fell before him, never to rise again. Not a shred of mercy did he show to those cruel creatures who had caused such pain to so many of the forest-folk.

Sophie grabbed the mirror from Joshua.

'You use your sword. I'll take this,' she cried.

Before he could argue his sister had disappeared into the thick of the battle. Weapons clashed, shouts and groans filled the air, smoke and dust choked her lungs, but Sophie ignored it all and made for the blazing castle. There was only one goal in her mind. She wanted to find the Crone herself.

Sprinting across the open ground she reached the walls and began to clamber over the rubble. A large Grog blocked her way almost immediately. With a growl of fury he raised a great broadsword and prepared to strike her down.

Without hesitation, Sophie flicked open Gilmere. The light blazed forth and the Grog at once shrivelled to a cinder. Sophie was not sorry. With a shrug she pressed on.

Moments later she was standing in the courtyard. Buildings blazed all around her and massive beams and towers fell in noisy showers of sparks and dust. Smoke swirled everywhere as Sophie's eyes darted about in an attempt to find her bearings.

The next moment, a huge, dark shadow fell across her. She turned and looked up in panic. There before her reared a gigantic Grim, like some prehistoric monster, with its fiercely taloned wings outstretched, and as black as night. Its eyes glared with bloodshot hatred and the long jaws snapped greedily, revealing its vicious reptilian teeth.

Sophie fumbled with the mirror. Her hands were trembling, and she almost dropped it. The light streamed out – and missed! Her mouth fell open with horror as the loathsome creature advanced on her. She screamed and the mirror fell from her numbed fingers, its light still blazing.

Then, just as the vile creature was about to strike, the ground shook once more and where the light of the mirror shone, a wide chasm opened. With a scream of rage the creature lost its balance and with its limbs thrashing wildly it tumbled into the depths. Sophie lay panting and gasping, her heart beating fit to burst. She shook with fear and her legs refused to hold her weight. Looking around for the mirror she realised, to her dismay, that it too had fallen into the abyss. She knew now that she had no weapon with which to face Hagbane.

Time seemed to stand still. The noise and chaos around her faded into the background. Sophie thought about home, about her mum and dad. Would she ever see them again? What would Joshua and Andrew say? She hadn't even said goodbye to them. If only they were with her now. But Sophie was by herself and in the Crone's lair.

Slowly, she rose to her feet. A firm resolve filled her heart. 'I shall face her alone, in the name of Elmesh!' she said.

A door hung from broken hinges and, heedless of the chaos about her, with no weapon except her own courage, Sophie stumbled towards it.

* * *

'Stiggle, Stiggle, we're winning!' Joshua grinned in triumph at the weasel as they struggled towards the castle.

'Yes,' he shouted in reply. 'I reckon we've got them on the run. Oswain must be behind this somehow. I wonder what he's done?'

210

'We'll find out soon enough now,' his comrade replied. 'Looks like those revelations were right after all.'

It wasn't long before all the Grogs had been dealt with and the noise of battle began to quieten down. Hagbane's castle was utterly ruined, making it easy for Joshua, Andrew and Stiggle to climb over the broken walls and enter the wrecked courtyard.

'Whew, what a mess!' Andrew exclaimed.

'I wonder where Oswain is? And Sophie, too,' said Joshua. 'They must be around here somewhere. Let's give them a yell.'

'Sophie? Oswain? Where are you?'

There was no reply to their calls. They stood in silence and waited.

'Hush! What's that?' said Stiggle.

They listened, and heard the sound of sobbing.

'That's Sophie. Quick, it's coming from over there,' Joshua cried.

Joined by Trotter, they ran across the yard and entered a large room. Although it was wrecked it had obviously been Hagbane's lair. There they found Sophie, begrimed with soot, sitting on the floor among smouldering spell books and broken furniture, sobbing her heart out.

That wasn't all. A deep chasm ran the length of the room. Gingerly, Joshua, Andrew, Trotter and Stiggle approached the rift and peered over the edge. It seemed to go down for ever but somewhere deep they could make out a dull, red glow and could hear a subterranean roar that was muted by the distance.

Sophie turned at the sound of their coming. She looked at them in anguish, with her tears making white streaks down her blackened cheeks.

'He's dead,' she wailed. 'I know it. And Hagbane too. They've fallen down there – into that awful pit.'

She pointed into the gaping hole.

'Oh, why did it have to end like this? He's destroyed her but he's died, too. We've won, but we've lost as well,' she cried.

With that Sophie burst into tears again.

The others edged towards her, aware of how dangerously close to the chasm she sat. Joshua reached her first and he stooped down to put his arm around his sister. Suddenly, he felt very weary. Together they gazed into the pit but it was too deep to see anything except the red glow.

Joshua spoke at last. 'Come on, Sophie, it's no use staying here,' he murmured, and gently he helped her to her feet.

19

To the Enchanted Glade

Sophie rose, still sobbing, and with the others stared hopelessly into the chasm. She shook her head and turned away.

Before she or Joshua and Andrew, or Trotter and Stiggle could say another word a deep rumble shook the room. Dust fell all round them and the half-burned timbers of the Crone's lair groaned ominously.

'Look out!' Joshua cried.

Masonry, great lumps of stone and rubble, began to fall, threatening at any moment to bury them alive.

'We've got to get out,' Stiggle yelled as he, like the others, ducked and wove to avoid the falling rocks and rafters.

Through the dust and confusion they saw the yawning chasm begin to close up. A final crash resounded through the ruined building. More debris fell. Then, only a jagged line remained to show where the pit had been. The rumbling and shaking had ceased as suddenly as it had begun. Everyone stood coughing because of the dust, staring in stunned silence at the crack running across the floor.

'It's closed up,' said Andrew rather obviously.

'That's that then, I suppose.' Joshua answered. 'Nothing more we can do. Though I wish I knew what that hole was all about. It seemed to go on for ever like some kind of hell. It was horrible.'

'I don't understand it,' said Trotter. 'Except that Oswain seemed to know what he was doing when he handed himself over to Hagbane. There may be more to it yet, but I am at a loss to know what.'

At that moment, one of the remaining roof beams began to groan and buckle.

'Come on' cried Stiggle. 'We haven't much time.'

Scrambling over the rubble, they made for the door as fast as their legs could carry them and escaped only just in time, before the rest of the ceiling and roof collapsed.

'Whew, that was close!' Andrew gasped as he stepped into the open air.

The moment Trotter and Stiggle and the three children came into view a vast cheer rose from the animals assembled in the courtyard.

'Hurrah for Stiggle! Hurrah for Joshua!'

'Hurrah for Andrew!'

'Hurrah for Sophie!'

'Hurrah for Trotter!'

Everyone began to clap and to stamp their paws.

The five stood together and smiled wanly at the company gathered before them. Then Trotter raised a paw to indicate quiet so he could speak. He stepped forward and cleared his throat.

'My dear forest-folk,' he began. 'You have every good reason to be happy, for a mighty victory has been obtained here today. All the Grogs and Grims have been destroyed thanks to your bravery and the assistance of Arca.'

Much cheering and clapping interrupted him – particularly for the eagle, who was perched high on a remaining part of the wall. Trotter waved for silence again.

'The best news of all that I have for you is that

Hagbane herself is dead.'

For a brief instant there was silence, then, as the truth sank in, the whole crowd erupted into a riot of cheering, stamping, shouting and whistling that looked as though it might go on for the rest of the day.

Trotter waited patiently until things quietened down a little. Even those who knew what had become of Oswain couldn't resist smiling as they saw the joy and relief on the animals' faces.

Eventually, Trotter was able to continue.

'We are free at last to live our lives in peace and without fear of arrest or death,' he said. 'I cannot put into words just how much that means to us all.' His voice trembled with emotion. 'But it has not been without its cost. I see that some of you have been wounded in the fighting, but I refer especially to our dear brave Aldred who longed for this day, and…and to Oswain.'

He faltered and a murmur ran through the crowd.

'Yes, I am afraid Oswain is dead, also,' he said at last. 'It appears that he died while destroying Hagbane, but we do not know what happened exactly. The truth is, we have received some remarkable help from Elmesh. Were it not for the earthquake things might have been very different. Part of that earthquake split open the ground in Hagbane's lair and it appears that both she and Oswain fell to their doom. We owe a great debt to Oswain's memory; he willingly paid the ultimate price for our freedom…for the freedom of Alamore.'

A solemn silence had fallen over the audience as the full meaning began to sink in. It had not been a cheap victory.

'Well,' said Trotter, doing his best to brighten up and not wanting the forest-folk to lose their happiness.

'What's done is done and I am sure it is what Elmesh wished. So, go to your homes. Tell your loved ones and your children that they are free to enjoy the forest once again. May Elmesh bless you all…and thank you for everything you have done today.'

The crowd slowly dispersed, everybody talking among themselves about the events of the day, and soon only the little band of five remained.

'We'll pull this castle right down,' said Stiggle. 'Then we'll erect a monument to Aldred and to Oswain's memory. It'll become a favourite spot to visit, I expect.'

'That's a good idea,' Andrew said. 'You could use the stones of the castle to build it.'

'I think I would just like to get away from this place at the moment,' said Sophie. 'Can we go?'

'Sophie's right,' said Joshua. 'Come on, everyone. We look as though we could do with a good clean up, let alone something to eat. I'm starving.' He felt guilty as soon as he said it.

They looked at one another's bedraggled clothes and grimy faces and then, seeing the sense of his words, nodded.

'We do look a sight. I wonder what Mrs Trotter will say,' said Trotter. 'Yes, let us get back,' he sighed.

Andrew spoke to Sophie as they trudged back to the cottage.

'Maybe that's all there is to it, Sophie. We've done our part and perhaps we can go home to Mum and Dad now. I know you're upset over Oswain, but he's done his part, too.'

'I don't know,' his sister replied. 'It feels so incomplete, so…well…so, not right, if you know what I mean.'

'Yes, I do. But you mustn't let it get you down. Come

on, race you back to the cottage.'

'Thanks. I'll try not to be too sad. But I think I'll walk back, if you don't mind.'

* * *

By the time they had eaten and cleaned themselves up, it was quite late. Exhausted by the day's events, nobody needed any encouragement to go to bed and before long they were all sound asleep. All, that is, save for old Trotter. The badger was perplexed and sat up long into the night, staring straight ahead, lost in thought.

Much later, he rose and went to his library where he began to pore over some dusty parchments.

'It doesn't make sense,' he muttered to himself over and over again. 'I wonder. I just wonder.'

It was not until the early hours of the morning that he eventually stopped and fell asleep in his armchair with the papers sprawled across his lap.

He awoke with a jerk at around five o'clock. Outside he could hear the birds singing and the sun was already up. Swiftly and silently, he rose and left the house. The air was fresh and sweet and he couldn't help noticing that the undergrowth was looking fresher than he could ever remember, even back in the days before the troubles began. Bright green leaves cast a delicate filigree of shadows over the path as he walked. He breathed deeply of the wholesome air, then made his way resolutely towards the Enchanted Glade.

Sophie had slept heavily without dreaming but she woke up quite suddenly, not long after Trotter had left. She, too, rose quietly, noting that everyone was asleep but that somebody had left the house, leaving the door ajar. She felt sure it was Trotter and that he was on his way to the glade. With scarcely a moment's hesitation she set out to follow him.

Trotter sat on a moss-covered rock in the Enchanted Glade. The air seemed electric all around him and he felt a tingle of happiness running through his old frame. It was as though the years were falling off and he was young again. He wrinkled his snout and wondered if he actually looked younger.

Just at that moment he heard a rustle behind him. He leapt to his feet.

'Oh, it's you, Sophie,' he said with a slight tinge of disappointment in his voice. 'I had expected someone else. But then, I am not surprised that we should be here together again.'

'Hello,' she whispered. 'I just had to come. I've got this feeling that, well…that something very wonderful is going to happen today. I can't explain it.'

'There is no need to try, my dear. I feel exactly the same. That is why I am here. There are things I did not understand when I read the old writings last night, but when I woke this morning I knew that I must come here and wait. Hush! What is that?'

He placed his paw on Sophie's shoulder.

'It came from over there, from Elmere itself.'

They gazed in the direction of the pool, but nothing seemed to have changed. Still the pearl-like droplets dripped from the overhanging ledge with their musical plip-plop. Then Sophie cried out: 'The water! Look it's moving!'

They stared at the pool and, sure enough, its surface was in a tremendous turmoil. It began to boil and bubble like a cauldron and then slowly a watery shape began to rise from its depths.

The two watchers stood transfixed as the shape, at

first formless, became the figure of a man who rose splashing from the water as it cascaded from his head and shoulders. An aura of light seemed to surround him and he was magnificently clothed in purple and gold, glistening with wetness. He rubbed his eyes with his hands and shook the water from his face. The full morning sun revealed his strong tanned features and penetrating eyes.

He looked at his surroundings and then, fully risen, he stepped from the pool.

'It's Oswain!' cried Sophie. 'It's Oswain! He's come back!'

Sophie raced towards him and leapt up to throw her arms around his neck.

'Oh, Oswain, it's you! It's really you!' she exclaimed.

For a moment the man looked surprised and then he laughed.

'Sophie! I thought you were dead! Yes, it is me. As you can see, it has all come to pass as promised.'

'So I was right,' breathed the badger. 'Welcome back, Oswain, son of the High King of Castelfion – and rightful ruler of the Great Forest of Alamore.'

He made to kneel but Oswain swiftly reached out a hand and lifted him to his feet.

'Oh, no, Trotter, old friend, I will not have one such as you bowing before me. I am a King, as it was prophesied, but I count you as an equal, not a servant.'

He gave them both a warm smile. 'To find you alive, Sophie, is so delightful. Your brothers, too, I guess? I can't tell you how happy all this makes me.'

He laughed again and soon all three were delirious with joy, dancing round and round with their arms thrown about each other.

'What a wonderful morning! The winter is over.

Springtime has come at last!' Oswain exclaimed as they came to a panting rest.

B…b…but how? W…what happened?' Sophie asked breathlessly when at length they quietened down. 'How did you kill Hagbane? How did you get here? And…and…'

'Enough, Sophie,' Oswain laughed. 'I shall tell you all just as soon as everyone is gathered. It won't do to spoil it now, will it? How are Joshua and Andrew? Is everyone all right?'

'Yes, everyone is well except for…but I will tell you later,' declared Trotter. 'They will all be overjoyed to meet you again. Why, this is truly amazing. I can hardly wait to hear your explanations myself.'

'Well, that will not be long now, and then I will hear of your own exploits. But there is more to happen yet. Come over here. I want you to see this.'

Oswain led them across to the pool and plunged his hand into the water. Slowly, he drew out a glittering jewel and held it up in the light for Sophie and Trotter to see. The stone glowed with a brilliant fire that seemed to shine right through each one of them. Were it not for Oswain's presence, Sophie felt she would have been burned up by its power. She stared in wonder, too entranced to speak.

'The Merestone,' sighed Trotter. 'You have the Merestone. After all this time.' His eyes filled with tears to see it again.

'Yes,' replied Oswain. 'And now I restore the Merestone to its rightful place. Let it never be removed again while a king reigns in Alamore.'

So saying, he placed the jewel upon the rock to the side of the pool. There was a hissing sound and the stone fixed firm. He tapped it.

'There. It is done. From this day the forest will be blessed by its presence and the future days will be as glorious as the former.'

The three gazed reverently upon Elmesh's stone, captivated by its beauty and power.

'Can we go now?' asked Sophie. 'I'm just dying to tell the others.'

'I think we may,' Oswain replied. 'Listen though. Someone is coming.'

20

Explanations

Joshua's eyes opened; he blinked and looked around him. Sunlight was streaming through the leaded windows, lighting the old oak furniture with a mellow glow and making the brass ornaments sparkle. The new day smelt so fresh that he just had to get out of bed.

'Hey, come on everybody,' he shouted. 'Wake up!'

He gave his brother a shove.

'Wassermarra?' Andrew groaned sleepily. 'What time is it?'

'Getting up time! It's a brilliant day. Come on!'

Andrew wasn't yet convinced. He snuggled into the blankets while Joshua went into the other room to wake the rest.

'Hey, where's Sophie and Trotter?' he called. 'They're not here.'

'Oh, they've gone out, my dear,' called Mrs Trotter from her room. 'To the Enchanted Glade, I expect, if I know them.'

'The Enchanted Glade? We'd best go after them. Don't want to miss anything. Come on, Andrew. Get a move on. We'd better hurry.'

By now, Andrew was wide awake, too.

'All right, but how do we get there? I don't think I know the way.'

'Nor do I, but I reckon we'll be OK today. I just feel it.'

'Huh, you sound just like Sophie!' Andrew joked.

'I'll have breakfast waiting for you all.' Mrs Trotter called as they made for the door. 'Mind you're not too long now.' She smiled to herself as she busied about the kitchen.

Outside, the dew shone in the early sunshine and birds chirped in trees fresh with newly opened leaves. The sky shone blue, the air smelt clean and it felt good to be alive.

'I can't believe this,' cried Andrew. 'Yesterday, we were fighting Grogs and Grims and upset about Oswain, but today I don't feel tired or aching or…or even sad.'

'Yes, I feel the same,' his brother replied. 'Something special has happened in the night. Perhaps it's just that Hagbane is dead and the curse is lifted. Anyway, Trotter's bound to know. Come on. The path starts here. Race you to the glade.'

So off they ran and, sure enough, they did find all the right paths and it wasn't long before they arrived, puffing and panting, at the great sentinel stones that marked the entrance to the glade. Joshua made it only just ahead of his brother.

'Come on, loser! Let's find the others.'

'Oi, you only just beat me,' Andrew protested.

They stepped into the glade just as Sophie, Trotter and Oswain turned at the sound of their coming.

'Hi Sophie! Hi Tro…'

The boys stood speechless with their mouths hanging open in amazement. For a moment they just stared and stared. Andrew was the first to regain his voice.

'Oswain! Oswain! It is you, isn't it? B…but, we thought you were dead.'

'But I have returned from the darkness,' he replied with a smile. 'Hello Andrew – and Joshua. I'm so happy to see you again.'

Slowly, the two boys came forward. Actually, they both felt just a little bit awkward, though afterwards neither could explain why. There seemed to be something very special about Oswain that they hadn't felt before and it put them in awe of him.

'It is you, Oswain,' Joshua whispered. 'I'm so glad. We really did think you were dead and...and that was all. It was really so horrible.'

There were tears in his eyes as he spoke.

'I have a lot to explain to you and I'll do that just as soon as – well, just as soon as we've had breakfast. To tell you the truth,' he said, 'I'm very hungry.'

He laughed and the awkwardness was broken. They all began to laugh together and because the idea of breakfast appealed to each one of them the party set off on the familiar track back towards the cottage, enjoying the freshness of the new growth all around them and listening to the birds singing in the treetops.

Andrew kept them laughing all the way back by cracking daft jokes like, 'What did the egg say to the sausage?'

'I don't know,' said Joshua.

'Do you want to hear a funny yolk?'

Sophie groaned.

'What about this then? How do you keep little cornflakes happy?'

'Go on,' she said.

'You tell them a serial story,' Andrew chortled.

Trotter looked bemused. 'I don't understand that,' he said. 'What are cornflakes?'

The children laughed.

'It's a kind of breakfast food in our world,' Sophie explained.

'Here's another one,' said Andrew as they meandered

224

along the trail. 'Where do monkeys cook their potatoes?'

'I don't know,' said Joshua.

'In a chip pan, see!'

Sophie groaned.

'I've got one,' said Joshua. 'Where do baked beans go for their holidays?'

'Go on,' Sophie answered. 'Where?'

'To the Windward Isles!'

Sophie slapped his arm playfully. 'Trust you!' she said.

Laughing and joking the little company soon found themselves nearing Trotter's cottage.

When they arrived they found Stiggle waiting for them. He bowed low before Oswain as soon as he realised who he was. The poor weasel couldn't cope with Sophie's garbled explanations and stood, as the boys had done, quite speechless with wonder.

'Stiggle, I am glad to see you, but where is your brave captain, Aldred?' Oswain asked.

A solemn hush fell on the room.

Trotter explained.

'I am sorry to say, but Aldred has died. He gave his life to save the children when they were about to be burnt alive by Hagbane.'

Oswain was silent for a long time upon hearing this news.

'He was a courageous leader,' he said at last. 'We shall not let his name be forgotten. You must tell me everything and I will ensure that he is honoured throughout my kingdom,' he declared.

They were interrupted at this point by Mrs Trotter who came bustling through the kitchen door. Trotter hurried across to his wife and briefly explained what had happened. She advanced slowly and curtsied low before Oswain.

'I've already laid an extra place for you, sir. I rather thought you might come back,' she said knowingly.

Oswain smiled.

'Come now, great and noble lady of the forest!' Oswain cried. 'The king should bow before the cook, not the cook before the king. Let us honour you by doing justice to your labours. To the table, everyone!'

Mrs Trotter hid her face in her apron with embarrassment but was really very pleased.

After an enormous breakfast, during which little was said to interrupt the serious business of eating, everyone went outside and sat in a circle on the warm grass. Sophie made sure she sat right next to Oswain. Eager to listen, they all looked to the king as he gave his promised explanation of what had taken place.

'You all know the early history of the Great Forest,' he began, 'including the time when Hagbane seized the Merestone and began her evil reign. But I must take you back to a time before that, to the time of my early youth in the lands West of Alamore.

'My father, Argil, is the High King of those lands, and it has been a great kingdom for many an age. He is both wise and good and he ensured that my upbringing would fit me one day to succeed him. Now it is the custom in my country for the wise to speak words of good counsel to the young and, on occasion, to predict their path. Such was my case; it was told that I would not only inherit my father's kingdom but that in time I would become the legal ruler of the Great Forest of Alamore beyond the mountains.'

Trotter nodded thoughtfully.

'They said this was the will of Elmesh and that he would make known to me when this should happen,'

226

Oswain continued. 'The wise also told me that it would involve sacrifice and suffering to achieve this. I may say that I did not relish the idea at all. Then the day came – or I should say the night, for it was given to me in a disturbing dream. Elmesh spoke in a vision and I knew this was the moment. So I set out for my unknown destiny.'

'That would be when I also heard from Elmesh,' interrupted Trotter.

'Yes, and Arca, too. When the time is right Elmesh speaks to many, so that there need be no doubt.'

'Then we came through the Passway!' exclaimed Andrew. 'But we didn't know why until Trotter explained things to us. It all seemed so weird.'

'I'm sure it did.' Oswain laughed. 'It is strange enough when you know something of Elmesh's ways but even more so if you haven't even heard his name before.'

'You saw something in the Star Pool,' said Sophie. 'I think I know what, but please tell us.'

'Ah, yes, Sophie.' He looked at her with a smile. 'You have a special gift indeed. Much like the wise of my own land. Be careful you do not grow too old to recognise it any more, for it is given to very few.'

Sophie's cheeks coloured and she looked thoughtful.

'Now, when I reached the forest – which I only managed after strong opposition from evil forces – I discovered that Hagbane was the foe, but I was unprepared for what would follow. I gazed into Elmere – the time that you found me, Sophie – and I saw the truth. I had known Hagbane before.' He paused before continuing. 'She was the one that I was to marry.'

Everyone present except Sophie gasped at this.

'Whew! No wonder you didn't want to talk about it,'

Joshua murmured.

'So she was not always like that?' queried Trotter. 'Surely?'

'No indeed,' Oswain answered. 'She was once the fairest maid in the Westward lands. In those days her name was Dorinda. I loved her so much that my heart was lost to her. She was to become my wife and the future queen of my kingdom.'

'What happened?' Stiggle asked.

'I spoke to you before about the unrest that seemed to fall upon the land. It was a time of disturbance and fear. Strangers, wanderers, began to travel in great numbers through our country and it was one of these who poisoned my beloved's heart. Some evil seed of pride and greed took hold of her and she became a changed person. My Dorinda began to behave strangely. She grew hard and arrogant. She wanted things – gold, silver, servants who would grovel and do anything she asked even if it was wrong. People became afraid of her because of her temper. She became unbearable and my heart broke as I saw the change.'

Oswain paused for a moment.

'In the end, I knew it wouldn't work. I discussed it all with my parents and we knew that she was unfit to be my bride. It was very painful but I had to break off our engagement. Dorinda was furious and swore vengeance on us all, but then she went away and we thought that we had seen the last of her.'

'That must have been when she came to the Great Forest and stole the Merestone,' said Trotter.

'Indeed. Then she returned with it to my land, more evil than ever. She knew, of course, about the prophecies concerning my rule over the forest and I think this was her vengeance, that she should possess it for herself.

'My mother, Queen Talisanna, who is a wise woman, worked this out and confronted Dorinda. This was also shown me in the Pool. She attempted to wrest the Merestone from her but failed. It seems that Dorinda had gained some power which my mother could not resist. She was defeated, but in the conflict the Merestone fell and a fragment broke off. My mother had this mounted in a ring and placed it upon my finger, sure that the day would come when the Merestone would be reunited. Little were we to know how that would come about,' he said sadly.

'So Hagbane – I mean, Dorinda – left your land?' Joshua asked.

'Yes, and she came to dominate this forest. Here the evil seed fully possessed her heart and she became the Hagbane whom you knew so well.'

'But if she was so young, how come she looked so old?' asked Andrew.

'I think evil makes people grow older more quickly than they should,' Oswain replied. 'You can hardly imagine how I felt to see such a beautiful young woman turn into the horror of a Crone.'

'It must have been terrible for you to know that she was your enemy,' Sophie said.

'You knew you had to meet her, which is why you let yourself be captured,' said Trotter, nodding with understanding.

'That is correct, though I never imagined that it would be in such horrifying circumstances for you children. Now you must tell me what happened after that, because I was carried away by Hagbane in great anguish for your safety.'

Between them they told Oswain what had followed. When they came to Aldred's sacrifice, tears filled

Oswain's eyes. They spoke of the battle and of how they had discovered that Oswain must have died. Everyone was eager to know about the events within the castle, and Oswain described Hagbane's terrible sceptre and how she had tried to conquer him with it.

'I pleaded with her to give up this madness but she had gone too far. I saw that nothing would change her and knew that I could love Dorinda no more. She had become Hagbane for ever.' He shook his head. 'That was when she made her mistake. She brought out the Merestone to add power to her sceptre.' He smiled grimly. 'The stone came from Elmesh and now it was time for the prophecies to be fulfilled. The stone was made whole and Elmesh took his vengeance on Hagbane's wickedness. The room burst into flames and a mighty earthquake split the floor apart. Just as you thought, Sophie, we fell together into the abyss, locked in mortal combat.'

'Then why didn't you die? I mean, why are you here?' Andrew asked, frowning. 'I don't understand that at all. I mean, it just doesn't happen, does it?'

'I cannot fully explain all that took place in the terrible depths of that pit, but we did not die, as you understand death. Great forces were unleashed, light against darkness, good against evil, life against death. We ceased to be bodies as you know them but the battle continued until with my spirit I grasped the Merestone as mine by right and Hagbane...Hagbane was destroyed. That is all I can say.'

He paused for a moment.

'I was exhausted by the struggle and wandered as a spirit through the darkness beneath the earth, only the light and hope of the Merestone guiding me. It was a strange existence that I do not fully understand, but none dared touch me in that shadowy realm and slowly my strength returned and I was renewed.' He smiled. 'Then I heard the voice of Elmesh himself call me back to life. I came at last to the Star Pool where the light of Elrilion met that of the Merestone once again. Such glorious light and colour – you couldn't imagine it,' he mused. 'Anyway, in the midst of that splendour I received my body again and came up from the waters – as you two saw.' He looked towards Trotter and Sophie.

'Yes,' Trotter spoke. 'I *knew* that something must happen. The prophecies had been right all along and I could not believe they would fail now. I studied them again until sleep overtook me. When I woke I knew the answer lay in the glade and so I came to await whatever should come to pass.'

'I think it's utterly amazing,' Joshua declared. 'I mean, I've never heard of anything so...'

'Hey!'

Stiggle cried out and leapt to his feet. Before anyone else could move, he shot into the bushes and began crashing around.

Moments later he emerged carrying a torn piece of green cloth in his paw.

'Pah! Too late. They got away,' he growled.

'What was all that about?' asked Andrew in consternation.

'Hey, I recognise that cloth,' cried Joshua.

'It's the wizard's!' Sophie gasped.

'Yes,' Stiggle replied. 'I heard a rustle in the bushes. We weasels have excellent hearing, you know. They must have been listening. Pity I wasn't a bit quicker.'

'Never mind,' Oswain said. 'They heard little to their good. I guess two wizards are at this very moment fleeing for their lives. They know now that the Great

231

Forest is no place for the likes of them. Poor shadows!'

*   *   *

Deep in the undergrowth, two figures scuttled along as fast as their legs could carry them. The taller one slapped the other around his bald head.

'You stupid idiot. Why can't you keep quiet? They'll be after us now.'

'It's not my fault, you gawky old fool. I don't know why we had to go spying again, anyway. It would have made more sense to have tried getting on their side.'

'Bah! You know nothing.' Terras scowled. 'You don't think that they would want people like us, do you? Come on, let's get out of here before it's too late.'

So, still grumbling at each other, the two wizards fled the forest to seek their fortune elsewhere. But, high in the sky, a pair of fierce eagle eyes watched their going and their direction with great interest.

21
Celebrations

'Can I go out now, mum?'

'Mavis, my darling, you can go out as much as you like! Everything has changed for the good.' laughed the rabbit's mother. 'And take all your brothers and sisters with you. It'll give me a chance to clean the burrow.'

Nobody had quite believed it at first, but once the news had started it spread like wildfire. It was a miracle. Oswain had returned – and Hagbane was dead.

Young Mavis, along with many others who had flocked to see him, had gazed in wonder at the sight of the king seated beside the Enchanted Pool where the Merestone now shone in its beauty and power.

'That's Oswain, our new king,' she explained to her wide-eyed brothers and sisters. 'Mum says he's really good, and I reckon he is, too.'

So the tale is nearly told. The Enchanted Glade was more wonderful than ever and the Great Forest of Alamore began to prosper and flourish under Oswain's reign. Animals walked without fear; the young played wherever they liked; flowers and fruit grew in plenty and everyone said it was the happiest place there ever was. All traces of Hagbane's rule were swiftly and thoroughly erased – the stones of her castle became all sorts of useful things, such as a new jetty for the river, paths, house walls and millstones. Elmere became again the place for wisdom, for healing, and even for love.

All this came about after some time, but there was one early event that formed a topic of conversation for many years to come. It was the great celebration.

During the days following Oswain's return there was much planning and busyness on the part of the forest-folk. Even the children were drafted in to help Mrs Trotter with the baking. Rumour had it that this was to be the biggest feast ever! Expectations ran high.

At last the appointed day came and everybody gathered in the old clearing. How different it was from their last meeting! The sun shone upon the fresh, green grass; trees proudly displayed their blossomed finery; flowers, gorgeous in colour and sweet in fragrance, filled every available spot. The air buzzed with excitement as the multitude came together. Young eyes looked with longing at the heavily-laden food tables and hoped that the formalities would not take too long.

Then a long, clear trumpet call sounded. Everyone turned their attention to the platform that had been erected for the occasion. Trotter stepped forward and spoke.

'My dear forest-folk,' he began, 'I want to welcome you all to this great occasion, this time of celebration, this day of thanksgiving and of feasting.'

He paused as everyone cheered wildly. Smiling, he held up his paw for silence.

'For a number of years now I have had the privilege of being your leader. Those years were hard and sad, and only by the help of Elmesh was I able to keep going. My hope lay in the promise of deliverance that was given way back in the elder days. Good folk, that deliverance has come and we are once more free. Elmesh be praised!'

More cheering rent the air.

'Now, my time as your leader is completed. My task is done. So it is my joy and privilege to appoint one to succeed me – a ruler whom we can trust utterly to be wise and just in his government.' The aged badger paused and drew himself upright before continuing. 'To you who dwell in the realm of the Great Forest of Alamore, I present, Oswain, the son of the High King of the West, whom I declare our King by the will of Elmesh!'

Oswain rose and stepped forward, resplendent in his royal robes of purple and gold. The sun shone upon his noble features and he seemed bathed in an aura of light. Trotter bowed low before the new king and all the forest-folk followed his example.

Oswain smiled upon the crowd. When he spoke, his voice was deep and clear.

'Rise, forest-folk, for I will not have you in fear of me. My reign must be one of love and friendship, of justice and truth, not pomp and ceremony nor threat and fear. We shall begin as we intend to continue.'

'Hear, hear,' said an old rabbit who was probably Mavis' great grandfather.

'Soon we shall eat and drink and celebrate together.'

More cheers, especially from the younger element in the crowd.

'But first,' he continued. 'we must express our gratitude and thanks to those who have brought us to this happy day. The foremost is old Trotter himself. For a long time he has been a faithful adviser and friend to you all. It was he who foresaw the time of Elmesh's visitation. He is the one who so fearlessly campaigned against Hagbane's evil devices. None can put into words how much he has done for the forest.'

A ripple of applause ran through the crowd.

Oswain's eyes scanned their faces. 'He has stood down from leadership but I cannot accept that fully. Friends, I wish to appoint Trotter as my chief and personal advisor for the rest of his days – and may they and those of his wife be long and happy. They shall be known henceforth as Lord and Lady Trotter.'

The whole crowd rose as one and applauded this announcement for all they were worth, while Trotter looked a bit abashed, but nonetheless obviously pleased.

'Next,' Oswain continued. 'There are three very brave mice whom we wish to thank. Fumble, Mumble and Grumble, come forward!'

There was a rustling at the front of the crowd.

'Ouch! Silly clot! Can't you do it right even today? Get off my foot!'

'Sorry,' Fumble replied, still standing on it.

'Common yew toe, beehive prop alley.'

'Oh, shush!'

The three mice made their way up the steps and bowed low before the King; except that Fumble bowed so low he fell over in a somersault and landed on his back, with his legs waving in the air. Everyone burst out laughing, much to Grumble's indignation.

'Fumble, Mumble and Grumble,' Oswain continued, once order had been restored. 'In recognition of your bravery I appoint you, hereby, knights of honour to accompany me wherever I go in the forest.'

The mice swelled with pride, while Trotter looked more than a little alarmed.

'Don't worry,' Oswain whispered to him. 'I shall send them to the Enchanted Glade until their, um, difficulties have been sorted out. But they are of fine heart, old friend, do not fear.'

He turned to address the crowd once more.

'We have had a mighty ally, without whom we could not have achieved this victory and we must thank him, also.'

So saying, Oswain looked up and whistled long and shrill. From his lofty domain Arca, the mighty white eagle glided to land gracefully before the King. Although the animals knew him to be a friend they, nonetheless, drew back before his awesome presence.

'Arca, we thank you for all you have done. I give you no reward for I know you would take none. And I ask no allegiance of you for I know you serve Elmesh alone. Yet, I bid you always welcome among us and would have you know of the honour with which we hold you in our hearts.'

'It is well,' the bird croaked in reply. 'Elmesh's will has been done. May his sun warm your days and the light of Elrilion guard your nights. Farewell, Oswain. May your reign be long and peaceful.'

With a shrill screech, the eagle rose from the ground and soared upwards towards the sun until not even the keenest eyes could follow him.

'And now, good folk,' Oswain declared. 'Last but not least I give you the children, Joshua, Sophie and Andrew Brown.'

The three children stepped forwards and mounted the steps. The crowd rose as one and cheered and stamped so enthusiastically that they felt really quite embarrassed and even Andrew reddened.

'These three came from far beyond the forest, in fact from another realm altogether,' Oswain said. 'They are here at Elmesh's bidding and they found themselves unwittingly caught up in our battles. They have faced many fearsome dangers in their bid to help us and have proved their bravery and loyalty to us all. I would bid them stay among us and be honoured by everyone, but it is not within my power to do so. Soon they must return to their own land and time. Yet I want us to remember them always with warmth and affection as we enjoy the freedom they helped us earn.'

Oswain motioned to Trotter and the latter brought forth a velvet covered tray upon which there lay three translucent pearls of crystal. Each had a chain of gold so fine as to be almost invisible.

Moving from one to the other Oswain took each of the jewels from the tray that Trotter carried and in turn placed them around the necks of Joshua, Sophie and Andrew.

'These are solidified droplets from Elmere,' he explained. 'At least, as near as can be called solidified, for you will find that they possess a life and a power more than sight or touch can tell. Take them as our token of thanks and in memory of your adventure.'

Sophie and Andrew looked at Joshua and nodded to him to say something. He turned to face the assembled forest-folk, blushed, coughed, cleared his throat and began:

'Er, um, well I don't know what to say really, but, er, thanks for everything. It's been a wonderful adventure but scary too and, um, well, I'm, I mean, we're glad it turned out all right in the end. And we think you really are wonderful and...and we're really glad this happened to us.'

He finished, still a bit flushed. The crowd applauded loudly as the three returned to their places and sat down.

'Well done, Josh,' Andrew whispered. 'I wouldn't have known what to say.'

'Look at these jewels,' Sophie said. 'Why, you can hardly see them they're so clear.' She fondled the jewel, grateful that she could take something of the magic of Elmere with her for the rest of her life.

Oswain was speaking again.

'There is one more person to mention,' he declared. 'I have left him to last because of his importance. His name is Aldred. Alas, he is no longer with us, as you all know. He gave his life to save the children as selflessly as he had lived and fought. We mourn his loss, of course, but his name shall always be honoured and remembered in our midst. Some of you have been busy making this possible and now we can reveal the result of your labour.'

He pointed to a large structure covered with a white sheet. Everyone had been wondering what it was but great secrecy had surrounded the project, although the sound of hammering and chiselling had been heard for many days. Oswain motioned with his hand and four young stoats tugged at the sheet.

It fell off amid wondering gasps. Revealed in shining stone was a larger than life statue of Aldred mounted upon a pedestal of rough-hewn rock. It really was a most magnificent sculpture and a worthy monument to the brave leader.

'From now on,' cried Oswain. 'This clearing shall be known as Aldred's Park and so his name will be immortalised for ever.'

A heartfelt round of applause greeted this proclamation.

'And now,' he smiled at the folk gathered before him, 'the time has come to end the formalities and to begin the feasting. Let us then make merry!'

Possibly the loudest cheer went up at that moment,

especially from the younger ones, and the crowd descended as one upon the food-laden tables.

* * *

Joshua, Sophie and Andrew were sitting together on the grass in the shade of a beech tree. For the past two hours they had eaten their fill of goodies and spoken to many animals who had wanted to thank them personally.

'Whew, I feel blown,' declared Andrew. 'Any more food and I'll probably explode!'

'Me too,' his brother agreed. 'It's been a great party. I wonder how long it'll go on for.'

'I don't know,' said Sophie. 'Probably until quite late, I should think.' She frowned and pulled her knees up to her chest. 'But I feel it's finished for us now, anyway. We've done what we were sent to do and I kind of feel, well, an outsider again. Do you know what I mean?'

'Yes, I agree,' Joshua nodded. 'I think we should go soon. It feels a bit sad but I suppose we really must get back to our own home.'

'I suppose we can do that,' said Andrew, a little anxiously. 'I mean…'

'Oh, of course we can,' his sister interrupted. 'If Elmesh got us here he can get us back. I'm not worried, anyway.'

'You know, it seems bad, but I've hardly thought about Mum and Dad, I guess they'll be terribly worried about us. Do you think they'll be angry when they see us?' Joshua said.

'No, just relieved,' Sophie answered.

'I bet they've had the police out, and tracker dogs and helicopters and the army and everything,' Andrew enthused.

'Oh, I do hope not,' said Sophie.

'Well, we'll find out soon enough now,' Joshua observed. 'Here come Oswain and Trotter and I have the feeling it's time to say goodbye.'

They rose to their feet as the King and the badger drew near.

22

Return to the Passway

'Goodbye, everyone.'

'Take care of yourselves.'

'Hope to see you again.'

The afternoon shadows were lengthening, and the air was warm and sweet with the scent of honeysuckle, as the little company made its way through the forest paths. They had decided in the end that only a few should see the children off and so, after touching farewells to the animals and especially to Fumble, Mumble and Grumble only Oswain, Trotter, Mrs Trotter and Stiggle accompanied them on this last walk through the forest.

Their route took them first to the monument to Aldred where they stopped to pay their respects to the brave stoat.

'I wish he were still alive,' said Sophie. 'He would have loved to see how things have turned out.' She sniffed back a tear.

Mrs Trotter stood next to her. 'Maybe he's more alive than any of us know,' she said quietly. 'The loss is ours more than his. Elmesh knows.'

Led by Oswain, they left Aldred's Park and took the route to the Enchanted Glade. They found it more wonderful than ever now that the Merestone was restored.

'You can feel it in the air!' Andrew exclaimed. 'It...it's

as though the air is alive.'

'Just look at the pool and the way the drops of water are falling. It's like liquid light...like living diamonds...' Joshua whispered, his eyes shining in wonder.

Sophie laughed. 'You have changed, Joshua!' she marvelled.

'Yeah, well, it's just this place...'

'You don't have to explain it, Joshua,' said Oswain. 'We all feel the same.'

'I'd like to stay here for ever,' he replied.

Trotter coughed politely. 'There is just the matter of you getting back to your own world,' he murmured.

Reluctant to leave the glade as they were, they all agreed and so set off on the last stage of their journey to seek out the old Passway.

* * *

'Just around here, I think,' said Trotter, breaking the silence of the last few hundred metres.

They rounded a clump of hazelnut bushes and there before them lay the set of steps that led up to the dark stone-arched opening in the hillside. There, too, they found Sophie's piece of red ribbon that she had tied to the branch of a nearby oak tree. She ran across to retrieve it. Slowly, the rest of the party walked to the base of the steps.

'Well, here we are,' said Joshua with a sigh. He gave them all a wan smile. 'Time to go, I suppose.'

Everyone stood in an awkward silence for a few moments, until Oswain, sensing that words were needed, addressed the children.

'Joshua. Sophie. Andrew. What can we say? We have become great friends in the brief time that we have known one another and it is not at all easy to say farewell. It has been a great adventure and thanks to you the Great Forest is once more free. We will never forget the part you have played in ridding us of that evil tyrant. However, we all sense that it is time for you to return to your own realm, so we send you on your way with the blessing of Elmesh.'

'Oh, I wish I could stay here for ever!' Sophie exclaimed. 'I love it so much now that it's all changed. And you've become such dear friends. If only we could come back whenever we pleased, even though I know it's not like that.'

She bent and kissed first Mrs Trotter and then Trotter himself.

'I shall never forget you. And thank you for looking after us.'

'I don't know that I did much of that, my dear,' said Mrs Trotter. 'Seems to me that there were others who protected you when you most needed it.'

'Yes, but you made it all so warm and comfy.'

Stiggle she hugged. Oswain stooped and put his arm around her.

'Sophie, you and I have a special kind of kinship, for you possess the same gift as my mother. I want to remind you to guard it well and use it wisely to help others. Do not let the passing years take it from you.'

She looked into his eyes and nodded solemnly. Tears filled her eyes as he kissed her goodbye.

The two boys shook hands with the badgers and the weasel as cheerily as they could and they all wished each other well. Oswain put his arms around their shoulders.

'You boys have played a valiant part in this adventure, with courage far beyond your years, and you have learned many lessons about the ways of good and evil. Do not forget these as you grow up. It will not be the last time you are called upon by Elmesh, of that I am sure. Farewell, my good friends.'

Joshua and Andrew said their farewells, feeling suddenly very grown up.

'Right then,' said Joshua. 'Everyone ready? Let's go.'

So, without further ado, the three children mounted the steps. When they reached the entrance to the Passway they turned and waved goodbye to their watching friends, and then they stepped into the passage.

'Take good care,' called Trotter as the children disappeared from sight.

'Our world's still there,' cried Andrew. 'Look, you can see it!' And with that he ran on ahead while Joshua and Sophie followed more slowly.

Suddenly he stopped and uttered a cry of alarm.

'What is it, Andy?' Sophie called.

'I…I can't seem to go any further,' he said. 'I don't get it. There's some kind of invisible wall, or something.'

Joshua and Sophie hastened to where he stood and Joshua experimentally pushed his hand forward.

'You're right,' he said. 'There's a barrier of some kind. We can't get out.'

Sophie looked alarmed. 'What are we going to do?' she asked.

Between them they tried again, first pushing, then a sudden movement, then feeling the air for a way through, but there was nothing.

'We're stuck,' said Andrew rather obviously.

'There's only one thing for it, we'll have to go back down to the others and see if they know the answer,' said Joshua. He turned and started back.

Except that, to his consternation, he couldn't, and for the same reason that they were unable to continue forwards. Another invisible barrier had formed.

'I...I can't move off one way or the other!' he exclaimed. There was just a hint of panic in his voice.

It took only seconds for his brother and sister to realise their predicament. They could proceed neither forwards to home, nor backwards to the Great Forest.

'We seem to be trapped,' Joshua said glumly. 'What are we going to do?'

All three pondered the question in silence.

'At least we can still breathe. I can feel the air moving,' Andrew observed. 'So we won't suffocate.'

'No, we'll just die of thirst and starvation!' Joshua replied.

'We've got to think,' Sophie interrupted. 'Look, where are we along this passage?'

'About halfway,' said Andrew after a moment. 'We're stuck halfway.'

'Then we're on the boundary between two worlds,' said Joshua.

'So why can't we go the other way? And why can't we go back the way we went in the first place?' Sophie furrowed her brow and thought deeply. 'Something must have changed,' she said.

'Like what?' asked Andrew.

'Well...I don't know...quite, but well, we're a bit different,' she replied. 'Perhaps that's it. Maybe we've been touched by the magic of the forest and we can't get back because of that.'

'But then we should still be able to return to the forest, and we can't do that,' Joshua countered.

'No, you're right,' Sophie answered slowly. She

absentmindedly fingered the neck of her T-shirt. 'I've got it!' she exclaimed suddenly. Her fingers had alighted upon the almost invisible crystal jewel that hung from her neck.

'What is it, Sophie?' Joshua asked.

'It's these jewels,' she explained. 'They come from a different world to ours. Just maybe they can't be taken into our world.'

'And we can't go back because we're from a different world to the jewels and the door back is closed,' Andrew added.

'So, we're at a kind of threshold,' said Joshua. 'I bet the jewels could go back down without us and we could go home without the jewels. We just have to take them off and leave them here, then.'

Sophie nodded but she was frowning. 'That's all very well,' she said. 'But I think Oswain meant us to keep them, like to remember what happened, and...and to kind of protect us, I suppose.'

Joshua agreed. 'It's more than that, though, I think,' he said. 'We should bring something back with us and maybe it's so we can help other people when they're facing evil.'

'That's it!' Sophie agreed at once. 'Well done, Josh.'

'So, what do we do?' Andrew wanted to know.

'I think we hold the jewels in our hands and...and we say, 'In the name of Elmesh',' Joshua answered. 'And if that doesn't work, we'll just have to leave them here.'

The others agreed, so with Joshua leading, they turned to face the direction of home.

'In the name of Elmesh,' Joshua cried, clutching anxiously at his crystal. He lifted his foot tentatively to take a step forwards.

To his immense relief it worked. He felt a strange

tingling sensation all over his body and the crystal in his hand blazed a shimmering blue for a few seconds. Then he was through and walking unhindered towards the entrance.

Sophie and Andrew did the same and moments later they stepped out of the tomb entrance and into the spring sunshine of their own world. Everything seemed surprisingly normal again.

'I wonder what day it is?' Sophie asked.

Joshua shrugged. 'Dunno,' he replied.

'Mum and Dad are going to be terribly worried,' said Andrew. 'I wouldn't be surprised if they're cross with us – at least, until we explain what's happened.'

'We'd better get back home as soon as we can,' said Sophie.

* * *

Quickly they rushed into the kitchen and Sophie ran into her mother's arms.

'Oh, Mum, we're so sorry we've been away so long! It's lovely to be back safe and sound. We've had the most incredible adventure but you must have been really worried about us. Have you been very upset?'

Sophie looked up appealingly into her mother's eyes.

'What are you going on about?' her mother said, stroking Sophie's hair. 'It's not even lunch-time yet. I don't call a morning a long time.'

'A morning?' they repeated incredulously. The children couldn't believe their ears. Perhaps Sophie was right and their mother had cracked up because they had been missing for so long.

'But we've been away for *days*!' Joshua exclaimed, looking puzzled. 'In the Great Forest of Alamore, fighting the Crone and…and…'

He tailed off, when he saw his mother was laughing.

'Oh, so that's it! You've been making up an adventure. What imaginations you children have!'

'But it's not,' Andrew declared stoutly. 'It really happened and we were nearly killed. And there was Trotter and Oswain and Arca the eagle and…'

'And lots of others too, if I know you,' his mother interrupted. 'So where is this Great Forest of yours?'

Andrew glanced at his brother and sister. Sophie nodded.

'It's in a cemetery. On the other side of the park. It's another world,' Andrew explained.

'Another world? You're telling me! It's high time they tidied that place up. I blame the council,' Mrs Brown answered. 'But what were you doing there? Not getting into trouble, I hope. It may be a mess but you should still respect the dead, you know.'

Sophie was hopping up and down with exasperation. 'No, mum, it really is another world,' she insisted.

'You have to go through the wall of a tomb to get there. Well not exactly through the wall, if you know what I mean. Through a special passageway,' Joshua explained.

His mother gave them one of those looks that said, 'you're pulling my leg and I'm not falling for it'.

'And I suppose there are monsters and witches and battles and outlaws,' she said.

'Yes!' chorused the children in all sincerity.

'I thought there might be!'

'Well…well, we've got medals to prove it, anyway,' Sophie insisted. 'Look!'

Mum looked.

'Oh yes. So I see,' she said shaking her head in

disbelief, for there was nothing that her eyes could see.

'Well, feel them then,' challenged Joshua. 'Come on, Mum.'

'That's enough playing about now,' said their mother firmly. 'Hurry up, all of you. And don't forget to wash those hands! I'll have lunch on the table in five minutes. Walking through the walls of tombs, indeed! Wait till I tell your father.'

'Parents!' declared Andrew as he went upstairs. 'Why can't they ever believe anything?'

'Kids!' mused their mother, smiling to herself.

*   *   *

That night, the children stood at the bedroom window, gazing up into the velvet night sky. Stars hung like jewels in the heavens and they stared in silence for a long while.

'Do you think we imagined it all?' asked Andrew.

'No, of course not,' his brother replied. 'I'm sure it happened, even if the grown-ups don't believe us.'

'What do you think, Sophie?'

'I *know* it was all real – and I don't think it's the last time we'll visit Caris Meriac, either. I can feel it somehow.'

Her brothers nodded.

Just then, one star seemed to glow more brightly than the rest. They all saw it. Then a dark shadow flitted across the sky. It was difficult to see, but the sound that followed was unmistakable. A high pitched, eerie screech pierced the gloom and sent shivers down each of their spines. They clutched at the jewels about their necks and almost felt them.

Unbelievably high in the night sky a great white bird

winged his way westwards and, far below, three pyjama-clad children whispered his name in awe.
   'Arca!'

The End – until the next time!

Next in the series...

Oswain's sister, Princess Alena, runs away from home wearing the Star Stone. She has no idea of its immense value or importance.

Gublak, a sly goblin, wants the mysterious Star Stone for himself. Loathsome pirates and vicious wolves aid Gublak in his greedy quest.

Once again, Joshua, Sophie and Andrew find themselves in Prince Oswain's world – this time in a desperate race to rescue Alena.

But there are deeper and darker powers at work. How will the children manage to save her, while battling evil forces that want the Star Stone at any cost?

Watch out for Gublak's Greed!

Visit the Oswain Tales web site to find out more
www.oswaintales.co.uk

Hagbane's Doom – The Musical

This exciting musical, based on the main elements of the story, is an excellent show for primary schools to stage.

The Director's Pack includes:

Director's Book with script, score and lyrics

CD with full vocal demonstrations by children for children and complete instrumental backing tracks for performance

Photocopiable pupil script and lyrics and a performing licence application form

Hagbane's Doom – The Musical 978-1-905591-19-0

Hagbane's Doom – The Musical (multimedia) 978-1-905591-20-6

Full details, including samples of all the songs and order details, can be found at
www.starshine.co.uk